Book 1

Seasons of Destiny

Paris in the Springtime

SUSAN AYLWORTH

Published Internationally by Susan Aylworth
Chico, CA USA
susanaylworthauthor.com

Exclusive cover © 2022 Bright Book Media
Inside design and formatting by Teri Barnett, indiebookdesigner.com

PRINT ISBN 978-1-955056-08-3
EBOOK ISBN 978-1-955056-07-6

Like Susan's Facebook Page
Follow Susan on Twitter: @SusanAylworth
Follow Susan on BookBub
Follow Susan on GoodReads

For Michele,

A good editor and a great friend to my books.

For Michele,

A good editor and a great friend to my books.

CONTENTS

Chapter One

P aris Cutler pulled into her grandmother's driveway and honked as she parked. "I'm home!" she called from the open window of her car. The breeze carried the rich scent of pine, spruce, and fir. Leaving the unpacking for later, she bounded up the back steps and turned the knob on the kitchen door, startled to find it locked. Only then did she notice the note.

Running a few errands. Back soon. Jess has your key at the school. Love, Gran.

Locks? Keys? When had that started? Though it wasn't the homecoming she'd hoped for, the setback was small and a detour to the high school no problem. She hopped back into her car and cruised a two-lane side street, the up-mountain side thick with evergreen forest, the opposite side home to the town's schools — elementary, middle, and high school built side by side, no more than six-hundred students in all three, and even that was an increase since she'd been a student here.

The next surprise came when she reached the high school parking lot to find it almost deserted, the only cars in the row reserved for staff and faculty.

"Hi, Mrs. Bailey," she called as she entered the front office. The school secretary seemed as permanent a fixture as the painted prospector grinning down from the wall of the gym. Mrs. Bailey had been the front office guardian for as long as Paris could remember. She still looked just as Paris remembered except for her graying hair.

"Oh, hello there, Paris. You're looking well." The secretary seemed genuinely pleased to see her. "Can I help you with something?"

"I'm here to see Aunt Jess. I guess this must be a staff development day?"

"Oh yes, right you are. Professional development today, staff only.

The students return on Monday." She turned the guest register toward Paris and laid a pen on its surface. "Go ahead and sign in, dear. The faculty should be finishing their afternoon session. I expect you'll find Ms. Kerr in Room 18."

"I remember." Paris signed her name. "Thanks, Mrs. Bailey."

"Have a good visit." The woman turned back to her computer screen and Paris closed the office door behind her.

Memories assailed her as she walked the familiar halls. She'd started here as a sophomore, fifteen years old and the new girl among students who'd known one another since preschool. Though she'd known them briefly, for most of sixth grade, she'd arrived again as a stranger, already bearing a chip on her shoulder because of her mother's cancer. Too ill to work, her mom had given up her job. That meant losing their condo in the valley and moving to Destiny in the Sierra Nevada foothills to live with Gran.

Torn from her home and friends and terrified for her mother, Paris had been prickly, introverted, and angry, putting on a tough-girl attitude that made her difficult to befriend. Amber Reyes had befriended her anyway. Paris smiled, remembering the kindness of one of the more popular girls in school, Amber had seen through her toughness, her 'who-cares' veil of indifference, and had done her best to bring Paris into her social group.

By junior year, Paris had begun to fit in. That was when she'd first embraced her love of writing, thanks in part to the encouragement of Mr. Frantz. He'd come to Destiny High as a student teacher in Mrs. Elam's English class. He sure didn't look like a teacher, at least no teacher Paris had ever known. Twenty-two, tall and handsome, he won the attention of every girl in school, including Paris, who couldn't help her crush. Little Petey Wells, the class clown, joked that if Paris and the teacher married, her name would be Paris Frantz. "Get it? Paris, France!" Other kids joined in the teasing, calling her Frenchy when they passed her in the halls. Thank goodness that ended when Mr. Frantz left at the end of the schoolyear.

She passed the art room and rounded the corner to room 18. Seeing her aunt at the desk was a bit like looking in a mirror. Jessica and Paris shared the same slender, long-legged frame of all the Kerr women, with the same brunette hair and blue eyes. "Hey, Aunt Jess! How's California's best math teacher?"

"Paris! It's so good to see you!" Jessica Kerr leapt up and slipped around her desk to clasp Paris in a bear hug "How was your drive up?"

Aunt Jess's concern was predictable, though disconcerting. "It gave me time to unwind."

"Are you okay?"

"Bruised but not broken. I just need to regroup."

"What she did to you was so wrong. I'm sure you have grounds to sue—"

Paris held up a hand. "Jess, if you don't mind, I don't want to talk about it. I don't even want to *think* about it."

"I'm sorry, sweetie. On to more pleasant things. Gran is over the moon that you're staying with us. Have you seen her yet?"

"No. She left a note about running some errands and said you'd have my key. What's that about anyway? I don't recall that kitchen door ever being locked."

Jess sighed. "The modern world has finally found Destiny in both good and bad ways. We've had some break-ins lately."

"Break-ins? Real home invasions?"

"Yep. No one hurt, at least not so far. There usually isn't very much taken, and the sheriff thinks it's probably kids messing around. People are starting to be more careful, though. Speaking of which…" Jess dug in her purse and came out with a keyring. "The square silver key unlocks the front door, the smaller silver is for the kitchen door, and the little gold one is—"

"The post office box, right?"

"Right."

"Still Box 214?"

"You remember."

"It hasn't been that long." Paris almost added that remembering one's post office box number was essential in any town too small to have mail delivery.

"No, I guess it hasn't." Jess gave her a long, assessing look. "Have you had lunch? We may have some leftover soup at the house—"

Paris grinned. "Don't worry, Aunt Jess. I'll be fine." She tucked the keys into her pocket. "I'll catch you later, okay?"

"Sure, sweetie. Welcome home!"

"Thanks." Paris leaned in for another quick hug, then threw a wave over her shoulder as she dashed out the door. Only six years older than Paris, Jess seemed more like the big sister she never had rather than an aunt, but that didn't keep Jess from trying to take care of her.

Would it be so bad to let Jess and Gran pamper her for a while? Paris turned that thought over. Maybe it would help her get over the stress left from her recent work debacle. Deep in thought, she smacked squarely into a solid wall of human muscle. Startled, she looked up into the man's face. "Mr. Frantz? What are you doing here?"

"Nice to see you too, Ms. Cutler."

Paris felt a blush heat her face. "Sorry if that sounded rude, and I'm sorry I smashed into you. Guess I had my head in the clouds."

"No worries. Hey, do you have a minute to catch up?" He inclined his head toward the quad.

Paris nodded. "Lead the way."

They sat on the half-wall that separated the school office from the student quad. Greg Frantz, now Destiny High's principal, filled her in on his last eight years. He'd completed his credential and begun teaching at an inner-city San Jose school. "Don't get me wrong, I enjoyed the classroom, and that feeling of being able to reach students one-on-one, but I soon realized I could have more impact elsewhere. I started taking night classes to prep for administration. Then I heard Mrs. Elam was retiring, and I applied to be the new English teacher."

"So you left a big school to come..." Paris gestured around her. "*Here*?"

"I had good memories here and enjoyed the school." He shrugged. "Easy choice."

"But you were planning to get into administration—"

"And Mrs. Elam was the part-time vice principal, so replacing her was a way in."

Paris frowned. "I still don't understand why someone working in a

big city would come to a dying Gold Rush town. I could hardly wait to get out of Destiny."

"Hey! Destiny isn't dying. Far from it. There's quite a bit going on…but you can hear about that later. What brings you back?"

"I'm not back. At least not permanently."

"I hear you have a promising career of your own. Technical writing, isn't it?"

She arched a brow. "How did you hear that?"

"Mrs. Bailey tries to keep track of all our alumni. Besides, your Gran is quite the cheerleader."

"Sounds like Gran." Paris quirked a smile. "But go on with your story. How did you move to the front office?"

"I'd only been year a few months when Bill Ross announced he was taking a teaching job in San Diego. I applied for the principal's job that same day. The school board interviewed half a dozen by telephone, then brought two other candidates and me in for personal interviews. The first one bowed out after she saw the town. I guess I impressed them more than the other guy. Rumor has it you're staying?"

Paris sighed. "Rumor. That's one constant about Destiny, but yes, I'll be staying a while. How long, I can't—"

Mrs. Bailey poked her head around the office door. "Mr. Frantz? You're needed on the phone. Oh! Sorry to inerrupt."

"No problem." Paris stood. "I need to get going anyway."

"Hang on, Paris." Mr. Frantz turned to the school secretary. "Mrs. Bailey, please tell the caller I'll be right there."

"Oh. Yes. Will do." She nodded and disappeared inside.

He turned back to Paris and grinned. "Hey, sorry to cut our chat short. Maybe we can get together soon?"

"Sounds good. I'll be around."

Mr. Frantz grinned, his eyes crinkling at the corners. "Great. I'll be in touch." He gave her a little wave and stepped into the office.

Paris ambled toward the parking lot, her thoughts buzzing. Who'd have thought the gorgeous Mr. Frantz would return to Destiny? As she drove toward Gran's, she was still befuddled. One thing was certain: The years had been good to him. Mr. Frantz looked every bit as marvelous as he did when he was a student teacher, even better. Back then, he didn't appear much older than the senior boys, but the years had given his boyish good looks a rugged maturity.

Mr. Frantz had always been kind and encouraging, especially about her writing. And he wanted to catch up? Paris wasn't sure whether to take his offer seriously. She sighed as she turned onto Gold Pan Road. She hadn't planned to stay more than a few weeks, just enough time to decompress and figure out what to do next. With her favorite teacher now living in Destiny, she would no doubt run into him again, and that made her feel better about coming back.

FROM HIS OFFICE WINDOW, Greg Frantz watched Paris leave, her shiny brown hair swinging behind her, the rest of her swaying attractively. His student teaching stint in Mrs. Elam's English class had been his first time in front of a classroom. He'd been so nervous, barely twenty-two and not that much older than the senior boys.

He remembered almost every student he'd taught then. Sixteen-year-old Paris Cutler had been a mixture of angry stay-away vibes and a vulnerable need to be sheltered and included. He remembered how prickly she'd been when she lost her mother in mid-year, orphaned at sixteen because of her father's earlier death. He also remembered her talent for writing. In his new-teacher idealism, he'd wanted to encourage and develop her ability.

Mrs. Elam had lectured him about the importance of maintaining professional distance, wisdom he had heeded. He knew the horror stories about teachers losing their jobs due to improper conduct with young students, or sometimes, just the kids' accusations.

He couldn't help feeling flattered when girls giggled as he walked by, but he'd kept his distance. When he started the lunch-hour writing club, almost all those who came were girls, and some went to great lengths to get his attention. He'd made sure to meet them in a group setting with the door open and always discouraged flirtation. Paris had never been among the gigglers and had generally withdrawn from the flirting and the who's-dating-whom gossip. He'd been drawn to her because of her sad situation, yet even in her sorrow, she'd been pretty with her lovely blue eyes and delicate features. Now that childish prettiness had matured into adult beauty.

He blew out a breath and flipped open his agenda, trying to recall the details of the phone call he'd just finished. He hoped to run into Paris again. Maybe he'd even try to arrange it.

Chapter Two

C omfortably ensconced in her favorite easy chair, Paris relaxed in contentment. The joy of delicious food and gentle pampering felt good. "Gran, that was the best dinner I've had in weeks. Thank you so much."

"You're welcome, sweetie." Annette Kerr beamed at her only grandchild.

"Your chicken pot pie is one of my favorite meals and you made it all from scratch, didn't you? Even the crust."

"Guilty as charged." Gran grinned. "Store-bought is never as good."

"She's been buzzing around here ever since you told us you were coming," Jess cut in. "Those peas were from Gran's garden, shelled this afternoon."

Paris clucked her tongue, shaking her head. "Chicken pot pie, fresh peas, hot yeast rolls—you really went out of your way."

Gran waved the compliment away. "Nothing too good for our Paris, is there, Jess?"

Jess grinned. "And you haven't even seen dessert yet."

"Dessert, too? Are you trying to fatten me up, Gran?" —

"I've always thought you could use a bit of meat on those bones, but no, this dessert won't do that. I bought fresh cherries at Gale's Produce Stand. We can eat them as they are."

"Oooh!" Paris sat straighter. "I'm crazy about cherries."

"I know." Gran brought out three bowls of plump cherries from the kitchen.

As they nibbled, Jess and Gran continued catching Paris up on the changes in town. Paris knew local news verged on gossip since people had little else to talk about but each other, but Gran also filled her in on plans for the Spring Fling arts fair. "We have artists and crafters from all around the mountains coming and even a handful from the valley. We're planning for nearly fifty booths in the park next month."

"We?" Paris asked. "Did you get drafted onto the committee?"

"She volunteered." Jess smirked like the Cheshire cat.

"Really, Gran?"

"I've enjoyed the arts fair for years. Seemed like time I started helping." She deterred further attention by adding, "Jess, why don't you tell her about changes at the high school?"

Jess nodded. "Since we got our new principal—"

"Mr. Frantz. I met him this afternoon, right after I saw you."

Gran chuckled. "Did you really? You know, he and Jess—"

"Gran, Paris knows." Jessica cut in. "That is, she knows there's always an adjustment period between faculty and a new principal."

"But—"

"Really, Mom, it wasn't that big a deal. Here, let me take your bowls, girls. I'll get rid of the pits." Jess buzzed about the room. To Paris, she added, "We disagreed about whether I could handle an Advanced Placement class on top of the regular curriculum. In the end, I taught both. It worked out fine." As she bent to take her mother's bowl, she whispered something in her ear.

Paris couldn't help wondering what that was about, but she shrugged it off. Whatever it was, she wouldn't be in town long enough for it to make a difference.

Long after Gran and Jess went to bed, Paris lay awake in her old upstairs bedroom, memories drifting about her. Looking back, she recognized how her junior year had been a hinge point, and how Mr. Frantz had taken a leading role in the change. A memory flashed, as fresh as if it happened yesterday. She sat beside Mr. Frantz's desk as he worked with her on an assignment in his lunch-hour writing group. One of their first tasks was to document a recent event, complete with description and dialogue. "You're really just trying to see if we know how to punctuate quotations correctly, right?" She pushed her paper forward, confident in her ability to place quotation marks and commas.

"That isn't all." He tapped the paper. "Paris, why did you pick this scene?"

"I dunno." She shrugged. "Because it was fresh in my mind, I guess."

"You are showing us the women in your family—you, your mother, grandmother, and aunt—talking about your mom's latest doctor visit. The news is all bad, yet you aren't showing any emotion. The dialogue is flat. I suspect you chose to write about this conversation because it has deep meaning for you, but you haven't shown us what that is. Why not?"

Again, she shrugged, dropping her eyes. "I don't know..." She couldn't go on because she *did* know. She barely whispered, "Because it hurts."

"I know it does. Show us the hurt. Get it out on paper."

"But—"

"You may even find it helps."

Looking back, she recalled how he'd had to work to convince her. Perhaps because she'd been crushing on him, she wanted to show how strong she was. She certainly didn't want anyone else to see her scribblings, so she'd talked him into letting her leave her new journal in a locked drawer in his classroom. Then she extracted a promise, practically a blood oath, that he would never read it, never even open the cover. And with that, she began to write.

She shared the unreasoning and unreasonable anger she felt toward her mother for being sick, and the guilt she felt for that anger. She raged about her father's death and the unfairness of being left by one parent with the second about to abandon her. She wrote about the days she didn't feel like going to school or doing much of anything, and about how the other kids' normal teen squabbles and crushes seemed trivial compared to the life-and-death drama in her family.

She'd written it all out and, as Mr. Frantz said, she discovered it helped. She felt more at ease dealing with ordinary, everyday stuff at school and less angry in her response to her mother's terminal diagnosis. She started trying to make things easier for her mom, for them all.

One day, near the end of the school year when her mother was gone and Mr. Frantz was preparing to leave, she brought him her journal.

"I thought you didn't want me to read this."

She pushed the book toward him. "Just the last two pages. Please?"

He held the pages in front of him and quickly scanned through. Paris watched him smile, blink a little, and smile again as he read her note thanking him for helping her through a rough time. He finished, put the pages down, and said, "It was my pleasure. I hope things work out for you. You have a good life ahead of you and great potential as a writer. I'd love to see you fulfill your dreams and be happy."

"I plan to," she said. "I'm going to." She longed to say all she truly felt, but caution stopped her. "I...I hope you have a good life too."

"Thank you, Paris."

She'd thought at the time that it seemed he also wanted to say more, but maybe she just wished it.

"Well, I'm sure you have things to do." He stood and the spell was broken, but Paris had clung to that moment. She had gone on to use his technique of journal writing to work through other difficult times in her life. Eight years later, she was glad she hadn't embarrassed herself with a declaration, but she'd always reserved a corner of her heart for the teacher who'd encouraged her and believed in her, helping her through the most difficult time of her life.

Chapter Three

For most people in Destiny, Saturday morning meant a visit to the Farmers' Market. Paris loved buying fresh produce at outdoor markets, something she did regularly in the Sacramento Valley. Although the markets there were larger, Destiny had some perks.

"Pick up some potatoes while you're there!" Gran called as Paris headed out the door.

"Will do!" Paris waved over her shoulder.

The weekly market had begun informally when a group of back-yard growers organized to sell surplus produce. The Gale family, who ran the produce stand, had seen the farmers as a threat and tried to shut them down. Then they came to an arrangement. Now farmers and crafters set up their stands in the back of Gale's parking lot each week and paid a small rental fee. In turn, the business at Gale's Produce Stand went up since people who came for produce often purchased other items at the store.

One thing Paris liked about Destiny was its sense of common purpose and community spirit. She couldn't imagine living here, since she preferred the excitement and energy of a big city, but she still could appreciate the positives of small town living.

She bought some fresh-picked broccoli and baby spinach from Mrs. Yang, who'd been her sixth-grade teacher the first time she and her mom moved to Destiny.

"I heard you're back in town," Mrs. Yang said as she passed her change.

"Not for long," Paris replied.

"That's too bad. You were one of my best and brightest. It's good to have you back." Mrs. Yang still had the sweet, motherly smile Paris remembered. "You know, I kept the card you made for me on the last day of school."

"Really?"

"It was lovely. You were always one of my more creative students. I hope you'll think about staying. We could use your energy!"

Paris was touched by Mrs. Yang's sweet words, and her gentle reference to energy. Mrs. Yang had been her most patient teacher. Sometimes, when Paris couldn't stop fidgeting at her desk, Mrs. Yang would whisper in her ear that maybe she could use a little walk in the fresh air. Paris generally ended up running and skipping around the school yard or climbing on the playground equipment. After a few minutes, Mrs. Yang would step out and wave her in. She always found it easier to focus after some time outside.

Paris chatted with other old acquaintances including Mr. Walsh from the hardware store, who sold her a pair of handmade abalone earrings, and Gran's neighbor Eleanor Heinz, who talked Paris into buying a batch of fresh baby beets.

Produce in hand, Paris paused to chat with Caroline Reed, listening to her mother's old friend update Paris on her daughters, Tegan and Teal. One year younger than Paris, the twins sang with their cousins in the rising country-pop band, Daughters of Destiny. Locals had followed the women's careers and Paris enjoyed catching up on their progress.

"Where are the ladies now?" she asked after hearing the band was on tour.

"They're in the southwest this week: Albuquerque, Santa Fe, Phoenix. Their concert venues are bigger since they hit the Billboard charts for the second time."

"When you talk with them again, tell them I said hello."

"I'll do that."

A "yoo-hoo!" from across the way interrupted them.

"Be careful," Mrs. Reed warned, dropping her voice. "Lucy Grimes wants volunteers for her Gold Rush Days committee. She'll draft you if she can."

Paris chuckled. "I don't think I'll be in town long enough for that."

Moments later, Paris told Lucy the same thing, not that Lucy seemed to listen. She was still talking about the various places where the committee could use her help as Paris backed away, waving her goodbyes.

Through the rest of the market stalls, Paris paused to chat with people she hadn't seen in years, speaking or waving hello to almost everyone. In her Sacramento apartment building, she didn't know people who lived in the apartments on either side of her. If that was because she'd been too busy or because she didn't make the effort, she didn't know. Being friendly seemed so effortless in Destiny where everyone knew everyone else.

She stepped out from the shade of the booths into the bright sunshine. Busy digging into her purse for her sunglasses, she wasn't watching where she was going when she walked into a solid wall of human muscle. Again.

"Easy there! We've got to stop meeting like this." A deep voice chuckled.

She knew that voice. An arm wrapped around her shoulders and steadied her, and it took a mortifying extra second before she drew away. How could she have been so distracted again? "Mr. Frantz! I'm so sorry! I didn't see you!"

He grinned. "I guessed that, and please, call me Greg. Are you all right?"

She wondered if her face looked as red as it felt. "Great. Good. Um…"

"Your grandmother told me I'd find you here. I had a thought to bounce off you. Can we talk? The park bench across the street?"

"Sure."

He took her elbow as they crossed Main Street, keeping up small talk about the weather. She tried to hold up her end of the conversation, but she couldn't help being distracted by the auburn glint of the sunlight on his hair; his eyes, still the color of dark chocolate; the wink of a dimple in his left cheek; his square chin and the way his mouth turned up at the corners…

She realized he'd asked her a question, something about the range of projects she worked on. She gave herself a mental shake with a firm reminder that she was no longer a schoolgirl crushing on the cute student teacher. "I, um, I worked on many projects, not just user manuals."

"Did you do any grant writing?"

"No. I did something like it, though. Our firm often acquired new clients through a bidding process. I suppose a Request for Bids like we see in business may be similar to a Request for Proposals."

"I suspect you're right."

Paris connected the dots. "Does the school have a shot at a possible grant?"

He nodded. "The Will and Melissa Bates Foundation has earmarked funds for foreign language classes in small, rural high schools and they've sent out a Request for Proposals, an RFP. Winning their grant would allow us to build a computer language lab. That way we could offer students access to online classes in Mandarin, Japanese, French, and half a dozen other languages we can't afford to give here."

"I remember. When I was in school, we had the choice of taking Spanish with Mrs. Delgado or commuting down the hill three times a week to the junior college—with permission, of course."

"And you took Spanish."

"I'm surprised you remember." The realization warmed her.

"It's not surprising, really. I was one of those who had to give permission. Well, Mrs. Elam was, and she assigned that job to her student teacher." He smiled, a look that said you-know-how-that-is. "You never requested permission. Besides, I sometimes heard you and Amber Reyes practicing in the hall."

Memories swarmed her. "Amber had a head start," Paris said. "Her grandparents spoke no English. Her parents spoke excellent English but tried to use Spanish at home. When I wanted to *practicar*, I went to the Reyes family. They always made me feel welcome."

"They're good people." Greg straightened. "But back to the RFP. Could we talk you into popping over next Monday or Tuesday to take a look?"

She hesitated a moment and then pulled her phone and checked her calendar for Monday. "Sure. I have a couple of things to take care of—banking, stuff like that. I can stop at the school office after."

"Great. I'll let Mrs. Bailey know." He stood and held out his hand.

Paris stood as well and took his hand, completely unprepared for the tingle that went up her arm. She hoped she didn't show how his touch had affected her, but she couldn't help noting the brief glimpse of surprise on Greg's face. Was it possible he'd felt the same rush she had?

"Well, um...I'll see you soon," he said.

"Yes, probably Monday." Did he seem reluctant to turn away? Now that she thought of it, she didn't have to do her banking on Monday. She turned toward her car.

"Paris? You forgot your vegetables." He retrieved her cloth bag and passed it to her.

"Thanks," she answered, face flaming.

All the way back to Gran's, she reviewed their conversation and that delightful tingle.

"Did Lucy Grimes draft you for her Gold Rush Days committee?" Gran greeted Paris as she entered the house. "Or maybe even for the Arts Fair?"

"Tell me you didn't sic her on me, too?"

"What do you mean *too*?" Gran looked genuinely confused, but then the light dawned. "Ah! I guess Greg Frantz found you."

Paris set her purchases on the counter. "Yes, he did. That was odd, him hunting me down on the weekend that way." She lifted a shoulder. "Maybe he wanted to get me committed to his school project before Lucy could talk me onto her committee."

"Maybe," Gran answered, but then her tone changed. "Or maybe he's an interesting, single man who has noticed an attractive, available woman."

Paris felt her face warming. "I don't think..."

"Why not? You know, when he was dating—"

"Paris! Glad you're back!" Jessica bounded down the stairs.

Gran glanced toward Jess, then turned to Paris. "As I started to say—"

Jess laid a hand on Gran's shoulder. "Mama, we talked about this. Paris has been away for a while. Let her form her own opinions."

"But—"

Jess short-circuited whatever her mother had meant to say by reaching for Paris's cloth bag. "Let's see what you got at the market."

Gran tossed a frown at her daughter.

Jess commented on the high quality of the broccoli.

Gran asked, "Where are the potatoes? Still in the car?"

Paris grimaced. "Oh Gran! I forgot! I didn't write it down and I guess I got—"

"Distracted," Jess filled in. "I'll run out and get them, Mama."

"No need." Gran shrugged, but disappointment tinged her words. "I thought potatoes would be nice, but we can make do with what we have."

"I'm so sorry. I didn't mean to for—"

"I know, dear." Gran patted her hand. "It'll be fine. There are plenty of lovely veggies here, and I have more from the garden."

Jess picked up her purse. "I'm going into town anyway. I'll stop by the post office to pick up our mail and I'll be near the Farmers' Market. I can easily get the potatoes."

"No, please, I can go back." Paris picked up her purse.

"No." Jessica's tone dissuaded argument. "I'll take care of it." She kissed her mother's cheek and strode across the kitchen. "See you soon."

Paris was still upset she'd forgotten. "Gran, I—"

"Don't worry about it, love. Jess will get the potatoes." Gran busied herself with putting the produce away.

Paris sighed as she helped Gran, frustrated with herself for forgetting such a simple item. Seemed she had a knack for getting easily distracted. She'd often returned from the store with a bag full of groceries, realizing she'd forgotten the very thing she'd gone out to buy. She recalled her mother gently teasing her when she was a girl. *"Paris, were you sitting in the clouds again?"*

How she missed her mom! Her memories of her dad were less clear, but she remembered seeing her mom and dad hug each other before he left for work in the mornings, and she recalled sitting at the dinner table, giggling with her mom over something funny her dad had said.

Was it possible her problems at work could have been avoided if her parents were still alive? Might she have gone to them with the problems before they got so serious? Might they have given her the advice she needed? She sighed. She'd never know.

Once again resolving to do better next time, Paris busied herself with putting away vegetables and tidying the kitchen. She might have forgotten before, but she could be useful now.

Chapter Four

Mrs. Bailey looked up from her computer with an exaggerated sigh. "Greg Frantz, will you *please* stop pacing? You're as nervous as a field mouse at harvest time. Is something going on?"

Greg turned from the window, carefully composing both his face and his response. "Remember I told you I've arranged for help with that grant for a language lab? I expected she'd be in this morning."

"Oh good! There's the spare computer station in the conference room and... Wait!" Mrs. Bailey's eyes narrowed. "*Grant writing. She.* This wouldn't have anything to do with a certain Destiny grad who stopped in last Friday, would it?"

"Yes, it does." Greg gave himself a quick mental kick. Miranda Bailey had been Destiny High's office manager for more than twenty years. She was a remarkable school secretary and knew every student by name, both current and past, but she also tended to gossip. It had been an issue in the past when it came to his personal life, something he had to address politely but firmly. He hoped he wouldn't have to do it again. "Paris is a *tech writer*," he said with emphasis. "She doesn't do grant writing per se, but she has related experience. We're going to try—"

The office door opened, presenting a gangly boy who looked nervously at Greg and Mrs. Bailey, clearly aware he'd interrupted. "Uh, Mrs. Bailey said I had to bring a doctor's note before I could come back to school."

Mrs. Bailey motioned the boy nearer. "That's right, Hayden. We can't be too careful with strep. Here, let me see that note."

Greg nodded to the student. "Welcome back, Hayden. I'll let Mrs. Bailey take care of you." He slid into his office, but he hadn't quite closed his door when he heard another voice, a familiar female voice that brought a smile to his lips.

"Hi, Mrs. Bailey. Mr. Frantz said you could use some help with a grant proposal?"

"We certainly can," the secretary answered. "Mr. Frantz is in his office. Go right in."

Greg pulled the door open, eager to see Paris, and noted the gleam in Miranda Bailey's eye. He sighed inwardly. *So much for a gossip-free zone.*

"I THINK I can take it from here. Why don't you let me scratch out a draft and then you can have a look?"

"Yeah. Sure. I'll leave you to it then." Greg stood and started for the library. Then he added, "We appreciate your help."

"Glad to be useful." She smiled.

He closed the door behind him.

Paris sighed with relief and began to format the document. She couldn't help wondering if something was off. They'd gone over pretty much everything in the first half hour, but Greg had stayed and seemed to keep repeating himself. She'd ended the meeting so she could finally get started. Was he unsure about her ability to do the job? She hoped she'd be up to the task. It would keep her busy and get her mind off her job woes. And it was good experience.

Despite her anxiety about the proposal, she couldn't help noticing how attractive Greg was. She needed to get away from those dark chocolate eyes if she planned to get any work done at all. After all, her days of being a silly schoolgirl were well behind her. She'd dated in college and had a steady boyfriend for a while after graduating from the university, but she'd been single for more than two years, and hadn't thought much about serious dating given how time consuming her last job had been. And yet Mr. Frantz... Greg... still had the power to make her pulse race and her body tremble. And he was a nice man, one who'd been kind to her at a time when she'd doubted her worth, when she'd carried so much anger.

She looked at the mostly blank screen and reminded herself that she'd come here to write a grant for the high school, not to crush on its principal.

Paris worked her way slowly through the rather simple Request for Proposals. The Bates Foundation seemed to be looking for projects exactly like what Destiny needed. In her previous job, she'd responded to Requests for Bids that were much longer and more complex, ones that required more twisting and massaging to show how her firm could fit the other company's needs. Those that required the most manipulation were the bids her company inevitably lost. It was far better when the needs of those writing the proposal and those funding it were in tune.

This proposal should be easy. The thought surprised her, yet what she saw in front of her made perfect sense. *I think I can do this!* The project would need a clear but catchy title. She decided to let that cook on her mental back burner and instead began with the project summary, a simple overview of what the high school proposed to do with a Bates Foundation grant. In half a page, she laid out the basics. Later, when she worked on subsequent sections, she'd weave in background information and demographics to add detail. By the lunch bell, she'd roughed out a skeleton draft. She was saving her document when Mrs. Bailey popped in.

"Ready to take lunch?"

"I...um...yeah, sure." Paris did a quick recovery. "What's the cafeteria serving today?"

"Not sure, but they always have a choice of two hot dishes as well as sandwiches and salads."

Paris turned back to her draft. Despite her misgivings, this project had proved interesting, even absorbing. She decided to work a little longer. "Could you bring me back a sandwich?"

"Any special kind?"

"Anything is good. Thanks, Mrs. Bailey."

Engrossed as she was, Paris barely noticed when food appeared next to her workstation. She even had to remind herself to refill her cup at the water cooler, putting it off until she felt overly thirsty. By mid-afternoon, when she realized she'd eaten only half her tuna sandwich, she became concerned about it sitting out and tossed it.

She went back to work, unraveling the specs for the RFP, filling in details, and further persuading herself that she really did know how to do this. She had almost reached the end of one section when the final school bell rang, making her jump in her seat. How had the time passed so quickly? She added a couple of sentences in brackets to remind herself of her intended direction and shut down the computer.

On the way out, as she passed Greg's office, she tapped on the door. When she heard no answer, she tapped again.

Mrs. Bailey looked up from her work. "Oh, he's not in there, Paris. He had to go take care of a student who fainted in the locker room."

"Fainted?" Paris felt the increase in her heart rate. "I hope she's all right."

Mrs. Bailey smiled gently. "Oh, it isn't a *she*. One of the boys overdid it running track and then spent too long in a steaming shower. He'll be all right. Coach Velasquez wanted Greg to check him out, just to make sure he didn't hurt himself from his fall." She looked at the clock. "The boy's mother is probably with them by now. Greg should be back any minute."

"Well..." Paris hesitated. "Tell him I'm done for the day and made good progress. I'll be back by mid-morning tomorrow."

"Planning to do more job hunting in the morning?"

Paris bridled. "Did Greg tell you that?"

Mrs. Bailey sat straighter. "Oh. Uh...no. I thought it was common knowledge that you're staying with your grandmother while you look for work."

Common knowledge, huh? "I see," Paris couldn't help but sigh at how the Destiny gossip mill worked. "I'll be in tomorrow by eleven or so. I'll hit the ladies' room now. If Greg comes back before I leave, I'll tell him myself. If not, please let him know."

"Oh. Oh yes. Will do."

Paris stepped down the hall to the women's staff room. Minutes later, she came out as Greg entered the front office. She followed him in. "How's the patient?" she asked.

"He's fine. Just a bump on the head. He slumped against his locker instead of falling on the floor, so he should be okay. I think Coach Velasquez and I explained what happened so his mom won't need to run him to the hospital. She should probably have his doctor check him to be sure he's okay, though."

"Poor woman, she must have been worried."

"Terrified when she first got here, but I imagine that kind of phone call would disturb any parent. She's okay now. Did I hear you're done for today?"

"Yes. I told Mrs. Bailey I should be in by eleven tomorrow."

"Thanks for your work. I hadn't expected you to stay this long."

Paris arched a brow. "I hadn't expected to. It's just — well, it's interesting stuff." Right then, her stomach growled, its protests embarrassingly loud.

Greg frowned in concern. "Don't tell me you worked through lunch…"

"It was fine. Mrs. Bailey brought me a sandwich."

He sniffed the air. "Tuna?" At her questioning look, he added, "Mrs. Bailey said you didn't get much to eat."

"I was busy," Paris answered, uncertain why she'd gone on the defensive.

"Busy on our behalf," Greg added. "Seems to me the school owes you a meal. Let me get you—"

"I'm sure the cafeteria is closed by now—"

Greg chuckled, a deep, delicious sound she could listen to all day. "For a favor as big as the one you're doing, I think we can manage something better than the cafeteria. How about Louie's?"

"Broadway Louie's Kosher Mexican? Best enchiladas this side of Tijuana?" Her stomach growled again, making its own demands.

"The very same. Are you up for it?"

"You bet!" Then she added, "I'm surprised Louie's is still open. Doesn't seem like there's enough traffic here to keep them in business."

"You may be surprised. People have started coming up from the valley to check out the 'quaint little Gold Rush towns.' We're seeing good tourist traffic lately. Of course, it's mostly weekends and holidays until summer, but local business keeps Louie open in between."

She nodded. "Good to hear."

They continued chatting as he led the way toward the parking lot.

A few students in the halls gave them speculative looks. Despite some new move-ins, Paris still knew most of the local families and hoped there wouldn't be any rumor mongering. After losing both her parents, she'd been the subject of more than her fair share of gossip, both at school and in the community. When people looked their way, Greg gave them an amiable smile and continued chatting. Paris tried to calm her concerns, reminding herself that she wouldn't be here long enough for the gossip to make any difference, but she couldn't help feeling the stares following them as they left.

She paused in surprise when Greg led her to a clean, sensible, mid-size sedan. "You drive a family car?" She lifted her eyebrows.

He tilted his head to one side. "I didn't think of it that way. I wanted a vehicle I could use for driving a prospective teacher around town or to welcome a vendor or—"

"…take a grant writer for a late lunch?"

He chuckled. "Yes. Exactly." He escorted her to the passenger side and closed her door, then zipped around the back and slid into the driver's seat. "Glad to see you've buckled up."

"Glad to know you're safety-minded."

"I have to be. I've subbed in too many driver's ed classes."

"Ooh. I remember those movies."

"Then you know what I'm talking about. Thank goodness we don't show the scare-tactic films anymore—not here, anyway." He started the engine. "Broadway Louie, here we come."

Chapter Five

F rom its front door sculpture of a stylized Chinese lion to the full-size replica of a Central Park carriage pulled by a plastic horse, Louie's was every bit as quirky and eccentric as Paris remembered. "I've often wondered: Do tourists come here for the food?" She gestured around her. "Or for this?"

"A little of both, I suspect. And maybe partly for the great views of the valley you can see from the parking lot. I often see people shooting pictures from there."

"Good point."

He drew out a chair and held it for her as she sat. He'd barely seated himself before a server appeared, a young man in blue jeans and a scarlet t-shirt with the slogan, "Louie Sent Me." He set down their menus. "Welcome to Broadway Louie's. What can I get you to drink?"

Greg ordered a soft drink and Paris followed suit.

Louie's menu also looked as she remembered. "My favorite has always been the shredded beef enchiladas with red sauce." She laid her menu on the table.

"Hmm. You like it hot."

"You betcha, and Louie's red chili is some of the hottest around."

"As you said, the best this side of Tijuana." He set his menu atop hers. "I had those recently, though. I think I'll have the signature tamale pie."

She smiled. "My second favorite."

The server returned with their drinks and took their food order. "I should have that to you soon," he said.

After he left, an awkward silence ensued, as if neither knew where to start. Paris knew her memories of Greg's year as a student teacher were surely different from his, and probably best kept to herself. But after a few minutes they were chatting easily, almost like old friends catching up.

Paris cautiously kept some details of her life in the valley to herself, but she found Greg so easy to talk to that she shared more than she realized.

"It sounds like you had a great job. Why did you leave?"

She glanced away, considering how much she wished to reveal. "Creative differences," she finally replied. "When they began to disrupt the working environment, I decided to look elsewhere."

"You're submitting resumes?"

"I've been selective, but I respond to a couple of ads every day and I've sent emails to my network, asking if they know of anything." She squirmed. "It's tougher out there than I thought."

Their food arrived and the conversation slowed as they ate. "You worked on the proposal today," Greg said after a time. "What do you think of our odds?"

"That may depend on who else applies." She hedged, not wanting to get his hopes up needlessly. "But it looks like the Bates Foundation wrote this RFP with Destiny in mind. Foreign language training is high on their list of priorities, and they state a need to serve underprivileged and low-income communities. All things considered, I think your chances are good."

"I'm glad you think so. Any idea how long it may take you to finish?"

"Why?" She quirked a smile. "Are you afraid the school can't afford more late lunches?"

He grinned. "If the school can't, I can. But I know the deadline is coming and—"

"No worries. We have eleven days before the final draft is due and I expect to be done by the end of the week."

His brows shot up. "*This* week?"

"You're surprised?"

"And impressed! This is what happens when you find a pro. It would have taken me the rest of the month. Even then I'm not sure I'd have come up with an acceptable draft."

"You don't give yourself enough credit."

"And *you* don't appreciate how grateful we are to find someone who knows what she's doing."

They chatted as they finished their meal and returned to the school. He led the way, his hand brushing her back as they passed through the parking lot, smiling at the students—and some adults—who gave them curious glances. When they reached her car, he waited until she was belted in, then leaned on the open door. "Thanks again for your work today."

"Thank you for the lunch."

"My pleasure." He closed her door and waved. Paris drove away, feeling better about a workday than she had in months.

THAT MONDAY BEGAN a pattern that lasted through the week. Paris started her job search early each day, going through the online job boards and applying for positions that seemed a good fit. She put out feelers with her contacts, hoping something might come that way. By mid-morning, she arrived at the high school and went to work on the draft proposal. Then Greg took her out for a late lunch after school let out.

On Tuesday they returned to Broadway Louie's. Paris chose the tamale pie and decided it was no longer her second favorite but tied with the enchiladas for first. Wednesday found them at Aubrey's Burger Grill, conspicuous at an outdoor table where every passerby could see them. She reminded herself that she wouldn't be around long enough to be affected by gossip.

The possibilities for buzz about town got worse on Thursday when Greg picked up their order at Joe's Sandwich Stop and they ate on a bench in the park, the weather barely warm enough to be comfortable. Paris thought they must have seen half the community wander by. A few stopped to chat, while others waved or nodded. In a community the size of Destiny, being seen eating a sandwich together in public created prime fuel for the gossip machine.

By the time she shut down her computer Thursday, Paris wondered if her daily outings with Greg might be making things more complicated. They were starting to feel more like lunch dates rather than lunch with a colleague. She remembered the way Gran taught her to limit the zucchini harvest by pinching off the blossoms. "Nipping it in the bud" kept the blossom from growing into a squash and besides, the flowers made a pretty addition to a summer salad.

Despite Gran's advice, she didn't want to offend Greg. She wouldn't want to hurt him by building up false expectations either. She'd sometimes read people wrong in the past and ended up causing needless misunderstanding. Could she be reading Greg wrong? Was he just being friendly or was there something more in his interest? Funny, back when she was in high school, she would have been thrilled by all this attention. Greg was funny, charming, handsome, and super smart. But she was all grown up now, and life was more complicated than worrying about a crush on the student teacher.

By Friday morning, she'd applied for several more jobs and decided she wouldn't be in Destiny long enough for any misunderstandings. What would it hurt to hang out with Greg while she was here? Besides, she had been clear from the beginning that Destiny was only a temporary stop. She worked late that afternoon, hoping to complete the project.

When five o'clock came around and she wasn't done, she called it a day. She knew Greg was waiting, so she shut down the computer and met him in the parking lot. He drove them to Berman's Mesa, a top-notch steak house nestled on a ridge overlooking the Sacramento Valley. "The school owes you for everything you've done, but this one's on me," he said as she balked at the prices. "Order anything you like."

Paris hesitated, finally settling on the vegetarian option, one of the least costly. The idea that had been nibbling at her thoughts and stirring her emotions finally rose to the surface. After the server took their orders, she spoke it aloud. "Greg, I appreciate your generosity, but you don't have to keep taking me out to eat as a thank you. I'm trying to help the school, and maybe help myself a little too. Call it a selfish motive."

"Selfish? How?"

"If this proposal is a success and you get the funding, I can add grant writing to my resume."

"I'm glad. It means your work is serving you as well as us."

She took a deep breath. "Is it all about the school?"

He had just picked up his water glass, but he set it down again. "Is *what* all about the school?"

"This." She gestured to the table. "You, taking me out every day. Us spending so much time together."

He raised his hands. "Okay, you caught me. I've been enjoying our outings. In fact, I'd like to extend them."

"That should be easy. This proposal could take me much of the day on Monday as well. How about I treat for Monday's meal?"

"That's not exactly what I mean."

"Oh?" She set down her glass.

"How about a hike and picnic tomorrow? I'm thinking noonish. I'll bring the picnic. There's something up Herbert's Mountain I'd like to show you."

As a child, Paris had chewed her fingernails any time something unnerved her. The habit had been difficult to break and she had to hold onto her water glass to keep from reverting. "I..."

"If you have other plans—"

"No. No other plans. At least, nothing more important than catching up on my laundry." She managed an awkward smile. "It's... You realize I'm not staying, right? I've applied for one or two jobs almost every day this week. None of them are in Destiny."

Greg straightened. "I know, you've been plain about that from the beginning." He laid his hand over hers. "Look at it this way. You're an interesting, attractive woman. I'd enjoy spending more time with you while you're here."

Paris hesitated. The tingling sensations evoked by the touch of his hand made it hard to think let alone speak. "I'd like that too, but can we keep it casual?"

"Of course." He smiled as he gave her hand a gentle squeeze. "So... does tomorrow work for you?"

"Make it 11:30. And I'll bring fresh strawberries. Gran's are starting to come on."

"Sounds great. I'll pick you up at 11:30... or a bit after. I'll head to Joe's as early as I can, but they're busy on Saturdays."

"I won't watch the clock," she promised, wondering if it was true.

Chapter Six

Greg prepared for the picnic with the same care he put into a Parents' Night or a presentation to the school board. He stopped by Joe's after school on Friday, placing his order and making sure to get the same type of sandwich Paris ordered the day they ate in the park. She'd liked that. At the grocery, he picked up sparkling water, as well as insect repellant. At home, he chose the backpack he was going to use and organized how he'd pack everything so he could carry it all. He even thought about what he was going to wear, not something he ordinarily did. It mattered today...but would it matter in a month or two when Paris landed a job in Sacramento or farther away? Was he so drawn to her that he was willing to risk getting his heart broken?

PARIS WOKE EARLY, filled with anticipation. Vague bits of a dream floated through her mind, images of her with Greg. Maybe this was about their upcoming picnic? She wondered where he was taking her and what he wanted to show her. Did he want to talk about their budding friendship or...whatever it was? That part stretched her nerves. Paris couldn't get close to Greg or anyone else, not until she found another job.

The silent house told her Gran and Aunt Jess still slept, and the clock showed she had hours before Greg turned up, so she followed her usual routine. She went downstairs, turned on the heat, opened her computer, and found...

...the perfect job!

It's exactly what I've been looking for! Her pulse quickened as she scrolled through the job description. An up-and-coming software firm was looking for a junior technical writer "with upward mobility." The east-side location in the city suburbs seemed ideal; the firm had cornered a growing niche market and had four years of steadily increasing revenues. The salary and benefits package equaled or topped others she'd seen.

Scrolling through the job requirements added to her excitement. All she had to do was make a few tweaks to her resume and she'd be good to go. She clicked on the file and went to work. A half-hour later, Paris was polishing her cover letter as Aunt Jess made her way downstairs.

"You seem excited." Jess poured herself a cup of coffee.

"I've found a great job listing. I'm finishing my application." Paris looked up. "Ooh! New haircut. I like it."

"I'm not sure if I do." Jess grimaced as she looked in the mirror. "She cut it too short on top. I look like I'm channeling Rod Stewart."

Paris grinned. "You're beautiful, Jess, as you've always been."

Jess rolled her eyes and started some toast while Paris finished her letter. Gran came downstairs, greeting them with a cheery 'Good morning,' just as Paris clicked "Send."

"There. I've applied for my dream job."

"Sounds promising," Gran prompted. "Tell us about it."

"Over breakfast." Paris hopped up. "I hope you're both hungry. I feel like cooking!"

"I'm having toast," Jess said, "but I'll sit with you while you eat."

"Good enough," Paris said. Over French toast and grits with cheese, which even Jess nibbled, she told them about the job. "It's perfect, just what I've been looking for."

Jess raised the delicate question. "You said you need a recommendation letter. Will your former supervisor give you one? I mean, under the circumstances…"

"She will," Paris answered. "She'd better. I told her I'd go quietly and not make a fuss over what she'd done, but that I'd kept good records, and I warned that if she didn't recommend me, my attorney would be in touch with her H.R. department."

Gran looked skeptical. "Are you prepared to go through with something like that?"

Paris set down her fork. "I hope I don't have to, but I can't let that...that *woman's* actions keep me unemployed. Let's hope it doesn't come to that." She pushed away her half-empty plate

"Oh dear." Gran's brow furrowed. "I hope I didn't ruin your appetite."

"Not at all," Paris calmed her. "I overdid the portions. That's all."

"Looks like it's going to be a great day," Jess said in a clear attempt to change the subject. "We had a little rain last night, but the sun's poking out."

Gran persevered. "Are you sure you had enough to eat, love? I didn't mean to upset you."

"I'm fine, Gran," Paris stood and picked up her dishes. "Besides, I want to leave room for Greg's picnic."

"Oh yes," Gran also stood. "You'll want fresh strawberries, of course."

"I'll get them, Gran. Enjoy another cup of coffee."

"Thank you, dear," Gran said, pouring a second cup as she looked out the window. "Jess is right. Looks like it's going to be a pretty day for a picnic."

"It's going to be a beautiful day," Paris declared. It was already off to a great start with her application for a dream job. Spending the day with Greg would be whipped cream atop the sundae.

Greg picked up the sandwiches early. Joe had done a great job and the food looked and smelled fantastic. The familiar streets passed in a blur as Greg focused on his plans for the day. With a sigh, he admitted that his interest in Paris had gone beyond attraction. He *liked* her, liked the woman she'd become, and he wanted to know her better. Something in her called to him and had since he'd seen her again.

What was it about her? From that first day he'd seen her again, he'd been captivated. Yes, she was beautiful, smart, accomplished, but he'd known many women who qualified on all those counts. What made Paris stand out? He didn't know the answer yet. But he wanted to find out. What he did know was that she lingered in his thoughts, and he found himself thinking about her even throughout his busiest workdays.

He saw plenty of lovesick kids at work. Sometimes he had to step in and offer guidance to help one through a broken heart. Would he recognize the signs in himself? He shook that thought away. He was a grown man with plenty of life experience. If things didn't work out with Paris, he wouldn't fall apart. He pulled into the Kerr driveway and set his brake, his mind reacting to the awkwardness of this situation. The last time he'd been here...

But there was Paris, peeking out the front window and waving. Anticipation lifted his heart rate as he parked his car and bounded up the stairs to the kitchen door.

PARIS HURRIED to the side door to meet Greg. Her grandmother caught her as she passed. "I saw the weather report on the news. It's likely to rain this afternoon, love, and lightning can be bad on the mountain."

"I know, Gran. Don't worry. We'll be careful." She flashed Gran a reassuring smile as she opened the door for Greg. "Hi. Would you like to come in while I grab my jacket?"

Greg said, "Sure," and stepped inside. He greeted Paris's grandmother, calling her Annette, and said hello to Jess. Then to Paris, he said, "Here, let me help you with that," and held her jacket while she slipped it on.

"I expect we'll be back before dark," Paris said to Gran. "I'll call if I'll be later."

"Keep an eye on the weather," Gran reminded.

"Will do!"

Gran's warning brought memories of her high school days when Paris rebelled against telling her grandmother or Jess where she was going or when she'd get home. Oh, how bratty she'd been! As an adult she knew to check in as a courtesy. That's what people did when they cared about each other. And that's what she and Greg were, she decided, adults who cared about one another. As they drove toward the mountain trailhead, she told Greg about the perfect job she'd discovered that morning.

PARIS LOOKED around as they hiked. The path Greg chose was lined with new growth on the trees, and thimbleberries just beginning to raise their central stems. She spotted a wild rose near the walkway leafing out and flaunting a few new buds. She inhaled deeply, enjoying the mingling fragrances of flowers, damp moss, recent rain, wet tree trunks, and sweet evergreens. She loved the ocean and hoped to retire near the beach one day, but the high Sierra had its appeal. "It's so lovely here. Thank you for bringing me."

"Give it a minute. The best is yet to come."

A few minutes later, they veered off the main path and approached a fence. As Greg began to climb over, Paris reached for his sleeve. "Are you sure we should be doing this?" Paris pointed to a *No Trespassing* sign. "It's private land."

He grinned. "Don't worry. I have permission."

"You're sure?" Paris looked around nervously.

"Do you think I'd risk it if I weren't sure? How would it look for the high school principal to be arrested for trespassing?" Greg dropped the wire and placed his hand on his heart. "I solemnly swear I have the owner's permission to be here." He picked up the wire again, holding it for her. "Let's get going before that rainstorm your grandmother predicted."

Paris stepped through the fence and followed. At the top of the trail, Greg stopped and put down his pack. Paris turned, taking in the scene. A boarded-up mine shaft signaled the effort someone had made to dig a living from the earth. Someone had also cleared an area near the mine and used the cut logs to build a small cabin. In its time, it must have been a solid, if simple, refuge — its walls sturdy, its metal roof secure. The cabin's door had slipped on its hinges but still held its place, keeping out small animals that had left their tracks on the wide porch. "Plenty of little critters must like this place."

"Um," Greg agreed. "They like it too much, I fear. I'm glad the door keeps them out."

Beside the porch was a heavy table made of a single slab of cut fir, its bench a smaller plank set on two wide stumps. A hawk screeched overhead, the only interruption in the symphony made by the trickling spring and the wind sighing in the trees. Paris tipped her head back, the sun on her face and the breeze against her skin. "This is heavenly," she murmured.

She followed the pathway a few steps to where a pipe tapped into a mountain spring, its open end spilling a steady trickle of clear water into the hollowed-out log that served as a trough for the miner's live-stock. The far end of the trough dribbled into a rock-lined streambed, joining the creek that ran down the hill. Larger animals had left their footprints there.

"It looks like the deer come here to drink." Paris examined the sharp hoof-prints near the trough's lower end, "and something larger too. What do you think made this print? It's almost like a human foot, but…not."

"Don't be alarmed," Greg answered, "but I think it's a bear."

"A bear?" Paris looked up, unable to hide her concern. "Are we in its space or is it in ours?"

Greg smiled back. "I imagine we can easily share the space, so long as we aren't trying to use it at the same time."

"Sounds good to me." She closed her eyes. Tipping her face toward the sun, she spread her arms wide and turned a slow circle, breathing deeply of the pure mountain air. She stopped to find Greg watching her. "This place is so beautiful. How did you ever find it?"

"It wasn't so much a matter of finding it," Greg said. "Come sit at the table. I'll tell you about it while we eat."

"Sounds good." Paris helped him spread a checkered tablecloth and set out the food he'd carried. They sat side-by-side.

"Do you remember an old sourdough prospector who used to live in the area?"

"Do you mean Herbert the Hermit? Everybody wondered where he lived."

"He lived here," Greg answered, "and he was my great-uncle, my grandfather's brother."

"You're kidding!"

"No kidding. His name was Herbert Frantz, although he stopped using the family name when he and Gramps parted ways."

"A family feud? Sounds like a good story. Maybe a sad one too."

Greg nodded, looking thoughtful as he bit into a fresh strawberry. "A little of both. They came here together, maybe sixty or seventy years ago, planning to make a go of the mining claim and homestead my great-grandfather left them." He lifted another berry. "These are great."

"Gran raises good berries." Paris nodded as she selected one. "So old Herbert really was a prospector."

"He thought of himself as a miner. He said his pops had done the prospecting."

"They had a productive claim?"

Greg tidied the remains of their lunch, tucking their trash into a paper bag for the trek down the mountain. "Ever hear of Destiny Diamonds?"

She shrugged. "Just the stories the kids told. I wasn't sure whether to believe them. It sounded like what the locals might tell a new kid, like taking a first-year camper on a snipe hunt."

He grinned. "It does sound a bit fantastic, but it's all true."

"Really? The whole thing? Even about the diamond cartel that bought and closed the mine?"

"The whole thing." He opened the package of chocolate cake he'd bought at Joe's Sandwich Shop and offered her a piece. "Have some dessert and I'll tell you about it."

They each dug into a slice of Joe's Death-by-Chocolate while Greg talked. Paris promised herself she'd stick with half, though the first mouth-watering bite told her restraint would be difficult.

"My great-great-grandfather, Elias Frantz, was the first to homestead here. He came at the end of the Gold Rush when miners were stumbling on Destiny and established a small claim. Later he homesteaded the land as well. He didn't get rich, but he pulled enough ore out of the mountain to buy up some deserted claims and a few abandoned homesteads."

"He must have been one of the founding fathers of the community."

"You'd think so, but the old man didn't much like people. He left others to build the town while he stuck to the hills."

"Interesting guy."

"So they tell me." Greg gathered the dessert plates and Paris was surprised to realize she'd eaten her whole slice.

"He's the one who found the diamonds?"

"Nope. That was my grandpa, Ralph Frantz. That old man knew gold when he saw it, but he didn't recognize the other mineral vein that ran through the same mine. Besides, he was more of a farmer than a miner. He took his dad at his word that the mine was played out and didn't bother looking. Neither of them recognized the treasure waiting to be found—not for a long time, anyway."

"Real gem-quality diamonds?" Paris pulled her jacket close against the chilly breeze.

"Exactly."

"That's hard to believe. Diamonds aren't mined in North America, are they?"

"There's the Crater of Diamonds Mine somewhere in Arkansas, but other than that, no—at least, not to my knowledge. The few mines that produced diamonds have mostly turned up industrial-quality stones and not many of those. That's probably why the old man didn't know what he was seeing."

Paris helped pack up the remains of their lunch. "So how did your grandpa know?"

"Gramps—"

"That would be Ralph Frantz."

"Right. Ralph Frantz was at the university when his father, Elias Frantz, died. He'd heard his dad's stories about the mine and was curious, so he took some classes in mineralogy."

"If no one in North America was mining diamonds, how did he know what to study?"

"He always called it a stroke of luck. One of his professors got involved with a South African mining company. He brought back stories and pictures to share with his classes. Gramps was sharp enough to realize that what he saw in the pictures matched what he'd seen at the old gold claim. He invited a rep from a mining company up to look."

"And they found diamonds."

He nodded. "They did—and as soon as the word got out that they'd found real, gem-quality stones, the diamond cartel came in and made Gramps an offer he couldn't refuse."

"So that was when they bought out your family's claim and sealed the mine shut."

"Right."

Paris nodded thoughtfully. "I'm with you so far, but where does Herbert come in? And if the mine was sold and closed, how did he manage to stay here? And why?"

"That's where the feud comes in. Gramps, that's Ralph, and his brother Herbert had come to this area together, and they planned to reopen the mine together. Gramps was the older brother and the family had agreed to send him to university first. Herbert would get the chance later if all went well."

"Then your grandfather, Ralph, found the diamonds—"

"Yep." Greg tucked the last of their picnic waste into his backpack. "Once Gramps knew the diamonds were there, he arranged to split with Herbert the land and the claims their father had left them, separating into what seemed to be two equal pieces, but keeping the open mine for himself. He managed to keep the diamond discovery quiet, so Herbert didn't know he was being cheated. When the cartel bought and closed the mine, it was Gramps' land they purchased. Gramps had a university education and millions of dollars—"

"And Herbert had nothing."

"You've got it. There's little question that Gramps cheated his brother and did so knowingly. Neither spoke to the other for the rest of their lives."

"I'm so sorry." Paris remembered how it felt to have stress among loved ones. "Secrets and betrayal should never happen in a family."

"I agree. Family comes first, or at least it should."

"How did you get involved?"

Greg sighed. "I loved Gramps. It took me some time to realize what a scoundrel he was and how he'd cheated his brother, but I loved him anyway. By then Herbert was living up here on the mountain, looking for 'color' in the rocks around him and surviving on what he made herding a few head of cattle. He was bitter and angry and wanted nothing to do with our family—or anyone else. He'd become a true hermit."

"So...?"

"So I hiked up the mountain and pretended to be an interested nature-lover. I didn't back down when Herbert threatened me with his shotgun, and I didn't admit I was family. I told him what a beautiful place he had and that I'd like to come up and visit sometimes. I offered him the canned goods I'd carried up and he softened a little. Over time I befriended him."

"And when he found out you were family, he didn't feel betrayed?"

"I never told him. He figured it out for himself, said I looked just like my grandfather. He asked me once why I'd looked him up. By then I knew that he knew, so I told him, 'Because you're my great-uncle and we're family.' He nodded, like he'd known it all along."

"How about your Gramps? How did Ralph take it?"

"I never told him, and he was too self-involved to notice. By the time he died, he'd squandered his millions and alienated the family. Grams went to his funeral out of a sense of obligation even though they'd been divorced for years, and my dad went to support his mother. I was the only other person there, and I'm pretty sure I was the only one who mourned."

"I'm so sorry, Greg."

He shrugged. "I'm also the one who took the news to Herbert. All he said was, 'Good. It's about time the old toad croaked.'"

"It sounds like a morality play."

He nodded. "I suppose it is."

She paused. "Wait! I'm putting this together. I assumed you came to Destiny for your student teaching because it was where you were assigned, but you had roots here." She hesitated as another piece fell into place. "That's why you wanted to come back. It's why you applied when Mrs. Elam retired. You were more invested in this town than anyone thought."

"Maybe more than you know," he answered, gauging her reaction.

The realization hit her. "Herbert left his share to you, didn't he? This cabin is yours."

"This whole side of the mountain is mine." He watched her carefully as he added, "And there's a possibility that Herbert's old mine connects to the other end of the diamond vein."

Chapter Seven

P aris stilled, absorbing what she'd heard. "Greg, that's...that's amazing. Do you plan on pursuing that? Looking for the diamond vein, I mean."

"I've already had a couple of mining experts up here looking at the place, sharing their findings."

"That helps me understand why you wanted to come here. And it's a lovely place. I can see why you love it up here on the mountain. But Greg? Why tell me this? Why did you want me to see this?"

"Because I want you to understand that Destiny has a future, not just a past."

She nodded thoughtfully. "I remember you saying the town has growth potential. Opening a diamond mine would surely change things. There's one thing I don't understand. Why did you want *me* to see this?"

"Because—" He sighed in frustration and drew close. He smelled of ginger and lime and clean, male skin. He leaned in and kissed her.

From the moment Greg's lips touched hers, Paris drifted in a world of sensation, of magic. After several heart-stopping moments, she opened her eyes, returning to the world.

"I've wanted to do that for a while," Greg said.

"That was—" She paused, drawing in a deep breath, and expelling it slowly.

"Wonderful? Inspiring? Totally repeatable?" Greg prompted.

"Unexpected."

"You must have felt the attraction between us."

"I felt it, but I wasn't sure *you* did." She sighed. "I'm still a little... in awe of you."

A bemused smile curved his lips. "In awe? Of me?"

"You know, the favorite teacher thing."

He touched her hand. "It's been a long time since then."

"Eight years." Paris thought of the job application she'd turned in that morning. "Why are you doing this now, when you know I'm not staying?"

"Because I like you. A lot. Because there's something good starting between us and I don't want you to leave before we have a chance to see where it goes."

She suppressed a sigh. "If the job I just applied for comes through, I could be leaving very soon, possibly within days."

"How far away would this job be?"

Together they calculated a travel time of roughly ninety minutes. Greg said, "That's doable."

Paris said, "Is that far enough away to be considered a long-distance relationship? Those usually don't work."

"It's not that far," Greg argued. "But let's worry about that later. We have time together before anything changes. We'll focus on that."

Paris didn't realize she'd been holding her breath until she slowly released it. "Okay. I'd like that."

He stood and held out his hand. "Come on. I'll show you around."

She popped up. "Good. I'd like to see what your family created here."

They spent another hour checking out Herbert's homestead. Greg showed her where his uncle had grazed cattle. He carefully wrenched open the cabin door and showed her inside—the wood stove Herbert used for both cooking and heat, the board-and-rope bed he had built against the far wall, the cupboard that constituted his kitchen. "He had a privy outside," Greg explained, "but I knocked that down when I first moved back."

"Very nineteenth century." Paris fingered the kerosene lamp Herbert had used for light.

"Yes, even into the twenty-first. I've got a more up-to-date latrine around the corner."

"Show me the mine?"

"I can show you the entrance, but it isn't safe to enter. That's why it's boarded up. But I had enough of Herbert's ore to interest the mining company. They came a couple of weeks ago and used a robotic device to collect samples. If what they find looks promising, this place could soon be back in business."

Paris looked around her. "It would be a shame to see this refuge covered with heavy equipment."

"That's one of the issues we discussed. The company rep left a brochure about the latest techniques, care of the environment, and so forth. It sounds like they'd cause as little disruption as possible. And it would be a nice shot in the arm for the local economy."

"That's what you meant when we first talked about life in Destiny. You said you had ties here and you thought this town might have a future."

He nodded. "That's part of it, but the town has a future even if the mine doesn't. You saw Berman's Mesa. They're down the ridge a little, but their address is Destiny and they're so good they're fast becoming a destination restaurant. People come up from the Valley."

"It makes sense. Berman's couldn't stay alive on local business."

"The mine isn't the only venture that may be moving in." Greg carefully dragged the door behind them so it would keep out vermin. "Remember the old commune? There was a compound not far from where Berman's is now."

"The Children of Rah. I remember. That's why Amber Reyes had her cousins living with her. Their mom was involved in the Rah cult and wasn't doing much mothering."

"Sunny and Skye. I remember them, and I've seen them in town a few times—well, Sunny anyway. Skye isn't around much." He helped her down the steep front steps. "You know the commune closed a few years ago."

"I heard. The absentee owner came up to look. He didn't know the Rah people were squatting there, though they claimed they'd been there long enough to have property rights."

"That's how it began." Greg looked toward the lowering sun. Paris looked too. Dark clouds had begun to gather, and the wind was picking up. "The court case was settled last year," Greg said. By then the Children of Rah had pretty much disbanded. When the cult leader was jailed on drug charges, that wrapped it. The back edge of that property has a gorgeous view of the valley, even better than at

Berman's. The new owner is talking about putting in a destination health spa and resort. That would be another huge boost to Destiny."

"I imagine it would." Paris watched Greg shoulder his pack. "I guess I have a hard time imagining people wanting to drive up here."

"The busier the valley becomes, the more people need an escape. They come to Destiny for clean air, natural surroundings, our 'quaint' business district with its boardwalk and Victorian-era store fronts."

"All four blocks of it?"

He smiled. "All four blocks. Five if you count the old stone church."

"Honestly, Greg. I have mixed feelings about all this. I guess I've always held a grudge against Destiny because I never *chose* to come here, y'know? It was always the place we *had to come* when the rest of our lives fell apart. The first time was a couple of years after my dad died. Mom had been scrimping, living on her small earnings and whatever savings she and Daddy had built and then, a few weeks into my sixth-grade year, things got bad and we had to come here to live with Gran. I don't know everything that went on, but Mom got another job in the valley and we moved back down before I went to seventh grade. Then the cancer..."

She paused. "There's an old quote by poet Robert Frost: 'Home is the place where, when you have to go there, they have to take you in.' That's what Destiny was to me, always our last resort." Thinking of her current situation, she shrugged. "Still is. At the same time, I don't like the thought of this place changing. Not big changes, anyway. It's like it's a last resort, but it's *my* last resort, just as it is. Know what I mean?"

"I believe I do," he said, taking her hand and holding it gently.

Paris blinked back tears that had come unbidden. "Don't get me wrong. Gran and Jess are great. They've always been welcoming and have made me feel loved and cared for, as if they could hardly wait for me to move in."

"Maybe that's exactly how they feel."

She laughed. "Oh, I doubt that! I've never exactly been convenient to have around, but Gran and Aunt Jess have always made Destiny feel like home, even when I didn't want it to be." She gave herself a good shake. "I'm probably not making any sense at all."

"I think you're making good sense. Destiny has made you strong. It has helped to shape the woman you are."

"Maybe." She sniffed, watching him through a veil of unshed tears. "Don't mind me." She wiped her eyes. "Talking about the past is making me emotional."

He stroked her hand. "You have every right to get emotional about your family. I went through some emotion of my own when I found out what Gramps did to my great-uncle Herbert. The thing is, we can't dip towns in plastic and keep them on the mantle. They either grow and change or they shrink and die."

"You're right. Destiny will become a ghost town if something doesn't change. And California already has a wealth of Gold Rush ghost towns."

"That's the way I see it too." They started down the trail. Greg said, "There's a concentrated effort to give Destiny a future, and people you may know are investing in it. I assume you've been chatting with Amber."

"Amber Reyes?"

"Um-hm. She's the principal at the elementary school."

Paris stopped still. "Here? I mean, in Destiny?"

"You didn't know? I was sure you'd spent some time with her by now."

"I'm amazed she's here. She was as eager to get away as I was."

Greg grinned. "She moved back a couple of years ago. I'm sure she'd love to see you."

"I'd love to see her too. I'll reach out to her when we get back."

PARIS ENTERED the kitchen an hour later bare moments before the storm broke. "That must have been some picnic," Jess said. Jess and Gran sat at the kitchen table, shelling peas. The looks on their faces suggested both had seen the farewell at the door, including Greg's brief goodbye kiss.

"We had a great time today." Hoping to hide her blush, Paris turned her back to them and began emptying her tote onto the counter.

Gran spoke. "Did I hear him say he's going to call?"

Paris clucked her tongue. "Gran, were you eavesdropping?" She chuckled at Gran's discomfiture. "But you're right. We're spending time together while I'm here."

Gran said, "And this right after you find the perfect job."

"Yeah. Weird how life works, huh? Give me a few minutes and I'll be back to help with dinner." Paris hurried up the stairs, eager to end that conversation. Minutes later, she returned, glad to find the topic had changed.

GREG CALLED that evening and arranged to take her out the next day after church. Sunday morning came and Paris attended services with Gran and Jess as she always did when in town. She'd seen Greg there before, but this time he met them and sat beside her on the pew.

Their congregation met in the historic stone church built by the town's first minister. Religious or not, everyone in Destiny honored Reverend Lewis, the bold and brawny man of God who came to reform the lawless gold town and served as its first sheriff. He also had skill as a stone mason, as evidenced by the walls of black basalt embellished with rows of green, and the altar of river rock. As she left the building, Paris smiled as they passed the reverend's portrait in the entry. Reverend Lewis was always the honorary grand marshal of the Gold Rush Days parade, no matter which town luminary rode in the convertible and waved to the spectators.

After church, she considered trying to get in touch with Amber, but it felt off. The two had once been close, but they'd drifted apart when they went to different colleges. Over the years, they'd lost touch. Paris thought about calling or finding out where Amber lived now and showing up at her door. Both seemed awkward, especially since she didn't have long before she was to meet Greg. She put off the reunion, deciding to find Amber in her office on Monday.

By mid-afternoon, Greg arrived and drove her downhill to what had once been the compound of the Children of Rah. The last of the storm clouds had passed and the day shone sunny and clear.

"There isn't much left, is there?" she observed, as they entered the clearing where a few makeshift buildings had once stood.

"No. As soon as the court case was settled, the owner hired a contractor to flatten and remove everything. I think that's all they left." He pointed to a rope swing hung from a giant oak. "New construction is set to begin this week, so even this could go. Want to swing?"

"You're kidding."

"Nope."

"I haven't been on a swing since I was eight or nine."

"Then you're long overdue." Greg got out of the car and came around to open her door. "Come on. I'll give you a push to get you started." Greg tested the swing, using his own weight to check the ropes, ensuring all was secure. "These ropes look new. Ready?"

"I guess go," Paris said, sliding onto the wooden seat.

"Hang on!" Greg called, pulling the seat back, getting ready to let it go.

"Wait! Wait!" For one panicky moment, Paris remembered the fear she'd felt as an anxious child approaching swings and slides. Other kids had been merciless in their teasing. *I'm not a child anymore,* she told herself firmly. She took a deep breath. "Okay. I'm ready."

The next minutes were among the most joyful Paris had known in some time. Greg pushed, she pumped, and the swing soared higher. Surprised she wasn't frightened, she pushed until she disappeared into the low hanging leaves before she let the swing slow and finally stop.

"Your turn," she said as she slid off the seat.

"I don't think I can go as high as you did." He grinned as he took her place.

Paris had even more fun with Greg on the swing. She set her hands on his strong back and gave him a push to start. After a few minutes, he slowed and stopped the swing. Then he suggested they walk out to look at the view.

"Oh!" Paris gasped in surprise as they reached the cliff. "What a view! You mentioned you can see the whole valley from here, but I hadn't realized how amazing it is. I can see the Sutter Buttes."

"Right. And clear across to the coastal range."

"And everything in between. This is spectacular." She looked out over the green rice fields, the blossoming orchards, and in the distance, the tall buildings of central Sacramento.

"You can see why a spa and resort might make a go of it here."

"Indeed." Paris turned back, embarrassed as her stomach growled. "The bowl of cereal I ate this morning won't hold me much longer. I don't suppose you brought another picnic?"

"Nope. I'm going to cook for you."

She cocked an eyebrow. "Now you're showing off your domestic side. You're pulling out all the stops, aren't you?"

"You bet. I'm determined to impress you." He said it with a breezy air, but Paris heard steel beneath his words. Knowing Greg wanted to impress her warmed her to her toes. Maybe her teenage hero worship hadn't vanished completely after all.

Chapter Eight

G reg kept the menu simple: steaks grilled outside despite the evening chill, a tossed green salad with cucumbers and grape tomatoes, baked potatoes with all the trimmings, and a loaf of French bread. His home was modest, but well-appointed. The main floor wasn't expansive, but it featured a large, modern kitchen that opened out to the living room. Greg clearly enjoyed cooking. He had all the accoutrements of a chef's kitchen, but Paris could see it wasn't for show. His chopping block had many nicks in it, and he had an array of spices and herbs organized neatly in glass jars with tidy labels. Best of all was the huge window with a lovely view of the forest that grew beyond the perimeter of his backyard.

"This is perfect, Greg. I don't know when I've had a more enjoyable meal." Paris smiled, pushing her empty plate to the side. "You have a nice home, too."

"Thank you. When I moved to Destiny, I knew I was in it for the long haul." He stood. "Would you like a tour?"

"Sure. Let me help you clean up first."

Together they cleared the table and rinsed the dishes, stacking them in the dishwasher. The cleanliness and order in Greg's kitchen impressed her too. Greg had cleaned up as he cooked so there was little left to do.

"Come on," he said, taking her hand. He started by walking her onto the back deck and pointing out the boundaries of his yard. "My little piece of heaven," he said, emphasizing how his land backed up to the national forest, so there'd be no development on the acres behind him. "You've seen most of the first floor," he said, leading her back inside. He made the walk around the lower floor brief, pointing out the laundry area and mud room and the entrance from the garage. "Now the upstairs."

He guided her up the staircase. Three good-sized bedrooms opened onto the landing. One had a desk with a laptop and a comfortable looking office chair. "I use that room for my home office. It works for now."

"Don't tell me you bring your work home too?"

"Well, I try to maintain a good work/life balance." He grinned sheepishly. "But it doesn't always work out that way. How about you? How do you manage the whole work/life thing?"

Paris paused, wondering. Would this be a good opening for discussing her work problems and how they'd impinged on her life? She decided that particular subject would bring the mood down too severely. "I guess I'm like most people," she said. "I try to keep a balance and find that I'm better at it sometimes than others."

"Yeah," he agreed. "I guess most of us are like that."

On the other side of the landing was the master suite. She noted the king-sized bed covered in a simple white bedspread. The master bath was open, so she peeked in. Greg had a huge, walk-in shower with a jacuzzi spa tub beside it. "That's it," he said. "The whole tour."

"It's lovely, Greg." She meant it. There were no frills—many of the walls were bare and there were no decorative pillows or houseplants or other feminine touches—but it felt like a comfortable home, a good place to start a family. Where had that thought come from?

"Thanks," he said as he led her back downstairs. "It's my haven, the place I can unwind after a tough day at school, and I love that it borders the forest, so I'll always have that peaceful view." He had laid a fire in the living room, and he lit it as she watched. "Come sit with me," he said, leading her toward the couch. She inhaled the fragrant blend of the crackling fire mingled with his warm cologne. "More kisses?" she asked without thinking. Then her eyes widened. "Oh! I didn't mean—"

He chuckled. "Don't worry." He ran his hands through his hair in a boyish gesture that made her knees wobble. "Kisses sound great, but I also have something else in mind. I thought we might look at some of the old Destiny High yearbooks. I have them starting with the class before yours and every year since."

"Old yearbooks?"

"It'll be fun. You'll see."

It was. Mostly. Paris remembered most of the upperclassmen—most had been kind, but a few were merciless with their needling and ignorant teasing about her being an orphan and living with her grandma. She smiled and nodded, trying not to think of the cruel jabs and barbs. "Some of those kids were good to me, but others…well, bullying is nothing new."

"No. Kids can be mean sometimes." His voice was gentle. "Often kids become bullies to hide something terrible going on at home."

"True. When I look back, I can see that, but some of those hurtful words stayed with me for a long time."

He slipped his arm around her shoulders and gave her a quick side hug. It felt good, kind, and supportive. She tucked her head into the crook of his arm as they moved through the next yearbook. When they flipped through the ones after she graduated, she was surprised by how many of the students she recognized, mostly younger siblings of people she knew.

After they'd finished with the yearbooks. Greg surprised her with a decadent dessert—more of Joe's Death-by-Chocolate. "I guess you can tell I'm a chocolate fan," he said as he handled her a slice.

"We certainly have that in common." She licked the dark fudge frosting from her fork. "Yum!"

"That does look delicious," he said, and he leaned to taste the chocolate on her lips. "Um, yes," he said. "Delicious indeed."

Over the next few minutes, they enjoyed the dessert, occasionally pausing to share a taste or two. At the end of the evening, he drove her home and gave her another sweet treat on the back doorstep, a kiss that took her breath away. "You know, Paris," he said. "Our choices aren't always between good and bad. Sometimes they're between good and better."

Even though Paris had to be up early on Monday, she had a hard time falling asleep that night, thinking about Greg's kisses, the lovely time she'd had at his home, and choices between good and better.

She had never thought of Destiny as *her* destiny. The town held a lot of bad memories for her. *But it also holds good ones*, her inner voice reminded her. When she finally slept, she drifted away on dreams of swings, chocolate, and a man with soulful, chocolate-brown eyes.

MONDAY MORNING, Paris managed to get up early, despite her lack of rest the night before. She checked her email and was delighted to find a response from the software company asking to arrange a video conference later in the week. She replied, accepting the slot they had open on Wednesday and adding a note about how much she looked forward to talking with them. She was shutting down her computer when Gran came down the stairs. "You look happy."

"I am," Paris answered. "TriTech wants to interview me. They're the ones that make fund accounting software for non-profits."

"That's great!" Gran said. "What's the job?"

"Technical Writer. It means learning new software accommodated to a specific organization and then creating manuals for the end users. It's a challenge, but the kind I love. It's what I've been working toward since I started my writing major at the university."

"And the accounting part? Do you understand that too?"

"Enough. I took a few classes as part of my degree. The rest I can learn on the job, since I won't be doing accounting, just describing how to use the software."

"Sounds promising." Gran paused. "I didn't have a chance to talk to you last night. I went to bed early so I could finish reading that mystery for book club."

"Ah. Did you guess the killer?"

"Well, yes, but then the author made me think it was someone else, so I was surprised when it turned out I'd been right the first time."

Paris chuckled. "Sounds like you read an enjoyable mystery."

"Maybe." Gran settled into a chair. "How did your date with Greg go?"

"Great. He has a beautiful home and he's a fine cook."

"Have you talked with your Aunt Jess? About Greg, I mean,"

"Not really. Why do I need to talk to Jess?"

"It would be a good idea." Gran looked around. "How do you feel about Greg?

"I like him. A lot." Paris paused. "At first there was this leftover crush from high school, you know?"

"I can guess."

"But I'm getting to know him now, including his cool family history. Do you remember the stories about a diamond mine here in town?"

"Yes, but I've always wondered if there was anything to them."

"The stories are all true. That mine was owned by Greg's grandfather and his great-uncle Herbert. Part of it belongs to Greg now."

"Impressive. I knew he had family here from generations ago, and lots of us remember Herbert the Hermit. But I had no idea he was sitting on a gold mine."

"Or diamond mine?"

"That too. Well, you learn something new every day," Gran said. "So our high school principal is also into mining, not to mention he's one fine-looking man."

"Gran!"

"Well, I may be old, but I still have good eyesight."

They both giggled.

"Come on, kiddo. Let's cook some oatmeal while we talk." Gran led the way into the kitchen. "Where do you think you and Greg might be headed?"

"Honestly, Gran." Paris measured water into a saucepan and added a touch of salt. "If Greg lived in the valley or was interested in moving there, I would want to see where this relationship can go. As it is…"

Gran touched her shoulder. "Sweetheart, tell me what it is about the valley that makes it so important to you."

Paris sighed as she leaned against the kitchen counter. "I'm not sure I can put it into words. I know it's tied up with the way Daddy died doing blue collar work all alone in the canyon. And then Mom had to work to support us, and she didn't have an education either." She felt her body stiffen. "I put on blinders. All I could see for my future was earning a good degree and getting meaningful work that paid well. I promised myself I'd be successful."

"And have you thought about what that means to you, being successful?"

Paris huffed. "It means that job at TriTech and a nice apartment in the valley."

"And what else? Does a husband and a family figure in somewhere?"

Paris relented with a sigh. "I suppose so. I've always had this vague image of me married with a couple of little ones, maybe even a mini-van." She smirked. "He'd have to talk me into that, though."

"And when were you going to work that into your life?"

"Later." She started toward the stairs. "I've got to get going. I'm trying to finish that grant proposal today."

"And that means you'll be spending more time with the high school principal?"

"Gran…" Paris paused on the bottom step and arched an eyebrow at her well-meaning grandmother. "I have to grab a shower and get going." She turned and jogged up the stairs.

Behind her, she heard Gran calling, "You really need to talk to Jess."

THREADS of that conversation dangled around Paris as she parked in the staff lot and made her way to the conference room. It didn't make sense. Why should she talk with her aunt? It wasn't a conflict of interest for her aunt if Paris went on a few dates with Greg. Paris didn't work for the high school; she was only doing some volunteer work while she was in town. Besides, Jess was getting into one of the busiest times of her schoolyear. Paris had hardly seen her for days.

Soon Paris was setting up her workstation in the school conference room.

Her phone pinged, reminding her of her promise to call Amber. She dialed the elementary school only to learn that Amber was visiting classrooms and would be away much of the day.

"Can I make an appointment for tomorrow?" Paris asked.

"Not tomorrow. She'll be in the district office."

"This visit is personal. Perhaps if I come at the end of the day?"

The secretary seemed hesitant to commit but agreed on an after-school time slot. Entering the time into her phone calendar and satisfied that she would see her friend again soon, Paris went to work.

~

ALTHOUGH HIS CLOCK seemed to move very slowly, it finally ticked past noon and Greg knew that meant time for lunch duty. Before he went to the cafeteria, he wanted to speak to Paris about a meal at the end of their workday. He stepped into the conference room, but Paris was in deep concentration and hadn't noticed him. He smiled at how focused she was when she worked. It was like she tuned out everything around her. As he made his way to the cafeteria, he pondered on his life since moving to Destiny. Although he'd enjoyed his bachelor lifestyle for many years, lately he couldn't help thinking about setting down real roots, filling his home with a woman's love and children's laughter.

And then Paris came back to Destiny and thoughts of her seemed to fill every moment of his day. He thought of the stack of paperwork piling up on his desk. Low-priority work that could be put off a week or two. But what about his feelings for Paris? Could he put those off too?

~

PARIS'S APPOINTMENT TO register her car at the Department of Motor Vehicles was at two o'clock in the county seat, so she left the high school a little before one. She made the trip, arrived minutes before her scheduled time, and then waited in line for an extra half-hour before she got to see anyone. Once she got her turn, everything went smoothly. The only glitch came when she needed to give a current address and had to give her grandmother's. *Not for long,* she promised herself as she left, her duty to the state fulfilled.

She reached her car and decided to ask Gran if she needed anything from town. That's when she realized she must have left her phone at the school. A quick pass by the conference room wouldn't alter her plans much, and if Gran needed shopping, she could handle that tomorrow. As she drove, she thought about Greg and the application to TriTech, mentally thumbing through all her reasons working in the Valley. Over and around all those thoughts loomed Greg's reminder that sometimes choices were between good and better.

Arriving at the school, she parked in the visitors' section, hustled in, and reached the office in time to hear her name. She paused in the hallway as she heard Mrs. Bailey say, "Do you think Paris will finish that proposal? You know she left early today."

"She had another appointment, but she's almost finished already."

"That's good. But what about follow-through? She isn't always dependable—"

Paris swallowed a gasp. Her hand rose to the center of her chest. That's when she heard Greg say, "You're remembering her from high school and a very bad time in her life. She's an adult now and a professional—"

He was interrupted when a woman Paris didn't recognize rushed past. "Greg, you're needed by the goal post on the practice field. A couple of the older boys are squaring off. Looks like a brawl in the making."

"Coming," Greg said. Then to Mrs. Bailey, "Don't worry. Paris will come through."

Paris stepped backward, hoping Greg would be so focused on the situation ahead that he wouldn't look back. When the door closed behind him, she hurried to the drinking fountain, waited five minutes, and then swept into the office as if just arriving. She spoke briefly to Mrs. Bailey, keeping her voice polite and choosing not to make eye contact. Then she hustled to the conference room, snatched her phone off the desk, and hurried back the way she'd come.

She drove toward Gran's, her mind buzzing. Was her reputation *that* bad? She'd certainly had a rough couple of years in high school, but she'd outgrown those times. Hadn't she? Then she thought of Gran's disappointment when she forgot the potatoes. For the hundredth or thousandth time, she wondered why these things happened to her.

As she reached Gran's house, her phone rang, and she saw Greg's number. Though she didn't feel like talking with him, she liked even less the idea of disappointing him — of failing to follow through. She took the call.

"Hi," Greg said. "How about dinner tonight? We can celebrate finishing the proposal."

"But I haven't finished. Not yet."

"You'll finish soon though, won't you?"

"I hope so." A bitter voice in her mind wanted to ask if he feared she'd prove undependable, but she reminded herself that Greg didn't know what she'd overheard, and he'd spoken in her defense. She scrambled for something to say. "I'm kind of stuck on the budget."

"I thought Mrs. Bailey gave you the rundown."

Hearing the secretary's name tightened her throat, but Paris made a quick recovery. "Yes, she did, but there are some lines under Administrative Costs I don't understand."

"Like?"

"It looks like there's a space for a grant writer's fee."

"Probably is. Go ahead and claim it. You deserve it."

"Oh no! I didn't take this job for pay. I just wondered…is that how grant writers get paid?"

"You've got me there. We're just starting to apply for grant money, so we don't know much about norms. I did talk to one grant writer, though. She was going to charge us a fee up front because she didn't want to depend on getting paid only if the grant funded."

"Makes sense."

"That's why we were trying to do it on our own, and that explains why we are so grateful to you. At least you know what you're doing."

She snickered. "I guess we'll see."

"Anyway, I want to take you out, and I thought we might do something different."

Paris had been planning a long bubble bath and a longer sulk, but as she started to tell Greg she had other plans, she remembered him referring to her as a professional. Her emotions rallied. "What did you have in mind?"

Greg suggested they drive up the road to Bedford Falls, a high Sierra ski resort some forty miles away. Though Paris had given up her sulk, she didn't feel like making the lengthy trip Greg proposed, not when she needed to be at the school promptly as promised in the morning—if for no other reason than to rub it in Mrs. Bailey's face. "The state highway has a few exits with nice places to eat. Surely we can find something closer than Bedford."

"I know the perfect place," he said. "Pick you up in thirty minutes."

Paris ran a quick inventory of the tasks she needed to complete. "Give me an hour," she said, clicking off with a silent promise to adjust her attitude for Greg's sake.

～

GREG ARRIVED as promised and drove her up the state highway out of Destiny and past Reed Orchards toward Bedford Falls, but he stopped only a few minutes later at a highway exit with a gas station, a couple of homes, and a small restaurant called Heaven on Earth. The fragrance of sweet-and-sour sauce tantalized as they made their way toward the door of the restaurant. "Chinese food? Out here?"

"One of our new hidden gems. I'll introduce you to the Lees. Their son Todd attends our high school."

They entered and were instantly greeted like visiting royalty, with Mrs. Lee bowing frequently as she led them to her best table. "Please, Mr. Principal. Order anything you like. Your food on the house tonight." She bowed again as she hurried to the kitchen to return with water glasses and flatware.

Paris opened her menu but quickly closed it again. "I have no idea what to order. Do you have favorite dishes?"

He closed his menu as well. "I can recommend almost any dish, but the walnut prawns are especially good, as are the peach buns—any of the dim sum really, and you have to try their scallion pancakes."

"Sounds great. Why don't you order for me?"

He raised a brow. "You trust me with your dinner?"

"If I don't like it, I can always order something else." She settled against the back of her chair. "I won't let them comp my meal, though."

Greg lowered his voice and leaned nearer. "It's a game we play every time I come here," he said. "They always say they'll comp my meal and I always pretend to let them. Then I calculate a tip that's big enough to cover the cost of the meal with a tip on the side and leave the cash on the table. The next time I'm here, we do the same thing all over again."

She chuckled. "Tell me about the Lees?"

Greg told her what he knew, about the third-generation American-born husband who ran the kitchen and how his parents had sent him to China to live with distant relatives and learn his "home culture" first-hand. "That's where he met Ting," Greg said. "He told me about it once when we were chatting about Todd. He said marrying Ting was difficult because of the international politics, but he'd readily do it again. He told me finding the right companion is worth whatever it takes." Their eyes met and Paris felt a warmth infuse her cheeks at Greg's smile. She was relieved when Mrs. Lee returned.

"You decide?" she asked.

Greg gave Paris a look that said, *Yes, I have. Now I'm trying to talk her into it.* Then he rattled off half a dozen dishes from the *a la carte* menu and Mrs. Lee bowed again as she hustled to the kitchen.

When they were alone again, Paris spoke. "Greg?"

"Um-hm?"

"When I first arrived back in Destiny, you said you'd like to spend time with me while I'm in town. But after our dinner at your place last weekend, it feels like something's shifted."

He took a deep breath, let it out slowly. "The more time we spend together, the more time I want to keep spending with you. We don't know each other well, but I think we could come to care deeply for each other, and I'd like to find out."

"Greg, I—"

"Please, don't give me the memorized answer. Tell me what you feel. If we spent more time together, do you think you could… feel the same way?"

"Are you asking if I could, maybe, fall in love with you?"

He gave her a long look. "Well, yes. I guess I am."

She sighed and looked away. All her experience was telling her this was a good time to hedge, but her instincts were screaming to be honest even though that meant taking a risk. She straightened her spine and focused on Greg's eyes. "I feel much the same way. I think I could…just maybe…come to love you."

"Then let's not count us out yet."

"But Greg—"

"I know it's complicated, but we'll figure it out as we go." He touched her hand. "Deal?"

She bit her lip but knew the time for hedging had passed. "Deal," she answered, "but there's something you should know."

Chapter Nine

"**O**kay, are we talking one or two skeletons in your closet?" Greg grinned.

Paris rolled her eyes. "Very funny." She told him about the phone interview she had scheduled for Wednesday and how the opportunity seemed to be exactly what she wanted.

"Well," Greg sat back in his chair. "I'm happy for you. You certainly have all the skills they're looking for. I hope it works out. But it doesn't change a thing between us. If we both believe that what we have is worth pursuing, we'll find a way."

She shivered as a tiny thrill ran through her. "You don't discourage easily, do you?"

He gently stroked her hand. "Honestly, Paris, if you're not interested, I'm gone. But when you say you could fall in love with me, I won't let a few miles come between us."

"You realize this isn't a *few* miles, right? Given traffic in the valley, we could be talking two hours each way."

"You'll be coming up to visit your grandmother and Jess now and then—"

"My average is about every two months—or it was until the last job." She frowned in concentration. "Now that I think about it, I haven't been up for a while."

"Okay. We can work with every other month, if you think you can manage that, and I can come to see you too. I have—"

He paused as Mrs. Lee arrived with their food. It all smelled and looked magnificent. "My taste buds just went on high alert," Paris said. She dished up some of the walnut prawns and a small serving of two dishes she didn't recognize that smelled divine, passing them to Greg.

He reached for the prawns. "I started to say I can come down occasionally, maybe as often as two weekends a month—except when things get hectic around graduation."

"Greg, you don't have time for that, and you don't have a diamond mine yet either," she teased. "I like you too much to put you in the poor house."

He smiled at her touch of humor, but sobered when he said, "You keep coming up with reasons why we can't see each other. Are you changing your mind?"

Paris steadied herself. "Not at all. I'm trying to be practical."

"Then stop worrying. I have a college buddy who lives in Carmichael and says I have an open invitation any time I want to stay in his guest room. He stays with me when he needs to escape the crush in the Valley." Greg offered a reassuring smile. "Really, Paris. I hope you get the job, but when you do, it won't mean we have to stop seeing each other."

She picked up her chopsticks. "It wouldn't be every day, though, not like it's been.

"No, not every day. Then again, we can take our time. I'd like to explore this relationship, see if it has staying power, but it only works if we both want it to."

Take our time. Staying power. Paris thought of how quickly their attraction had developed. She'd only planned for a few lunches. Then their outings grew to dinner and hiking. Now she was contemplating a long-distance relationship. It was overwhelming, but exciting too, and she liked his idea of seeing if they had 'staying power.' As she lifted another delicately flavored prawn, she offered a flirty smile, "I believe we both want the same thing." Something inside her shifted then, making her declaration feel real, even to her.

By noon Tuesday, Paris had finished the proposal's budget and cleaned up ragged or wordy sections. She started the spelling and grammar check mostly to see if she'd left any typos and was well into the process when the door opened, admitting Mrs. Bailey. "Paris?"

Paris paused the program, her voice cool as she answered. "Can I help you?"

Mrs. Bailey hesitated in the doorway, biting her lip. "Oh, well, I hate to ask, but—"

The woman's obvious unease caused Paris to soften. After all, Mrs. Bailey didn't know what Paris had overheard. "How can I help?"

The older woman wrinkled her brow, her face a mask of apology. For a moment, Paris wondered if somehow, she *did* know her remarks had been overheard. Then Mrs. Bailey glanced at the door to Greg's office. "It's confidential..." So that was it. Greg's assistant wanted something, but she didn't want Greg to know. Well, it wouldn't hurt Paris to harbor a secret.

"I can't guarantee I can help with...whatever is bothering you," Paris said, "but I can guarantee I'll be the very soul of discretion."

"Oh, thank you!" Mrs. Bailey closed the door behind her, crossed the room, and sat beside Paris. "I've got myself in a spot of trouble." She held a tissue in her hands, and she wrung it in twists as she rushed through a description of driving down the hill to an appointment, having trouble with her brakes, and going faster than she wanted. "It was faster than the limit too, and when the officer turned his lights on and signaled me over, I still couldn't make the brakes work. When I reached an incline and pulled over, the officer was furious. He added everything he could to that ticket, even a fix-it for one of my parking lights that wasn't out, just flickering a little."

Paris's defensiveness relaxed further. "That's awful. You're okay, though?"

"Well, yes, though that officer about scared the bejabbers out of me," Mrs. Bailey said, her tissue now in shreds. "I'm nervous every time I see a police car."

Paris nodded, her response all sympathy. "I know the symptoms, that nervousness you feel any time you see a police car near you. I call it black-and-white fever, and I've had it myself, but really, I don't see how I can help you."

"I've decided to go to court to fight the ticket," Mrs. Bailey said, "not claiming I wasn't speeding, you know, but explaining the extenuating circumstances. I saved the bill for having the brakes fixed and it's dated the same day as the ticket. Now I've written a letter to the judge. I thought I'd ask the new English teacher to proofread it for me, but I made up my mind too late and he's already gone for the day. I'm hoping, maybe, if you have a minute..."

"I'll be glad to," she answered. She was still hurt by Mrs. Bailey's comments, but she also wanted to help. She checked her watch, not wanting to be late for her appointment with Amber. "I don't have time right now, though. I'll look at it first thing tomorrow."

"I have court tomorrow morning." Mrs. Bailey's face filled with apology. "I'm sorry, Paris. I wouldn't bother you with this, but I only made up my mind today and I want the letter to look good. It would be a great favor if you can take a look. Of course, if you don't have time..."

Paris checked the time again. "It's okay. I can give it a quick look."

"Oh, thank you! You're a lifesaver." Mrs. Bailey left the office but returned almost immediately with a typed page. "I'll attach a copy of the ticket and a copy of the bill for the brakes. Let me know what you think."

"I will, but your school day is almost over, isn't it?"

Mrs. Bailey glanced at the wall clock. "I'm off for the day in twenty minutes, but please, take as long as you need. I'll be at my desk."

"Okay." Paris picked up a pen and went to work. She wanted to be thorough, but fast. She had less than an hour before her appointment. She read the letter once through first, then scanned it again line by line, making corrections and suggestions with a red pen. A few minutes later, she carried the letter back to Mrs. Bailey's desk.

The assistant's eyes widened. "Oh my! I see all the red. I hope I didn't misspell anything."

"You didn't," Paris assured her. "It's a very good letter, Mrs. B, only you didn't say anything about the way the officer shook you down."

"Oh, I didn't want to complain. He's a police officer, you know—"

"And the judge deserves to know that the officer got a little badge-heavy. The deputy didn't understand what was happening, so it isn't completely his fault, but you shouldn't have to go through all this nonsense either." She picked the letter up. "Here I've added a paragraph that explains all the extra citations on the ticket and asks the judge to waive the fines."

"Oh my! Can you do that?"

"Yes, ma'am. I surely can. That is, *you* surely can since this is your letter."

"Oh, my goodness." Mrs. Bailey finally looked hopeful.

"Let me re-enter and print it for you. I'll be back in a minute."

Paris needed little time to retype the letter, deleting Mrs. Bailey's qualifiers, adding emphasis, and inserting her own carefully worded paragraph. She printed out the final draft and handed it to the assistant.

"Oh Paris! This is lovely!" Mrs. Bailey reread the new paragraph. "You said that so well. Thank you!"

"No problem. Just win your case. Then tell me about it."

"I'll tell you everything." Mrs. Bailey stood, folded the letter, and put it in her purse. "Greg knows I'll be late tomorrow. Thank goodness my court appearance is at the county seat, not all the way down to the valley. I hope I can pull this off."

"You'll be great," Paris assured her, patting her arm. "Just don't let anyone intimidate you. Remember you're a taxpayer; that means everyone at the court is working for you."

"Oh! Goodness! I never thought of it that way. But I'm an ordinary person—"

"Not so ordinary, Mrs. Bailey. You've always had a commanding presence. That's what has made you so effective around here."

"Do you really think so?"

"I know so! Remember I was a student here."

"Oh yes, that's true. I suppose I won't see you tomorrow, you being finished with the proposal and all."

"Actually. I'll be in by noon or so. I'll probably see you then."

"Oh, I hope so." Mrs. Bailey gathered her things, then she paused, apparently gathering her thoughts as well. "You know, Paris, I've grown very fond of Greg these past couple of years working with him. I..." She hesitated, as if she wanted to say more but had thought better of it. "Well, I guess I'll see you tomorrow."

"Okay." Paris stepped into the hall, anxious to get going.

"Paris?"

Paris hoped Mrs. Bailey wasn't going to ask for something else. She took a deep breath. "Yes?"

"Thank you again."

"You're welcome." Paris nodded and started for the parking lot. She was almost at the door when she realized she'd left her cell phone in the conference room. Again. Frustrated with herself, she rushed back to the office, glad Mrs. Bailey hadn't yet locked the door. "I have to grab my phone," she explained. "You can go, Mrs. Bailey. I'll lock up when I leave."

"Well...all right." Mrs. Bailey didn't look happy, but she let Paris enter the office.

Paris rushed into the conference room and rifled through the papers, making even more of a mess before she finally found the phone under a file folder. She blew out a breath as she tossed the phone in her purse. She rushed into the front office and was startled to find a slender blond boy opening Mrs. Bailey's top desk drawer.

"What are you doing?" Paris let surprise turn her voice sharp.

"Uh, I thought..." The boy straightened. "Mrs. Bailey has a lunch ticket for me—"

Paris stepped forward. "You're not supposed to be in her desk. Tell me your name and I'll write her a note."

"No!" The boy's eyes widened. "It's okay. I can come back. Don't..." Then he turned and ran, disappearing down the hall before Paris could stop him.

"That was weird," Paris mumbled, but she put it behind her as she hurried out, locking the door.

A few minutes later, Paris arrived at the elementary school with a sense of relief. She checked the time and still had a minute to spare before her meeting with Amber. In the office, she found Amber leaning over a computer and chatting with the front office assistant.

"Ms. Reyes?" Paris said. "I believe we have an appointment."

"Yes, my assistant told me someone was com—" Amber turned. She hesitated. "Paris? Paris Cutler?"

"Yes, ma'am." Paris swung open the half-door that separated the office from the lobby. The next moments were full of hugs and "how are you" and "so good to see you again!"

Amber turned to her assistant. "I'm heading out now, Claudia. See you tomorrow."

"What about the—" Claudia began.

"Whatever it is, it can wait." She looked to Paris. "Give me two minutes to grab my purse and we'll be out of here."

"You've got it," Paris said as Amber stepped into her office. She realized she'd not only been nervous about being late, she'd also been uneasy about seeing Amber. She knew now that she'd unwittingly burned a few bridges when she graduated and went off to college, and maybe a few more in the years since. Had her connection to Amber been one of them?

"You look great," Amber said as she came back out, and Paris's worries dimmed.

"You look wonderful." Paris gave her old friend a quick once-over, noting her dark brunette hair, thick and shiny, and grown out longer than she remembered it; Amber's deep green jacket complemented her dark hazel eyes and olive complexion. She'd been slightly plump during their teen years, but was now fashionably slender. "Really wonderful," she added with emphasis. "The years have been good to you."

"And to you too, my friend. What do you say we grab at sandwich at Joe's? We have a few minutes to catch up." Amber moved toward the parking lot.

"Sounds great to me." Paris followed, the last of her worries vanishing with the mountain breeze.

"So you're the mysterious woman who's been seen around town with Greg Frantz." Amber made herself comfortable at their table in Joe's Sandwich Shop. "I've heard rumors about someone keeping our high school principal busy. I had no idea it was you."

"I had no idea you were here in Destiny, or even that you'd gone into education," Paris said as she picked up her vitamin water.

Amber's warm response had relieved her concerns. Now she could relax and enjoy this reunion.

Amber shook her head. "We haven't kept up well, have we?"

"No, we haven't, and I'm sorry for my part in that. Last I heard, you were at Fresno State, planning on a business degree and shuddering at anything that sounded like teaching."

Amber shrugged. "Things change."

"That's one huge change."

"True. It sort of…happened."

Paris nibbled a carrot stick. "What was it that happened?"

"It's not all that mysterious," Amber answered. "My second year, I began working with a professor who sponsored a high school club for future entrepreneurs. They were bright, creative kids. I realized how much I enjoyed working with them, teaching some of the principles I had already learned. One thing led to another and here I am."

Paris sipped at her drink. "But you're not working with high school kids. Do the same ideas apply with the little ones?"

Amber offered a cat-with-the-canary grin. "Bright, creative kids who don't give you too much attitude can be even more fun. How about you? What are you doing back in town?"

Paris gave the standard answer about changing jobs and staying with family while she looked for something new.

"That explanation may work for other people," Amber said, "but you've forgotten how well I know you. Something must have happened at your old job."

Paris glanced away. "You could say that, yes." She bought time with another sip of water.

"Do tell." Amber echoed Paris's words back to her.

Paris spoke carefully. "Amber, I once considered you the sister I never had, and I still love you for the way you stuck by me, but I'm not ready to talk about the mess at my previous job. I expect some of the sting will go when I'm working again. Ask about it then."

Amber's face fell. "You expect to leave soon?"

Paris explained the interview on Wednesday and how the job seemed a perfect fit.

"Then I wish you well. What about Greg? You know you'd be the envy of every girl who went to school with us if they knew you're dating Mr. Frantz. Is there a future there?"

"I don't want to be the object of anybody's envy—and I'm not sure you could say we've been dating, exactly..."

Amber laughed. "Then what do you call it? You've been seen together all over town, including every place there is to catch a meal. If that's not dating, I don't know what is."

"Okay, you're right." An embarrassed blush warmed Paris's face, and she absently touched her cheek to cool it. "It's not as if I feel that schoolgirl crush anymore."

"Ha!" Amber set her drink down with a thud. "Tell that to somebody who can't see your face! Girl, you are over the moon."

Paris's face grew warmer. She lifted her cold drink to her cheek. "It isn't like that."

"You can't tell me—"

Paris cut her off. "Please! Let me finish."

Amber's eyes widened at her tone.

"I'm sorry," Paris said, immediately regretting her abruptness. *Why don't I think before I speak?* She reached out to pat Amber's hand. "Let me explain."

"Go ahead." Amber sat back, smiling encouragement.

Paris had forgotten how understanding and patient Amber was. No wonder she'd gone into teaching; it must have been a perfect fit. Paris dug deep, hoping to find the right words. "Sure, I had a crush back then," she began. "Everybody did, but even in high school, there was more to it." She paused. "Greg was a sounding board. He listened to me and seemed to care how I felt. He encouraged me to write and express all I was feeling. Yeah, I had a crush, but I kind of hero-worshipped him too."

Amber nodded. "Okay. I can see that. What about now?"

"I admire him, trust him, look up to him—"

"Love him?"

Paris swallowed. "I think I'm falling for him, and I can't. It's silly, I know. We hardly know each other, but I think about him all the time. Sometimes I suspect there's still a bit of that schoolgirl crush left over, but other times..." She put her hand to her heart and sighed.

Amber chuckled. "I hear that," she said. "And, from what else I hear, Greg is thinking about you too."

"This town and its gossip." Paris shook her head.

"Trust me, it's all good," Amber said. "People think you're a great couple."

"Seriously?"

"Seriously. So, what's the problem?"

Paris sighed. "Greg is fully rooted here. He's been working at getting back here for years, and it's where he wants to be."

"And that's a problem because…"

"Because my life is in the city, Amber. That's where I find the kind of work I want to do. It's where I can develop the career I want and find the kind of life I want…away from the problems of small-town living. Like gossip."

"Yep, that can be a problem. But people gossip everywhere, including workplaces." Amber tilted her head and smiled. "I know long-distance relationships can be hard, but if you're both committed, you can find a solution."

Paris played with the saltshaker. "That's what Greg says."

"Greg's right." Amber checked the time on her cell phone. "Unfortunately, I have a spring open house in just over an hour, and a full list of things I should be doing to get ready. Let's get together again in a few days. I want to hear how your interview goes. And of course, I want a play-by-play for how things are going with you and Mr.… Greg."

Paris grinned. "I promise to tell you anything you can worm out of me."

"Some friend you are." Amber winked. "Soon, okay?"

"Absolutely."

The two women hugged, and Amber blew a kiss as she left.

Paris watched her go, her thoughts in turmoil. Was it possible Amber was right? Was she already in love with Greg? The more she considered it, the more likely it seemed. But what if they loved each other and still couldn't make it work? She didn't know what the stats were on long-distance relationships, but they weren't good. For Greg and her to be together, one or the other would have to give up plans and dreams, and that would burden their future with resentments and other emotional baggage.

The doubts were too many and too large to be easily dismissed. Paris knew she should think seriously, but she couldn't bring herself to do it right now. She also knew she was procrastinating, something she did all too often. *But what else can I do about it? Besides I haven't even had my interview yet.* She decided she'd wait to figure things out. Maybe after she found a job. For now, decisions—especially the painful ones—could wait.

Chapter Ten

Paris awoke filled with both excitement and anxiety. As she rose toward full consciousness, she pinned her emotions on the next day's interview, firmly quieting the inner voice that asked if she'd rather stay with Greg. That meant staying in Destiny, and how could she do that? What would she do for a living? What if things didn't work out? She'd be stuck in Destiny with no job and no prospects, living off her Gran's generosity. Again? *No way!* That had been her only option in her childhood when her mother dragged her up the mountain, but she had grown. She'd educated herself, developed skills, and she never wanted to coming crawling to Gran again.

Steeled for whatever, she went to check her computer as she did every morning. Moments later, Jess flew down the stairs, dressed for the day and obviously in a rush. "I don't know why I keep oversleeping."

"Being stressed and over-committed may have something to do with it. That and staying up too late."

"Smart-aleck." Jess grabbed a breakfast bar and dashed for the door. "If I don't rush, I'll be late for my early morning tutoring session. See you!" The door slammed behind her.

Watching her go, Paris mumbled, "So much for a chat with Aunt Jess."

Half an hour later, she had almost gone through the list of new job postings—none of which seemed like a good fit—when she heard her grandmother on the stairs. "Hey, Gran. How are you today?"

"I'm fine. Is Jess out the door already?"

"Yes. She rushed out some time ago."

"It's like this at the end of every school—" The sentence ended in a shriek as Gran missed a step and landed hard, bumping down two or three more stairs before stopping near the bottom with her head against the railing.

"Gran!" Paris reached her in seconds. Relief washed over her as she found her grandmother conscious and moaning, but she didn't dare touch her for fear of aggravating injuries. She tried to keep her voice even as she asked, "How bad is it?"

Gran sniffed. "Mostly, I'm embarrassed. What a dumb thing to do!"

"Anybody can miss a step."

"Thanks, sweetie." Gran sat straighter, groaning as her spine adjusted.

Paris gently slipped an arm around her shoulders. "Do you think you can stand?"

"I don't know." Gran wriggled until she had her feet squarely under her. She caught the banister and started to pull up. "Oh!" Letting go, she settled back onto the step.

"Gran?"

"I sat down pretty hard, and I'm afraid my tailbone feels it. Give me a bit before I try to stand again."

Paris straightened. "That does it. I'm calling an ambulance." She turned to grab her phone.

Gran caught her hand. "No, you will not."

"But Gran—"

"I'll be okay in a couple of minutes."

Paris had been through this before and she knew Gran wouldn't cave easily. She hadn't even allowed Paris to call the ambulance when she fell from her cherry tree and broke her leg in a compound fracture. The image of the shattered bone poking through her grandmother's skin had been one childhood trauma that still haunted Paris.

"Tell you what," she said, staring her grandmother down. "I'm looking at my watch. If you can't get up on your own in the next ten minutes, I'll call the ambulance and you won't be able to do anything about it."

Gran huffed. "Guess not if I can't stand up." She began grumbling under her breath.

Paris felt like grumbling too. Aunt Jess always kept long days this time of year, especially since she had become faculty advisor to yet another student club, but Paris wished she had backup for times like these. What would Gran do if she were alone?

She watched and waited. Gran attempted to stand a couple of times. Each time she groaned and slid back down. Eight minutes into her count, Paris said, "We don't need two more minutes, Gran. It's clear you aren't going to be able to get up without help. I'm calling."

"No need," Gran said. Biting her lip and grimacing against the pain, she slowly pulled herself to standing, leaning on the rail.

Paris applauded, giving credit where it was due. "That was really something. You're one tough cookie."

"It runs in the family."

Paris took her grandmother's arm. "How are you feeling?"

Gran pursed her lips. "Honestly? I think I broke my tailbone. How dumb is that?"

"I'm calling the ambulance."

"No." Gran shook her head. "No ambulance necessary, but I will let you drive me down the hill to the hospital."

"You've got it." Paris slipped her arm around her grandmother's waist and helped her to the car.

LUNCH HOUR CAME AND WENT. Destiny High was well into its afternoon class schedule when Paris arrived at the school. She had left Gran comfortably ensconced in a hospital bed, giving orders to the nurses and charming the students and interns. Although tests showed no broken bones, the doctors insisted the soft tissue injuries required healing time. Paris realized how much her grandmother must be hurting when Gran quietly allowed the hospital to admit her.

Paris parked and walked into the school, trying to refocus her energies for the upcoming project, but the image of her grandmother, pale and hurting, had embedded itself in her mind. "Sorry I'm late," she said as she entered the front office. She saw Mrs. Bailey at her desk. "I hope you got my message?"

"Oh yes, dear. Thank you for letting us know. How is your grand-mother doing?"

"She needs some healing time, but she's expected to make a full recovery." Paris only hoped that was true.

"By the way..." Mrs. Bailey stood. "Thank you again for that letter."

"It went well?"

"Oh yes! Very well. The judge heard my explanation and then she read your letter. She looked at the bill for having the brakes repaired and she noted that the brakes needed a complete overhaul that same day. Then she declared I had made all the necessary repairs and waived everything else. She smacked down that little hammer...what do you call it?"

"A gavel?"

"Oh yes, a gavel. I knew that. Anyway, she smacked down the gavel and that was that. She called the next case."

"I'm so glad."

"It might not have gone that way without your help. I can't thank you enough."

Paris flashed a quick smile as she moved into the conference room, pleased Mrs. Bailey no longer thought her unreliable, hoping she had enough energy and caring left in her to put the finishing touches on the proposal. The project that had fascinated her at the beginning had become tedious, even boring now.

An hour later, with the final spell-check almost complete, she took a last look at the document she'd created and smiled in self-congratula-tion. She'd hung in there and the proposal was finished.

"Almost done?"

She looked up, surprised to see Greg standing behind her. "I didn't hear the door open."

"I didn't mean to startle you. You were so intent on your work—"

She smiled. "I get like that, and you're also right that it's almost done."

"I know. I read the last draft you wrote, before you ran the spell-check."

"Well then, if you're ready to affix your electronic signature, I can email it to the Bates Foundation in the next few minutes."

"Sounds great."

She showed him where and how to sign and he did. Then, with a flourish, she pushed the SEND button. "Done. I hope it goes well for the school."

"It will." Greg's expression radiated confidence. "Whether we get the funding or not, you've taught us that we can take this road. The school will be better off for the time you've given us."

"Glad I could help." She smiled, delighted that he was so happy with her work. She reminded herself to act professional, even while falling for her client.

For a moment, they stood facing each other, the air between them humming. Then Greg said in a gentle voice, "If you're trying to keep me from falling in love with you, you're going about it all wrong."

Paris shook her head, feeling the heat of a blush. "Uh...what?"

"Mrs. Harkness told us why you were late coming in today."

"Who? Oh! That must have been the mother of the boy with the sports injury. She brought him into the E.R. while we were there."

"Braden turned his ankle running laps. He'll be on crutches for a while, but he's going to be fine. How's Annette—your grandmother?"

"She's going to be fine, too." Unexpected tears filled her eyes as the image of her grandmother unable to stand flashed to mind. She felt her chest tighten as though it was happening all over again. *I have to get a handle on my anxiety.*

"And you?" Greg stepped closer, touching her shoulder. "Are you okay?"

Paris swallowed hard. "I'm okay. It's—it's been a crazy morning."

"Taking care of your grandmother, taking care of Mrs. Bailey, coming back to take care of the school... You've been busy." He brushed her hair back from her face. "You're a good person, Paris." He leaned toward her.

"Greg—" Whatever she had planned to say was lost as he touched his lips to hers. The kiss was gentle, teasing, but it quickly morphed into something more urgent as Paris funneled pent-up emotion into their embrace and Greg responded in kind. Neither of them heard the door open.

"Oh!" Mrs. Bailey stood in the doorway. "I... I'm sorry. I didn't..."

"It's okay, Miranda." Greg turned toward his assistant, stepping in front of Paris to give her recovery time.

Paris appreciated his thoughtfulness. She needed that time to slow her breathing and overcome the whirling vortex that had sucked in her thoughts and emotions, leaving her dazed, amazed, and more confused than ever.

"I... uh..." Mrs. Bailey collected herself. "Mr. Frantz, there's a call for you."

Paris envied his even, calm voice as he said, "Take a message, please. I'll return it soon."

"Yes, of course." Mrs. Bailey closed the door behind her.

"Whew!" Greg turned back to Paris, sucking in a quick breath. "Wow. That was—"

"Yeah," Paris responded. "It was, and Mrs. Bailey is a witness. If the town wasn't already gossiping, that should do it."

Greg brushed a strand of hair from her face. "Do you mind? The gossip, I mean."

She'd always hated Destiny's gossip, but now... she recalled what Amber said about gossip, that it was everywhere, not only in small towns. "No not really," she answered. "I'm glad they're gossiping about us."

"You are?" Greg nuzzled her hair.

She stroked his cheek. "People think we're good together."

He tilted his head. "I agree. What do you think we should do about it?"

Paris sighed. "I wish I knew. I have that interview tomorrow—"

"I know. The perfect job."

"You don't have to sound so negative about it."

"Negative? Me? Not so. I want for you whatever you want most for yourself." He brushed the hair from her forehead. "Spend the evening with me?"

"I'd love to."

He leaned down to kiss her. Her response was immediate and

intense, and so was the kiss she returned. But she soon drew away. "Mr. Frantz, you have a phone call to make."

"You're right." He let her go. "Not that I want to leave."

She twinkled at him. "We have this evening."

"Indeed, we do. Pick you up at five?"

"Perfect," she answered, imagining a perfect evening and wondering about their odds for finding a perfect future beyond that.

THE SCHOOL'S minibus was filling as Greg prepared to leave school for the day. Jessica Kerr's academic decathlon team was on their way to a practice competition with another school. Ms. Kerr checked each student's permission slip as they clambered aboard, eagerly shouting practice questions at one another.

Greg saw an opportunity. "Ms. Kerr?" he called as Jessica started to board.

"Yes?" Jess looked back over her shoulder.

"Do you have a minute?" he asked, hoping she'd agree.

Jessica hesitated, then murmured something to the bus driver. Turning, she approached Greg in a few easy strides. "Okay, you've got a minute," she said with a smile.

"About Paris," he said. "Do you know what she has against Destiny? Why doesn't she want to live here?"

"I suspect it's complicated." Jess blew out a breath. Then, with a glance toward the bus, "I haven't much time, but her aversion to this town is almost a phobia. Unreasoning, you know?"

"Not really," he said, "but I do know how phobias work. Thanks, Jess."

He would have turned away, but she stopped him by catching his hand and quickly dropping it again. "Speaking of Paris—"

"Ms. Kerr, we've gotta go!" One of the older boys leaned out the window to call her.

Jess hesitated for all of two seconds. "Later," she said, and loped to the bus. "Okay!" she shouted as she closed the door behind her. Greg heard her say, "Let's show those Wildcats what they're up against!" The bus erupted in cheers as the driver pulled away.

"A phobia," Greg murmured as he went back to lock up. "How can I fight a phobia?" At least he had this evening to look forward to, and maybe Paris would give him a clue about how he could break through to her, once and for all.

Chapter Eleven

"Wow! You went all out," Paris said as she watched Greg sprinkle mozzarella over the lasagna and pop it in the oven.

"Ahh!" he said. "Think of the points I could make with a well-placed lie."

"What do you mean?" She sat up, crossing her arms over her chest. She didn't like talk about lies. Her last boyfriend had lied to her, and she'd been too naïve to see it. The company that employed her father had lied to everyone, creating much of the sorrow in her young life. Had she been too trusting again? Her inner voice answered, *You know Greg isn't like that. Can't you see he's joking?* Paris had been distracted by watching him spread cheese on the lasagna and his comment about lying had caught her unaware, but now that she looked at him, she could see his aw-shucks boyish grin and the mild blush suffusing his cheeks.

"Okay, full disclosure," he said. "I didn't make the lasagna."

"Who did?" Paris relaxed and reached for her water glass, now enjoying his banter.

"You remember Mrs. Winthrop?" He wiped down the counter.

"The really old lady who used to live by the post office?"

"That's right," he answered. "She's even older now and still there. She used to supplement her income by preparing meals for local families. People could swing by her place on the way home from work, pick up a dish or two to stick in the oven when they arrived, and have dinner on the table a while later. The income helped her, and we all appreciated her meals."

"I remember. But you said appreciated. Past tense."

"Yes." He opened the fridge and got out the ingredients for a green salad. "She still preps a meal for a favorite customer now and then —

especially when I tell her there's a lady I want to impress." He flashed another boyish grin.

Paris arched a brow. "You're trying to impress me?"

He closed the refrigerator door and stepped near her. "Is it working?"

"It just may b—" The thought remained unfinished as their lips met.

Greg's kiss was gentle, sweet, and Paris wished it could go on forever. She sighed. "Oh Greg. How did we get in this deep, this fast?"

"We can't call it love at first sight." He brushed gentle kisses along her cheek. "We've known each other more than eight years."

"True. I was attracted to you then, though. Does that count?"

"Sure, I'll count it. I can't admit to being attracted to you, though, since that would make me—"

"Yeah. It would."

He sat down beside her. "Paris, what happened at your last job?"

She drew in a sharp breath. "Whoa! That came out of nowhere."

"I've been waiting for you to tell me, but when you didn't, I thought I'd ask." He scooted back, giving her space. "I know you were badly hurt. You wouldn't have walked away from something that was going well. But you don't exactly open up about your problems."

"Not true," she said, feeling defensive. "I just about burned Gran's ears off railing about it—at least, in the beginning."

He hesitated. "Well, I wasn't referring to your grandmother."

"Oh." Now she felt like the sheepish one. "You're sure you want to hear this?"

"Is it going to make me want to rush down the hill to hurt some-body?" he asked with a ghost of a smile.

"Possibly. Not that it would do any good. Besides, you aren't the sort that settles things with violence."

"You're right about that, although there've been times when I would have loved to throw a tantrum." He drew a deep breath and let it out slowly. "Over the years, I've seen a few teachers and school personnel act like teenagers. As adults, we have to do better by our kids. Teach by example. It takes more thought and focus to hold your temper and be patient."

"You're a good guy Greg," she said softly. "You really care about these kids." She thought about the times she'd flown off the handle with friends and family, and how quick she was to get agitated. She wished she could be more like Greg, always calm and even-tempered. He sure had the right attitude for a school principal.

"Thank you. I appreciate that." He leaned in and gave her another sweet kiss, making her knees go weak. "Qualifier. I didn't say I *would* rush down the hill to hurt someone, just that I'd want to."

"I guess that makes a difference." She smiled. "How long 'til the lasagna is done?"

"Most of an hour. Why?"

"That lets me know how much I have to leave out to tell this story."

"We can keep the lasagna warm if necessary." He stroked her arm, his touch light. "Please. I want to hear it all. Let's sit at the table and you can tell me what happened."

Paris couldn't tell him everything, not the parts that were too ugly or embarrassing to share. Greg pulled out a chair for her at the dining table and he sat next to her, turning the chair so they faced each other.

She took a deep breath. "It started with a guy I dated when I was in the Roseville office. I don't think I went out with Raleigh more than three or four times before I told him I wasn't interested, but he kept asking—"

Greg stiffened. "A stalker? You should have gone to the police."

"It wasn't like that. He'd just call me occasionally or try to ask me out again if we saw each other in the hallway. Then the company transferred me to the midtown office, and I was relieved, thinking I wouldn't have to have run into him anymore. For a while, all was good."

He shifted in his chair. "What changed?"

"He got transferred to the midtown office too. I probably should mention that, although Raleigh isn't for me, he's the kind of tall, blonde, Nordic type that appeals to a lot of women. One of them was our boss, Alicia."

"Uh-oh. That's a potential minefield. She pursued him?"

"Yep, only Raleigh wasn't running away. Here's where the land mines started exploding. So, he was *dating* her—" Paris used air quotes. "If you can call it that. But he was still pursuing me, chatting me up, asking me out, that sort of thing. One day he backed me into a corner and tried to kiss me."

Greg's voice came out in a growl. "I hope you kicked him where the sun don't shine, stomped on his instep, something."

"I might have except the boss interrupted us. She screamed, actually shrieked like she'd seen a cobra or a decomposing corpse or something. People came running."

"Then everything was out in the open." Greg relaxed his stance.

Paris took in a deep breath. "You'd think so, wouldn't you?"

He sat straighter, his hands fisting on the table. "It *wasn't* obvious?"

"Maybe it was," Paris answered, "but my boss supervised almost everyone in that part of the building. There I was, literally backed into a corner with my side pressed against the water cooler, and she started screaming at me, saying things like, 'How dare you attempt to seduce a co-worker in the halls of our business?'" Paris's voice broke on the final word, and she wiped at an angry tear.

"How could anyone—" Greg grabbed the edge of the table, calming himself. Leaning in, he took a tissue and gently dabbed at her eyes, but his expression was fierce, as though he preparing for battle.

Paris swallowed, touched by his tenderness. "It was surreal, I could hardly believe it was happening. Alicia kept yelling, calling me all kinds of horrid names, blaming the whole ugly scene on me—on my being unwilling to 'give up' a man who didn't want me anymore, asking if I couldn't tell when a man had moved on… It was bizarre, real crazy-town stuff."

Greg scowled and his face flushed red. "Other employees saw it all, and nobody called her on it?"

"No." Paris shook her head, remembering her anxiety then. She couldn't sleep, couldn't eat, and she was constantly jumpy at work. "I suppose they were all afraid for their own jobs. I got a lot of sympathetic looks, but Alicia had proven how ruthless she could be. She'd already fired someone who stood up to her over another issue. and she transferred two others who she said weren't 'team players', which meant that didn't play her game her way. She's crazy, Greg, maybe even certifiable."

"I can't believe people like that think they can get away with what amounts to criminal behavior." Greg's stiff posture and fisted hands showed her how he struggled to hold his temper. "You say your co-workers knew what was going on and all you got was sympathetic looks?"

Paris opened herself to the memory, shuddering as the emotions rushed back. "They knew or could guess based on what she was screaming. But nobody wanted to draw her fury. When she finally finished, she took Raleigh by the arm, shouted that I'd 'better leave him alone in the future,' and marched down the hall. By then, I guess everyone was too embarrassed or too horrified to say anything. A few patted my arm or whispered 'Sorry' as they went by. Most disappeared into their offices to pretend nothing had happened."

Greg drummed his fingers on the table, his face tight. "How many people saw this…this incident?"

"I don't know," Paris answered. "I mean, I didn't get an exact count —I was a bit distracted at the time— but I'd guess at least eighteen or twenty. Probably more heard it all."

"Plenty of witnesses," Greg said. "What did you do?"

Paris paused, wondering if she should go on. Then, realizing that she'd already shared the worst, she plunged ahead. "Until this happened, I loved my job—really loved it, so I didn't give up easily. I kept going to work, giving it my best, and trying to stay out of her way."

She held up her hand as Greg opened his mouth. "Look, it wasn't the best possible response and I know that now, but I was upset and confused and that was the only approach I could think of. It wasn't as if a dozen coworkers or a company harassment officer came forward to explain what my options were."

Greg nodded, pinching his lips tightly together as he reached out, taking her hand in his.

Paris felt the warmth of his touch and his support behind it. "Everything seemed okay for a couple of weeks. Then one day Raleigh saw me in the copy room and stopped to say how sorry he was, only she walked in on us and went ballistic."

Greg took a deep breath and let it out slowly. "What happened then?"

"I interrupted her, actually shouted over her, which I'd never done before. I told her I'd meet her in her office in twenty minutes and we'd discuss the situation privately."

Greg attempted a tight smile. "Sounds like pistols at twenty paces."

Paris managed an almost-smile in response. "I think she expected a showdown. When I walked into her office ten minutes later, she looked ready to shoot before the count began."

"What did you do?"

"The thing is, I had been thinking about it for days. I had already made up my mind what I would do if it happened again. I held up my right hand with two letters. I told her they were both letters of resignation and I was prepared to turn in one or the other to her supervisor before the day was over. The first one explained that I had family responsibilities elsewhere and reluctantly had to give up my job. I promised I'd turn that one in if she signed a document promising a good recommendation letter and nothing negative in my employee file."

Greg snorted. "What did she say to that?"

"Alicia said, 'And if I don't?' So, I showed her the other letter, a much thicker one. I told her it detailed times and places along with the names of witnesses to each of her tantrums. I said I had sought legal advice—which was a white lie of sorts; I'd had lunch with a friend who's a legal secretary in a firm that specializes in employee law."

Greg gave an encouraging nod. "Close enough."

Paris nodded in gratitude. "That's what I thought. I told her I had a clearly actionable case against her for a hostile work environment, one of the worst my legal adviser had ever seen."

Greg relaxed his fighting posture. "You really laid it on. Good for you!"

Paris felt a surge of pride at his compliment. "I knew I'd probably get one chance to confront Alicia before she could scheme behind my back—if she wasn't already."

"Which she was clearly capable of," Greg added.

"No question! If I had waited, I'm sure she'd have sent me

packing on some drummed-up excuse. I'd seen her do it to others. So I laid it all out. I waved a thick manila folder under her nose and told her I had a detailed description of her actions that day at the water cooler along with eyewitness accounts. I flipped open the folder and waved it under her nose." Paris smiled, a sly twinkle in her eyes. "Of course, only that top page had anything to do with her. The rest was a thick client folder I'd picked up on a hunch as I left my office."

"A bluff." Admiration glowed in his eyes.

Paris nodded, his admiring look bringing a rush of heat to her cheeks. "It sure was, although I had plenty of material—not enough to fill that file, mind you, and most of it loose notes, but I knew I could follow through if necessary. I also have an electronic back up, which I told her was in a secure location, offsite. I promised that if she signed the document I'd drafted, I'd turn in the first letter, but I would keep the second. If she ever got in the way of my getting another job, I'd have my attorneys contact the HR department and we'd see her in court."

Greg nodded approvingly. "You think she believed you?"

Paris answered in the only way she knew. "So far, she hasn't made any noises to the contrary, but I haven't needed her recommendation yet. I may have to follow through on my promise if she doesn't come through on hers."

Greg traced a pattern in the tablecloth. "I hope it doesn't come to that—for your sake." He looked up. "It would be good for her to get some come-uppance, though."

"I understand she already has."

Greg sat forward. "Huh? How?"

"A friend who still works there told me Raleigh left for a management position in another department. On the day he left, he told Alicia he only went out with her to get ahead in the company, and he had no interest in seeing her again. People in the company knew about it because of the scene she created and the horrible things she shrieked."

"She's deranged." Greg's hard voice brimmed with contained fury.

Paris laid her hand over his. "I think she is. I've ended up feeling sorry for her. Anyone that insecure must be miserable all the time."

Greg added surprise to his admiring look. "You feel sorry for her? Really?"

"Well, yes. I mean, it's vindicating to realize Raleigh embarrassed her. But she's unstable, Greg, and obsessed with Raleigh. Of course, part of the blame lies on his shoulders too. He knew how she felt and manipulated the situation. Part of me wants to see him take a fall as well. Still, I can't help thinking neither of them is going to fare well in the future, and that makes me sorry for them both."

"You really are a good person."

"I don't know about that, but I know I'm glad to be out of there and away from all that drama. I hope to move on to a company where there are no Alicias or Raleighs misusing their power or the people around them."

Greg stroked her hand. With a catch in his voice, he said, "You're not only a good person, you've got the courage of a lion."

"I don't—" she began.

He stopped her with a kiss.

"Oh Greg," she whispered. "How can this work?"

"I'll show you," he said, and gave her another soul-searing kiss.

She sighed. "You do make a very convincing argument."

"I thought you might see it my way."

For a time, they simply lost themselves in each other. The oven had to beep a second alarm before they remembered the lasagna and settled down to eat.

Chapter Twelve

Despite some expected nervousness, Paris slept well, her dreams only occasionally haunted by images of a shrieking harridan or a handsome high school principal. She left the curtains open on her east-facing window, so she woke with the dawn. TriTech had scheduled a video call and she dressed with the same care as she would for an in-person interview. She also went through the notes she'd prepped about the company. When the call came through, she assured herself she was as ready as she could be.

A panel of three executives greeted her; all appeared under forty. Adele Rich, who'd scheduled the interview, introduced herself as the human resources specialist. The two men were George Sutherland from software development and Matthew Korda from customer relations.

The pleasantries ended abruptly when Korda asked, "How did TriTech get its start?"

It wasn't a question Paris had anticipated, but she was prepared. "Your former CEO, Barry Sinton, developed the software as a class project while earning his degree at Chico State. The company has been growing and developing that single product for the past fifteen years. You and George were the first student interns Sinton brought onboard and the heirs apparent when he chose to retire."

Korda nodded approval. "You've done your homework. Good."

"We need writers who are willing to do the necessary homework and background study," Adele explained. Jerking her thumb toward her colleague, she added, "Matt here likes to cut to the chase."

"Then I'm glad I read up on TriTech," Paris answered.

The tone became lighter, and the meeting ended half an hour later with Adele announcing they'd be settling on three people to invite for personal interviews the following week. "Should you be selected, can you make arrangements to come to our Sacramento offices?"

When Paris answered yes, her contact grinned. "I expect we'll see you next week."

Paris left the call more hopeful than she had been in weeks, and also hoping she could finally let go of any residual anger left from her previous job. An image of Greg popped into mind, but now was not the time. She pushed those thoughts to simmer on the back burner.

"They liked me, Gran," she reported when she visited the hospital later that day. Gran's doctors had found a suspicious-looking shadow on her x-rays and were keeping her another day while they decided what came next.

Her grandmother adjusted her pillows. "Of course, they did, darling. What's not to like?"

"Thanks Gran, for being my biggest cheerleader, but you know not every employer feels the same way you do."

"They need to know you better." Gran sat up straighter. "Have you told your young man yet? About the interview?"

Paris sighed. "He's not *my* young man, and no, I haven't told Greg."

"What do you think he'll say?"

"What he will *say* is that he's happy for me and hopes I get the job. I'm not sure he means it, though. He'd like to see me stay right here."

"And you? How do you feel about him?"

"I wish I knew. He's a great guy, but..." She let the sentence trail off.

"But you've been hesitant to commit to anyone since Erich broke your heart."

Startled, Paris took a moment to catch her breath. "I wish you weren't so perceptive."

"How long has that been? Three years?"

"About that."

"He promised you the moon and you were counting on him. Then—"

"I remember, Gran. I was too young, too naïve and trusting... We don't need to rehash it."

"It seems maybe we do." Gran leaned forward, taking Paris's hand.

"You haven't trusted any man since. And then after the fiasco with Raleigh—"

"It isn't just that." Paris breathed out a long sigh.

Gran waited.

"I saw what Mom went through when Daddy died. I was really young, but I remember how she struggled. She didn't have a job or career training. Daddy was going to provide for us, and Mom planned to make her career as a wife and mother. You know, she told me once that she'd have had another baby the next year if Daddy hadn't died. I'd have been a big sister." Paris averted her gaze, blinking away unexpected sadness. She regained control and went on.

"Those memories are still with me, Gran. Of Mom having to go out and find whatever job she could get to pay the bills, even while grieving her heart away. Being forced to sell our home and move into that small condo. Then when she lost her job, that was the first time we moved up here. I guess she had friends who helped her find another position, and another place for us to live, but of course, there was no health insurance, and when she got so sick, there wasn't anything to fall back on. Thank goodness for you and Aunt Jess. I hated that we had to sponge off you for so long. And here I am doing it again."

"Sponging?" Gran frowned. "Wherever did you get that idea?"

"You know what I mean. It wasn't ever Mom's idea to have to move back home to let her mother take care of us. She didn't have a choice."

"You have some very confused ideas." Gran looked upset, maybe even offended.

"I saw—"

"You were little, as you said. Maybe you didn't see clearly." Gran straightened her blankets. "I had been so lonely ever since your grandpa passed. Jess was here, but she had a life of her own...career, boyfriends—"

"Boyfriends?" Paris arched a brow.

"Of course, boyfriends." Gran sniffed. "Jessica has always attracted interesting men."

"I'll have to ask her about that. I haven't seen her with anyone lately."

"Yes, it's best if you ask her." Gran glanced away. "But we're talking about you and your mother. Having her here was a comfort, and it was a blessing to get to know you better."

"I guess I never thought..." Paris let her thoughts trail away.

Gran grasped her hand. "Paris, darling, family is the most important thing in life. I never fully understood what it meant to you when your father died, and I'm deeply sorry for what you suffered, but don't let those memories keep you from looking forward to marriage and a family of your own. Nor of staying close with us. You don't always have to go it alone."

"Gran—"

"No dear. This is important. Let me finish."

Paris waited.

"Maybe Greg isn't the one, but there has to be someone sometime, and I recommend you don't wait too long. Career is important. Knowing you can take care of yourself is important, but no woman ever lay on her deathbed pondering her wonderful career moves."

Stuck for a response, Paris squeezed her grandmother's hand.

Gran's voice softened. "Do you remember your mother's last hours?"

"I'll never forget them." Paris looked out the window. A blue jay bullied a sparrow until it dropped the insect it carried. "Mom was in hospice care. She had a hospital bed like this in the living room."

"Yes?" Gran encouraged Paris on.

Paris's eyes met her grandmother's. "She was raised up on pillows and her voice was so weak, but she kept—" As the memories returned, Paris felt her voice catch and she turned back to the window, watching the blue jay eat its stolen dinner.

"She kept reaching for your hand," Gran said. "...talking to you, telling you everything she hoped you'd remember...about her, your father, your family life together—"

"She was reaching for you too." Paris squeezed her grandmother's hand. "She talked about you and Gramps and Jess and the dog she had when she was a girl, an old sheepdog she called... what was her name?"

"Alice. Your mom got the puppy about the same time we read *Alice in Wonderland*."

"That's right." Paris smiled. "I remember her stories about wandering the hills, sometimes with Jess, but always with Alice."

"That old dog went everywhere with her. She grew up with your mom."

"Mom talked about her often."

Gran sighed. "That's the kind of life I want for you, darling."

Paris arched a brow. "Wandering the hills with a sheepdog?"

Gran huffed in exasperation. "Don't be cheeky, dear. I'd like to see you with a loving husband and a little girl of your own, maybe a couple of little girls and a boy too. I'd like great-grandchildren wandering the mountains with or without the dog."

"I don't know, Gran. I—"

"Think about it. That's all I'm asking." Gran yawned broadly. "Family is important. I've tried to convey that to all of you. Jess knows it. She'd like to meet someone and settle down."

"Aunt Jess?"

"Don't sound so incredulous. She isn't over the hill yet."

"But I've never seen her date. I didn't know she cared about having a family."

"She's had a couple of dating relationships that we thought might end in marriage—"

"Jess? Really?"

"Yes really. At some point, you should ask her about them. You really should." Gran's face sagged; she appeared drawn. "Now go talk to that nice young man of yours and tell him about your interview. The medicine they gave me is making me drowsy."

"Yes ma'am." Paris tenderly kissed Gran's cheek.

"You will think about it, won't you? About family?"

"Yes, Gran. I will." Paris started for the door. "And I'll be back to check on you tomorrow."

"Maybe the doctors will know what to do with me by then." Gran yawned and leaned her head against the pillow.

Paris tiptoed out quietly, closing the door behind her.

All the way up the hill, she considered Gran's words, mentally reviewing the few memories she had of her father, the pictures she'd seen of her mother with Alice, the way her mom had leaned so heavily on her own mother and sister during her final days. As much as she hated to admit it, Gran had a point. That was something else she'd have to consider. Someday.

~

"GREG FRANTZ, will you please stop pacing?" Miranda Bailey turned her disapproving stare on her boss. "You're going to wear out the carpet, and it isn't even a year old."

"Sorry, Miranda." Greg went into his private office where he could pace in peace. He glanced at the clock for the thirtieth time that hour: two-thirty p.m. He'd expected to hear from Paris by now. Hadn't she promised to let him know when her interview ended?

As he paced, he recalled what she'd said about them falling so hard so fast. He asked himself how that had happened, though he suspected he knew. After moving to Destiny, he had suddenly seen himself in a different light. No longer the happy-go-lucky, casually dating bachelor, he now felt ready to commit—and he wanted to find the right woman, the one who would make it all work.

The last woman he dated had seemed so *almost* right that it had been difficult admitting she wasn't, that they weren't good for each other. He didn't like it, but he could see the gaps, the problems that would arise down the road, as well as the immediate differences between them. Dating her had helped him clarify what he wanted, needed, in a wife. Since he was a kid, people had teased him about his habit of making lists, but list-making worked for him.

After that last break-up, he'd hiked to his place on the mountain. With a picnic lunch and a writing tablet, he spent the afternoon considering what he needed in a companion, lover, wife, and the mother of his future children. He created a list no human woman could possibly fill. Then over the next weeks, he'd whittled it down into three categories: 1. Essential qualities; 2. Important, but not necessary; and 3. It would be nice.

Since then, he'd measured every woman he dated against his list, always giving good candidates at least three dates before he compared them to his ideal. Even with some generosity in his comparisons, no one measured up.

Until Paris Cutler. His attraction to her had been instant and powerful—so powerful he felt certain he'd be disappointed if he got to know her better. The opposite happened. She had all of the "essential" qualities and most of those on the "important" list. Some of the "nice" qualities were there too. There were downstrokes of course, but he thought they could work on those together; after all, he had failings and foibles too. As he saw it, Paris was missing only one ingredient in his perfect recipe: Somewhere along the way, she would have to want him too—want him enough to give up her myopic vision of fulfillment by landing the perfect job.

He sighed. Paris was clearly interested, but if her interest didn't equal his, he was about to get his heart donkey-kicked right out of his chest. He wanted her to be happy. Part of him hoped she'd get the job. A more selfish part hoped she didn't. The *biggest* part hoped she'd get the position but choose him instead. That seemed highly unlikely. Another glance at the clock told him minutes still crawled like hours. He sat at his desk, trying to focus on the papers he found there, keeping one eye on his phone, willing it to ring.

PARIS REACHED for the office door and then dropped her hand. She took a deep breath—correction, *another* deep breath—and pushed. "Hi, Mrs. Bailey. Is Greg in?"

"Oh yes, Paris. He's in his office. Go right—"

The office door swung open, and Greg popped his head out, "Come in." As soon as the door closed behind her, he said, "I thought you'd call."

Paris frowned as she remembered the promise. "I'm sorry; I guess I was distracted."

"Uh-huh," Greg said.

"The doctors called this morning, so I went to see Gran at the hospital."

Greg's head snapped up. "She's still there?"

"Her doctors said they found a spot, a shadow—" And just like that, Paris was in tears.

"Paris? What's wrong?" He stood and went around his desk. Wrapping his arms around her, he held her gently, supporting her while she got her bearings.

"I'm sorry," she blubbered, embarrassed. "It's that phrase, 'a shadow on the x-ray.' That was the first thing the doctors spotted when my mom—" Her voice broke.

"It was cancer, wasn't it? That took your mom?"

Paris couldn't make her voice work, but she nodded.

"I see why that phrase frightened you." He stroked her back in sympathy and she welcomed the comfort. "When will you know more?"

"It's...hard to say." Paris spoke haltingly, but at least her voice was in gear again. "A couple of doctors are looking at the x-rays to decide what kind of imaging they should try next. She'll most likely have an M.R.I. in the morning."

"That should help them know what they're dealing with...if it's anything at all."

"I guess so." She paused. "I...I didn't mean to fall apart like that. I—"

"Emotion sneaked up on you."

She nodded. "You diagnosed that well."

"So... can I ask how your interview went?"

"That's the better news. It went great. They're going to choose three candidates for personal interviews and the H.R. specialist hinted I'll be one."

He squeezed her shoulder. "Good for you. I hope you get exactly what you want."

"I told Gran you'd say that."

"You told Gran, huh?"

"She asked me how you'd take the news—about the interview, not the x-ray—and I said you'd be completely supportive."

"Hope I didn't disappointment."

"You never do." As she said it, she knew it was true.

Greg sounded tentative when he asked, "Do you feel like having company tonight?"

Paris considered the idea. "If you don't mind, I think I'll pass."

He narrowed one eye. "Don't tell me: You need to wash your hair."

She laughed. "No, nothing like that. It's been a very… emotional day—a roller coaster day, you know? I have a few things I need to take care of—*not* including hair washing—and I'll probably make an early night of it. Still, I owe you a dinner. Maybe Friday?"

"Where? Your place? With Gran and Jess?"

"Not what I had in mind. I will cook, though. Count on it."

"I'll hold you to that," he answered… just before he kissed her.

Chapter Thirteen

Paris filled the hours before bedtime with useful work, yet her chores didn't take the time she expected. This would have been a good night to cook for Greg. With Gran in the hospital and Jess chaperoning her field trip, they'd have had the house to themselves. As she worked, she thought of everything Gran had said about marriage and family and began imagining a possible future with Greg. In fact, she thought of little else—except the shadow on Gran's x-rays.

Everyone had downplayed her mother's condition at first. Paris shuddered, remembering those painful memories; the times she found her mother bent, sobbing, over a stack of bills she couldn't pay, or studying the price tags in the grocery store. She'd never forget how broken her mother had seemed when she had to mourn not only the husband she loved, but the home they'd built together. And then the cancer...

Paris had sworn to avoid that kind of pain if possible. But who could say how her life would go? Unlike her mother, she had pursued an education, developed a sought-after skill, and begun a lucrative career. Even if she decided to walk away now, she could stay in touch with professional associations, keep up with where the industry was heading, and get back in the game if she needed to support herself... or a family.

When had she started thinking about a family? And why was she obsessing about her mother? Why couldn't she focus on the possibilities of a happy life instead?

She knew she had always carried a vague thought of a husband and children—someday. That someday had seemed closer, more substantial, after she met Greg, toured his home, saw the rooms he hoped to fill with children.

Our children? She shivered at the thought, both thrilled and terrified. But why should the thought scare her? Greg would make a great father, and his kids would be beautiful and as wonderful as he was. She shook the thoughts away, embarrassed at the direction they'd taken.

Still, the idea stubbornly refused to vanish, but kept sneaking back, intruding on the small tasks she'd set for herself. Even long after she'd turned in, she lay awake, thinking of a possible future with Greg and the beautiful children the two of them might make.

PARIS WASN'T the only one who lay awake. Across town, Greg tossed and turned in a large, lonely bed, a bachelor living in a family home, wondering what on earth had happened to his good sense. Why had he fallen for a woman who made it clear she wasn't staying? He felt tempted to jump up and beat his head against the wall.

He thought of the last time he'd considered commitment. They'd parted as friends, but things had been tense for a while. His inner voice warned that he'd walked into this new relationship with eyes wide open. If it failed, he had no one to blame but himself.

"I hate it when my inner voice is right." He groaned and buried his head under the pillow, rolled onto his stomach and thumped the mattress with his fist. Consciously changing the direction of his thoughts, he wondered how he could help Paris if her grandmother faced a serious threat. He lay awake until dawn, staring at the ceiling, knowing he was unlikely to find easy answers, but unable to stop the questions.

IN THE MIDDLE of the following day, Paris bounced out of the hospital with a much-reduced stress level. Further imaging had shown the shadow on Gran's X-ray to be a small fracture in her pelvis. Not cancer! Although it wasn't large enough to be spotted easily, the crack would take time to heal and would make walking difficult and movement painful. Gran's doctors had made a clear diagnosis but hadn't yet decided how to treat it. Gran would be all right, but she'd be hospitalized a little longer.

With Jess out of town for the weekend, this was the perfect night to have Greg over for dinner. For a moment, Paris considered whether that would be a good idea. Did she want to encourage a relationship that might keep her rooted here? *Stop overthinking.* Before she could change her mind, she called Greg, who eagerly accepted. Paris hurried to her car, already working on the menu.

GREG BUSTLED AROUND HIS OFFICE, busily rescheduling his evening. He was thrilled that Paris had invited him. It was the first time she had done the inviting and he didn't want to mess it up. Still, he'd need diplomacy to arrange for his science teacher and occasional vice principal to take his place at the P.T.O. meeting. Maybe he could get Ms. Delgado to report on the Bates Foundation grant proposal and what it could mean to their language programs. He rather liked that idea.

By five o'clock, Greg was ready to leave for the day. A glance in the mirror told him he could use a quick shave and maybe a clean shirt too. If he hurried, he'd still have time to stop by the corner store, so he didn't show up empty-handed.

He reached for the doorknob and realized his fingers were trembling. In fact, his whole body buzzed. He suspected this night might be make-or-break for him and Paris.

He sighed as he closed the door and headed for his car.

PARIS CHECKED THE PORK LOIN. She'd coated it in kosher salt and had it roasting at a low, slow temperature. It was coming along nicely. The pineapple upside down cake was cooling on the counter and her fresh spinach salad chilled happily in the fridge. Now for her signature dish, her spring risotto. She had sautéed the onion and garlic, added finely diced spring vegetables, and browned arborio rice. Next came the tricky part—concentrated stirring for twenty minutes, carefully adding a ladle of broth as needed until the dish was finished.

She had just begun the process when her cell phone rang, but she couldn't quit now, or the rice might be ruined. Then she realized this could be the call from TriTech. She checked the phone number, saw it *was* TriTech, and answered. Her sacrifice was rewarded when Adele invited Paris to come for a personal interview. Paris happily accepted as she juggled the phone in one hand while stirring the risotto with the other. In the end, she had both an appointment with TriTech and a successful rice dish—which she completed as Greg arrived.

"Come in," she called. "Dinner's all but ready."

Minutes later they sat comfortably at Gran's dining table, Greg exulting over the food while Paris admired his flowers. Then Paris announced, "TriTech called."

"Oh?" Greg set down his fork.

"I interview next Tuesday."

"Paris! That's… Congratulations."

Paris fiddled with the food on her plate. "I don't have the job yet—"

"But you have the interview, and you'll have the job as well…once they've had a chance to meet you."

"Greg—"

"I know. You always said you were leaving. You were clear about that."

"Greg—"

"Sweetheart—"

Paris warmed at the endearment as Greg took her hand.

"I told you I want you to be happy. If this job is what you want, then I hope you find it as rewarding as you want it to be." He kissed her fingers. "We've had this discussion. Let's see what happens."

Paris turned to him, taking his lips with her own. After a long moment, she drew away. "You always make a persuasive argument."

"I hoped you'd see it my way." He kissed her again. In the honeyed glow of that kiss, Paris could easily forget the differences, and the distance, growing between them.

Chapter Fourteen

P aris hummed through the morning as she tended the garden and prepped the downstairs room for Gran's return. The evening with Greg had her considering possibilities. Could a long-distance relationship work while they figured things out? Would Greg consider moving to the valley? She didn't want to live in Destiny, but maybe, if she and Greg...

She sighed. No use trying to work it out now. These questions could be put off.

Anticipating her departure, she and Greg had agreed to spend as much time together as they could, but today Greg had a lunch meeting with a faculty committee and the Spring Open House in the evening, the same activity that had kept Aunt Jess busy for much of the past week. Greg had asked Paris to call when Gran returned, but he'd be too busy to talk even then.

When she left for the hospital in the early afternoon, she already missed him.

She arrived at Gran's bedside to find her sitting up, packed, ready to leave. A nurse helped with medications. As Paris entered, the nurse helped Gran stand using a walker.

"You're going to be part of the walker set now, huh?" Paris meant it jokingly.

"It's temporary," Gran snapped.

"Mrs. Kerr will only need the walker while she's healing," the nurse explained. He put his arm behind Gran's back to support her while she took a step. "Careful," he advised. He continued to watch Gran as he spoke to Paris. "The fracture was not displaced, so her doctor recommended nonoperative treatment. She has prescriptions to manage the pain and appointments for physical therapy. She'll also need to return for further imaging."

"Further imaging?"

"Yes," the nurse said. "New x-rays."

Paris kept her frustration in check. "I know what imaging is. I don't understand why she will need it if they already know the fracture hasn't separated."

"Whoa there!" The nurse straightened, held Gran's arm to head off a fall, and looked directly at Paris. "There's always a risk of late displacement in a fracture of this kind. Frequent imaging can assure her doctor nothing is missed."

"I see."

Paris waited while the nurse helped Gran back to her bedside and gave her additional instruction about careful stepping to avoid putting torque on the break. "Looks like you're all set," he said. "I'll be back in a few minutes with a wheelchair."

"I'm sorry I snapped," Gran said as he left. "This thing hurts more than it has a right to."

Paris offered a conciliatory smile. "You have every right to hurt, Gran, and every right to be cranky if you feel like it."

"But no right to take it out on you or that poor man. He's been very kind."

They chatted idly while waiting. When the nurse was slow in returning, Paris excused herself to find a place with better cell reception so she could leave a message on Aunt Jess's phone. "I'll let her know you're coming home," Paris told Gran as she left.

"Little point in that," Gran groused. "She's never there."

Paris also tried calling Greg but ended up leaving a message. She returned to find the nurse helping Gran into a wheelchair. Paris collected Gran's things, including the walker which folded and rolled easily beside her. The two women were soon on their way home.

"I don't know how I'll manage this schedule they've set up what with physical therapy, hospital x-rays every couple of weeks, checkups—" Gran paused, her face lined with worry. "With Jess into her spring schedule and gone all the time and you getting a new job, I don't know how I'll get around. They won't let me drive."

"I don't have a new job yet, Gran."

"But you will. Your interview is Tuesday, right?"

"Yes, but even if they offer me the job, it won't start immediately."

"I know, but—"

"Don't worry." Paris squeezed her grandmother's hand. "It will all work out."

"I don't like to depend on other people." Gran lapsed into silence.

That's an issue for me, too. Paris bit her lip to keep from saying it aloud. She got Gran peacefully bundled into a recliner and called Greg again. When it went to voicemail, she chose not to leave a second message.

FRIDAY MORNING STARTED WELL with Paris finding two more jobs that looked like possibilities, should TriTech not work out. She completed the online applications for both before Gran woke. Then she took time to prep a nourishing breakfast for her grandmother. Afterward, she helped Gran through a simplified morning routine including recommended exercises. "Take it easy," she encouraged when Gran started across the room.

"I don't sleep well in the futon," Gran said. "I want to be in my own bed."

"Upstairs? No way."

"But—"

"I mean it, Gran. You even try to climb those stairs and I'll check you into a convalescent hospital. You about scared the life out of me when you fell. How do you think you'd manage those stairs on crutches?"

Gran flushed crimson. "A rest home? You wouldn't dare!"

"Don't push me, Gran. It would be a *convalescent* home, for while you are *convalescing.* And I'll definitely check you into one if you even try to manage those stairs on crutches."

Gran pouted. "They wouldn't take me if I didn't want to go."

"They would if you were incompetent to make your own decisions."

"Me? Incompetent? You listen to me, young lady—"

Paris laid her hand on her grandmother's shoulder. In gentle, firm tones she said, "No, Gran, you listen to me. I'd hate to take you anywhere but here. I want to take care of you myself, at least as much as I can for as long as I can, but you have to help. You were seriously hurt and it's lucky that you aren't down with a broken hip. Or worse."

She crouched in front of Gran, brushing her hair back with gentle strokes. "You scared me. I don't know what I'd do if I lost you. I know this recovery is going to be difficult and it will surely test your patience. But please, please give me this. Be the perfect patient until the doctor says it's okay to climb the stairs."

Gran's eyes twinkled. "And if I am? Since you're treating me like a child, are you planning to bribe me too? Give me an ice cream if I'm good?"

Paris sighed. "Okay. What kind of bribe do you need to behave yourself?"

"Just one thing." Gran beamed. "If I'm good as gold until the doc says I'm healed, you'll give serious consideration to staying here and marrying Greg Frantz."

"Gran!" Paris jumped to her feet. "No fair! You set me up!"

Gran smirked. "It was easier than I imagined."

"Please note that I haven't promised anything." Paris paused. "You may also want to note that Greg hasn't proposed."

"He will, if you give him any encouragement."

Paris shook her head. "I don't know what I'm going to do about you."

"I want you to be happy, dear. And I want him to be happy too. He's a nice man."

"Forgive my asking, but how would you know how nice he is?"

"We had him over to dinner a few times. When he first came back to town." Gran looked off into the distance. "You know, doing our part to welcome the new teacher."

'You're full of surprises, aren't you?"

"Stick around," Gran said. "There may be even greater surprises in store."

"You do keep me guessing." Paris helped her grandmother back into the easy chair.

An hour later, primped and primed, Paris parked at the high

school. Greg had asked her for an after-school meal, but he'd arranged to meet her here. She entered to find Mrs. Bailey busily working. "Oh hello, Paris. Greg should be back in a few minutes. Would you like to have a seat in his office?"

"I'll wait here if you don't mind." She pulled out a chair.

"Oh, well then, suit yourself." Mrs. Bailey returned to her organizing.

Paris sat watching the students walk by the office windows, leaving for the day. Things hadn't changed much in the eight years since she walked these halls. When a lone blond boy hurried past the window, she thought she recognized the one she'd found rifling through Mrs. Bailey's desk and realized she hadn't told anyone about the incident. Maybe she'd ease her way into it. As the traffic in the hallway began to clear, she turned to Mrs. Bailey. "I guess the petty cash fund has taken a beating with me around."

Mrs. Bailey frowned as she looked up. "Oh? Uh, what was that?"

"All these late lunches Greg has been arranging as 'payment' for my work on the grant. They must be draining the fund by now."

The secretary clucked her tongue. "Is that what he told you? Shame on him!"

"The school isn't paying?"

"I believe the first lunch came out of petty cash, but that's the only one."

"You mean Greg paid for the others himself?"

"Guilty as charged." Greg stepped in, raising both hands in a gesture of surrender. "You caught me."

Paris's face warmed. "You told me—"

"Whoa!" Greg took her hands in his. "I'll admit I implied that the school was paying, and I did let the school pay for that first meal at Louie's, but I never said the school was continuing to pay. Honest, I didn't."

"You—" But when Paris thought back, she couldn't remember any time he'd the school paid. Her temper had flared quickly—it always seemed to flare quickly—but this time it cooled as fast. "You let me believe it was the school's money," she said in a milder tone.

"You're right," he said, his voice gentle. "I let you believe that. Would you have gone with me if you thought otherwise?"

She narrowed her eyes. "You mean if I knew the truth?"

He answered with a sheepish shrug. "Well, yes."

"You wanted my company that much?"

"Do you mind?"

"I'm flattered."

He leaned toward her.

She leaned toward him, her eyes falling closed.

The kiss had almost happened when Mrs. Bailey cleared her throat.

Greg looked up as if roused from a trance. "Uh, yes. I think it's time for us to get going."

Heat flamed Paris's face, especially when she saw the students who gawked as they passed the windows. "Yes. I think you're right."

They waited until Mrs. Bailey left. Then Greg locked the office and led Paris down the hall. "Broadway Louie's sound good to you?"

She stopped. "Are you going to let me pay my share?"

"No way."

She pursed her lips, but let the expression soften into a half-smile. "You're spoiling me."

"I hope to."

"Okay," she said, grudgingly accepting that she loved the attention. "Louie's sounds great."

He swung the door wide. "Louie's it is."

Chapter Fifteen

They sat side by side, so close together their heads almost touched as they looked over the menu. They both picked their favorites, so ordering was quick and easy. As the server left, Greg spoke. "The first reports on the ore samples came back."

Paris set down her glass. "What? Really?"

"Um-hm."

"And you didn't say anything?"

He fiddled with his fork, his smile more of a smirk. "I'm saying it now."

"You're going to make me ask, aren't you?"

He grinned.

"Okay. What did they find?"

"Enough to want to do more checking. The matrix is the kind of stone where diamonds most frequently occur. And they found a few small stones too."

Paris drew back in surprise. "You're serious? They found diamonds?"

"Shh," Greg advised. "It's nothing we want to share yet, but yes, they found small ones. Industrial quality. It's enough to encourage them to keep looking, and they're willing to invest time and resources. They'll have a crew on the mountain by the first of May."

Paris smiled. "Were you nervous about telling me?"

"Nervous? Should I be?"

"Afraid I'll want to marry you for your diamonds."

"Is that a possibility?" His voice held the same teasing tone as hers. "Because if it is, I may go buy a few quality stones to salt the find."

"You're being silly. You know I—"

He frowned. "You're not going to start the old argument again, are you?"

"But—"

"You know if you keep arguing, I'll have to keep kissing you."

She grinned. "Sounds like a good reason to argue."

SATURDAY DAWNED SUNNY AND WARM. They took a picnic to Herbert's cabin. The walk entranced Paris with its beauty, the meadows decked in blossoming wildflowers. Greg paused to show her where people had mined for gold, the scars on the land visible more than a century later. They reached Herbert's clearing, unpacked lunch, and ate at the slab table. Paris breathed in the brisk, pine-scented air. "It's so lovely. I haven't always appreciated how beautiful Destiny is."

He arched a brow. "And you appreciate it now?"

"Yes." She smiled. "I do."

"Nothing like this in the city," he said. He licked his lips. "Here," he indicated a path. "Let me take you around the side of the mountain so you can see where the mining company wants to start exploratory drilling."

They hiked farther than Paris had imagined. "This is good," she declared when they finally reached the drilling point. "It's far enough from the cabin and the meadow that it shouldn't impact them."

"And the company thinks they can access it from the old logging road down there." He pointed to a thin strip of dirt a hundred yards below them. "So they won't be taking heavy equipment through Destiny. They're making every attempt to minimize environmental disruption, or impact on the town. Of course, employees may want to live there."

Paris considered that. "You told me Destiny had more going for it than I thought. Is this what you had in mind?"

"Yes, but the potential for a mine isn't all. The Destiny Spa and Resort could be taking its first clients within the year."

"That soon?"

"That's what I hear. The company is well capitalized. They'll have multiple crews working on various buildings, pools, spas, whatever. And they're already planning a huge advertising campaign in major metros across the western U.S. They want to create a destination spa that will draw big money from everywhere."

Paris raised an eyebrow. "Maybe there is something more to Destiny's future."

"Local farmers who haven't already gone organic are considering it now, and the organic farmers are creating a cooperative to sell 'mountain-grown' produce to tourists the resort may bring in."

"Some family farmers have had to sell because they can't compete with industrial farms in the valley, but an organic co-op and a fresh new market for their goods could change a lot."

"You see?" Greg held out his arms as if taking in the whole community. "Destiny may have a future for you too."

Paris rolled her eyes. "I'll believe that when I see it."

"Keep watching."

They worked their way back to the meadow. "Let me show you something." He led the way to a space in the meadow where he had carved one side off an old stump. "It's perfect for leaning back and watching the grass grow." He sat down, positioned himself against the wood, and beckoned her to join him.

Paris settled against him. The scent of fresh-cut wood swirled around them, mixing with the pungent sweetness of the evergreens, the grassy scent of the meadow, and Greg's ginger-lime aftershave.

"Peaceful, hm?"

"Wonderful," she answered.

For a time, they sat, soaking up the warm spring sunshine and enjoying the peace. Paris spotted a butterfly working the redbud blossoms near them. She was so caught up in watching its progress that she didn't notice what else was happening until Greg touched her shoulder, put his finger to his lips, and pointed.

She gasped, causing the young doe to lift her head and look their way. Apparently deciding the lumps by the old tree posed no threat, the deer went back to grazing, her spotted fawn at her side. They watched for several minutes until the flight of a hawk overhead startled the doe and both deer bounded from the meadow to seek shelter among the trees.

"That was amazing!" Paris stared after them.

"I've seen that doe in this area before, but this is the first time I've seen this year's fawn."

"She's raised others?"

"At least three I know of."

"How do you know it's the same deer?"

"She has a dark spot near her belly on her right side, maybe some kind of scar. None of the others I've seen here have that."

"You must come up often."

"I come a couple of times a month, almost daily during the summer. Of course, it's easier when I'm working in town, but I tried to come as often as I could even before Mrs. Elam retired and made a spot for me."

Paris gazed out with a new understanding. "You really love this place."

He looked around them. "What's not to love?"

Paris took in the meadow, the blossoms buzzing with honeybees, the forest beyond. She breathed in the fresh, clean air, scented by pines and wildflowers and Greg. "You've got me there."

They walked slowly back to the table where they'd left their things. Greg shouldered their pack. "Paris, what happened to your dad?"

"Oh my." She sat heavily. "Another zinger out of nowhere."

"I've heard enough to know it had something to do with his being out in the wilderness. I wondered if maybe that gives you concerns about…you know…being out here."

"Oh no! Not at all."

She stood again, taking the smaller pack. "You're right, though. His accident happened in the wild." She gestured toward the trail, and they started downward.

"Dad was working for the public utility. They had, and still have, small dams on the creeks up the canyons, each with a hydroelectric plant. Much of the power used in the valley comes from those canyon dams."

He nodded, encouraging her to go on.

"The power from one of those power plants dropped suddenly in the middle of a winter storm, lots of rain and wind, and the company sent Dad to see what was happening. Only they sent him alone. He was apparently crossing the creek, hopping from one stone to another, when he slipped on some wet moss and hit his head. He would have survived that injury except it knocked him out and his face was in the water."

Greg gasped. "He drowned?"

Paris nodded. "That was the official cause of death."

"I'm so sorry! I wouldn't have asked if—"

She swallowed. "It's all right. It's been a long time."

"Did your family file suit? Wrongful death, maybe?"

She lifted a shoulder. "The only family was Mom and me. I was a little kid and Mom was a timid soul who always figured the other guy had the upper hand. She wouldn't have dreamed of suing a huge utility company. Dad's brother checked on us later and found us living in...shall we say, much reduced circumstances?"

"He helped her file suit?"

"He encouraged, but there's a statute of limitations. By the time Mom started thinking about it, she was too late. She'd have won easily, I think. The company sent people in pairs after Daddy died. It was essentially an admission that they'd messed up by sending him alone."

"You call him Daddy."

She tilted her head. "I was little when he died. I always called him Daddy then. I guess I still think of him that way."

"And your mother never remarried."

"She dated a little. I remember her going out a few times, but after a while she even stopped accepting dates. She said she'd been blessed with a great husband and a great daughter and she'd be content to raise me and have me turn out well."

"I'm sure she was proud of you."

"I think she was." Paris blinked heavily.

"I didn't mean to stir up bad memories."

"It's okay. Really."

They walked in silence for a time. When the path became too narrow to walk side-by-side, Greg led, "in case there's a problem."

"It's still too cold for snakes, isn't it?"

"Pretty sure," he answered, "but who knows what else we might encounter?"

"Bears? Aren't they still hibernating too?"

He turned with a look that spoke volumes. "I'm more concerned about two-legged predators. Rumors about new mines can bring out the raiders."

"Oh, I didn't think." Paris followed closely, chastened but grateful Greg had been thinking when she had not. They reached the trailhead near the city park and Greg drove her home.

He walked her to the door, but as he leaned down to kiss her, he whispered, "We've got an audience."

Paris turned and saw two pairs of curious eyes, Gran and Jess watching from the dining room table. "I'll see you tomorrow," she whispered back. "Consider yourself kissed."

"Tomorrow," he answered, his look warm. "I'll cash in then."

GREG HUMMED as he drove home. He didn't recall the last time he'd started humming for no reason. But then he realized Paris was the reason. He loved being around her, loved how easy it was to talk to her, loved her look, her style, and the sound of her voice, even the quirky way she tilted her head when she was thinking. He could easily see her fitting into his life, his home, his future. Paris had begun taking the place of the faceless woman of his dreams as his wife, his lover, the mother of his children. *So much for taking it easy, Frantz. Face it: you're in deep.*

When he lived a bachelor's life, thoughts like these might have driven him to a panicked exit. Not tonight. Tonight he liked being right where he was.

PARIS WOKE Sunday morning with the image of the doe and fawn left from her dream. She hummed as she dressed for church and went to the kitchen to make breakfast for herself and Gran. With Jess out of town again, getting Gran to church would likely be a project. Glancing at the clock, Paris was glad she'd started early.

An hour later, Paris, Gran, and the walker struggled up the four steps to the church door. Paris quickly understood how big a barrier four steps could be. She started by lifting the walker to the landing at the top of the stairs. Then she had Gran lean on the handrail on one side while she stood on the other, balancing and lifting as they took one step at a time. They were only on the second when Gran slipped. It took all of Paris's strength to keep her from falling.

"Here, let me help." One of the men in the congregation, an older fellow named Harvey, caught Gran's elbow from behind.

A man named Grant stepped in front of them, taking Gran's free arm. "We can all help," he said. Grant lifted from in front while Harvey lifted from behind. Paris helped Gran balance and pull up on each step.

"There, we did it." Harvey smiled, patting Gran's shoulder as they reached the entrance. "You okay, Annette?"

"Yes, Harvey, thank you. Thank you too, Grant. I don't know how we'd have made it without you." Gran beamed at her helpers, both of whom assured her they'd done nothing and went to sit with their families.

For Paris, it was a reminder that Gran had a long history here. "Let me get the walker," Paris said, positioning it so Gran could take hold.

"Thank you, dear." Gran regained her composure and Paris admired her grace. Together they made their way up the aisle. Paris helped Gran get comfortably seated. She turned to adjust Gran's pillow and saw Greg slip in and take a seat behind them. The organ music rose in crescendo to a final dramatic chord and the meeting began.

During the sermon, Paris took every opportunity to catch a glimpse of Greg without seeming to look. Straightening Gran's pillow allowed her to turn half-way. Handing a hymnal to the young family behind her gave her an even better look. A still better opportunity came when a small sparrow chirped from the rafters and flew toward the back of the room. The congregation followed the bird's progress, so it seemed only natural for Paris to look as well.

She turned to fluff Gran's pillow again when Gran whispered loudly, "Paris, stop fidgeting! You're as nervous as a toothless man at a dental convention." Several people near them snickered quietly and Paris turned her eyes forward, her cheeks heating.

The sermon droned on. At its conclusion, Paris could not have said what it was about. When the final "Amen" was spoken and the postlude began, she helped Gran stand and stepped into the aisle. She looked toward the back of the room, but Greg was no longer there. Swallowing disappointment, she helped Gran down the aisle, hoping someone would help with the stairs. One of the men who'd helped earlier was angling toward the door and Paris pushed ahead to catch him. She arrived at the door to find Greg waiting.

"Where's your gran?" he asked, turning an expectant look behind Paris.

"Uh, coming. I'll… go get her." Flustered, Paris stepped inside. Had Greg really waited to help them? She was more than grateful.

"Is someone here to help us?" Gran asked. Paris heard a tremor in Gran's voice despite her composed appearance.

"Yes, Gran. Greg's here." She held the door.

Greg smiled broadly when he saw them. "Here, Mrs. Kerr. Let me help you down these stairs." He stepped up beside Gran and put one strong arm around her waist. "You don't mind a little cuddle, do you?"

Gran chuckled. "Been a while since I cuddled someone as young and handsome as you."

Greg held her with one arm, standing to her side and taking her other hand. "I've got you," he said. "I won't let you fall."

Gran beamed a grateful smile. "I'm sure you won't."

In four easy steps, they were down the stairs. Paris quickly positioned the walker and the three of them eased their way to Gran's car. Greg helped Gran take a comfortable seat on the passenger side and loaded the walker for Paris. Then he held the driver's door while Paris slid behind the wheel. The car wasn't quite out of the parking lot when Gran said, "You've got a good one, Paris. Don't be eager to throw away something that good."

Paris started to respond but bit her lip instead. She knew she'd have to think through all the questions sometime, and she'd begun to believe Gran could be right—though she still could not imagine how it could work. Some things could not be put off indefinitely and soon these questions would need to be answered. But not yet.

Chapter Sixteen

As soon as Paris got her grandmother settled, she was back in her car and headed for the address Amber had given. As a respected professional in the community, Amber was buying her own home not far from where she'd lived during the girls' high school years.

As Paris passed a home a few blocks from her grandmother's, she caught something odd from the corner of her eye. Was that someone climbing out a window? She shook her head, certain she could not have seen what she thought. Then she caught a glimpse of a slim figure disappearing around the side, dressed in jeans and a gray hoodie. He reminded her of the boy she'd seen in Mrs. Bailey's desk, and that reminded her that she hadn't told Greg about the scene she'd interrupted.

A honk from an approaching car reminded Paris that she was stopped in the middle of a public road. "Okay," she said aloud, waving to the driver while picking up speed. Should she call the sheriff to report a crime? Then again, did she know what she'd seen? Or that there'd been a crime? Shaking her head, Paris turned at the corner. By the time she reached her friend's home, she had put the incident behind her.

"Catch me up on everybody," Paris said as she sat down with Amber and picked up a mug. "How's your brother these days?"

"Tyler? He's married, with three cute kids and a dog, very settled."

"Huh. He was the playboy of the school the year before I got here. I never really knew him, since he was in college before I arrived, but everybody talked about him, and he brought some of his dates to town. What's he doing for work?"

"He's a social worker, a therapist for one of the big health insurance companies. He and his family live in the Bay Area."

"Sounds like he's doing well. How about the others? Your mom and dad, Sunny and Skye."

Amber smiled. "You knew Mom and Dad moved. They downsized, but they're still in Destiny."

"Yeah, I went by their old house. It doesn't look like them anymore."

"There's a young family there now, the Coopers. You'd like them."

"And the others? Your cousins?"

"You'd be surprised at Sunny. You know she wasn't much of a student when we were all in school."

"I remember."

"She graduated, barely, and swore she'd never enter a classroom again. Then she sort of fell backwards into leading tours at the State Capitol Museum and discovered she loved history."

"Ha! Mrs. Chang would be surprised."

"I'm sure she was. Sunny came back to ask for her recommendation when she applied to Sac State."

"You're kidding. Sunny went to college?"

"She's been slowly working her way through and she'll soon graduate. Last time I saw her, she was talking about grad school."

"I would never have imagined that. How about Skye?"

Amber blew out a breath. "That's a tough one. Skye is turning out like her mom—flighty, Bohemian, can't seem to settle on anything. I haven't seen her in a couple of years. I don't even think we have an address for her."

"I'm sorry to hear it, but I can't say I'm surprised. She was always off in her own little world. Really artistic, though."

"You got that right. But enough of the small talk. How're things with you and Greg?"

"Great. We see each other almost every day, sometimes more than once."

"He's sure going all out." Amber took a sip from her mug. "Has he mentioned marriage?"

"Only indirectly, but he talks about the future all the time. He's serious about having a family—sooner rather than later."

Amber looked thoughtful. "I guess that's to be expected. He's the sort of guy who makes a good family man. Now that he's in his thirties and settled professionally, it makes sense that he wants to settle in other ways."

"But why me? I've made it clear I'm not ready for that."

"Aren't you?"

"Amber—"

"Stop. I know what you're going say—all about how you don't want to live in Destiny, and you need a job in the valley. We've been there and covered that. What I'm asking is, if you weren't defending yourself so hard against this town, and if you had the job you wanted, isn't it possible you'd be ready for a husband and kids? And that Greg might be the guy?"

Paris pursed her lips, letting the question percolate while she swirled her cup. "Principal Reyes, you do ask the hard questions."

Amber sat back with a self-satisfied look. "That's what I thought."

"Then again, how can he be the right guy if this is the wrong time and place?"

"Aha. Now you're getting to the real problem."

"What are you getting at?"

"Doesn't it come down to a question of which is more important to you: the guy or the time and place? If Greg would be the right guy, given the right time and place, then maybe he's the right guy. You have to decide where your priorities are."

Paris set her cup on the table. "Were you always this perceptive?"

"No, but I wish I had been."

"You'll need to explain that."

"I had the same decision to make a couple of years back. I chose Destiny and the principal's job and gave up the guy. I absolutely love the job and being back here, where my family still lives and where I grew up. It's everything I wanted it to be, though I didn't realize I wanted that until I'd been away." She sighed. "Still, I wonder if it was worth it. Chad was…is a great guy. When I chose to come here, he took it as a sign that I didn't care enough. I hear he's moved on, that he's seeing someone else. And I sometimes I wonder…" She picked up her mug.

"I see," said Paris, the pieces coming together. "You wonder if you've blown your one chance, if you'll ever find anybody to fill that space in your life."

"Exactly." Amber swallowed hard. "Don't get me wrong. I'm not telling you what your choice should be, but you'll want to be very clear about exactly what you want. Sometimes, there's no going back."

"I hear that. Thanks for the warning."

"You're welcome." Amber cleared her throat. "Did I tell you about the kid who brought a gun to school?"

"No! Are you serious?"

"It was a toy pistol he got for his birthday. He brought it for show-and-tell in his kindergarten class, but the teacher saw it in his backpack and thought it looked real. We had a full sheriff's call-out and a school lock-down before we got things straightened out."

"Oh!" Paris let out a breath. "I'm glad everyone is safe."

"Me too! We don't expect problems like that in Destiny."

They went on chatting, the topic safely changed, but the discussion stayed with Paris throughout the day. It seemed everyone was asking the same question. She couldn't help wondering if they had good reason.

It wasn't late when Paris returned from her visit, but Gran was already in bed. "I think she was exhausted from the effort to get her to church," Jess said. "That sounds like something of a nightmare."

"I'm glad you were here to help get her settled. Have you finished with the big projects for this year?"

"Not remotely." Jess plopped into a kitchen chair. "I knew when I went into teaching that I wanted to be the very best teacher-mentor-helper I could possibly be. I didn't realize how much time and energy that would take."

The statement touched closely on what Paris had been thinking. "Aunt Jess? Have you ever had to give up a romantic relationship? Because of your career choice?"

"Hm. Good question." Jess ran a finger around the top of the salt-shaker. "There were guys I dated when I was in school and others in graduate school, guys who didn't like the idea that I wanted to move back to a little Gold Rush town in the mountains. I was never serious about any of them, though..."

"Who have you been serious about?"

Jess looked away, apparently becoming quite interested in the pepper shaker. "I'm not sure I want to discuss that. There are other... um, I'm just not...comfortable."

"Okay then. In general terms."

Jess sighed. "I've only been serious about two men. Ever. One I met here, believe it or not, but he wanted to move on, and I wanted to stay. So yes, I guess you can say that I lost that romantic relationship because of my choices of where and how to live."

"The other one?"

"The other I also met here. We broke up for... other reasons. We weren't right for each other. You really need to—"

Paris interrupted. "It wasn't Destiny that broke you up, though?"

Jess bit her lip. "No, it wasn't."

"That's good." Paris picked up the saltshaker. "Do you think I'm putting too much emphasis on a job in the valley?"

"Oh no! You're not pulling me into that discussion." Jess straight-ened her chair. "Listen, love. Only you can decide what you need to be happy. I know you have negative feelings about small town living—"

"An understatement."

"Okay. The question is whether that means more than whatever else you may want in your life. You are the only person who can decide. No one else's opinion matters."

Paris let that sink in. "You're right. I guess I have some thinking to do."

"I guess you do." Jess stood and pushed in her chair. "And you can't put it off too long, not if you don't want it to cost you. As for me, I promised a before-school tutoring session tomorrow, so I've really got to get my z's. Catch you later."

"Sure. Later." Paris watched her go. Then she got up and climbed the stairs to her bedroom, tired of pondering the unknowable and wondering what had made Jess so dodgy about her dating background.

~

HER CUSTOMARY WAKE-UP found Paris still drowsy, restless from a night of complex, confusing dreams. She could remember little of them, except for a vague feeling that she'd spent the night trying to solve difficult puzzles.

A bright, clear dawn encouraged her to get outside, so she dressed in her workout clothes and stopped in the kitchen for a breakfast drink before she took off for a run. Jess was there, grabbing a breakfast bar. "Guess I'll see you this afternoon!" she called as she went out. "Lock Mom in when you go out, 'kay?"

"Will do," Paris answered, though she doubted the precaution was necessary.

She'd jogged a little since coming back to Destiny, but today, she decided on a serious run. She took off at a good pace, rounded a corner a few blocks from Gran's house, and there he was again, that slim figure in jeans and a gray hoodie, slinking furtively around the side of the house where the Reyes family had once lived. Paris hesitated to enter the yard, even to make sure everything was okay, but no fence blocked her way and so she followed him but found no one there. She jogged back to the front of the house and was almost to the sidewalk when the householder stepped onto his porch, picked up his newspaper, and threw her a suspicious glare.

"Good morning, Mr. Cooper," she called cheerily, waving as she ran on.

"Hey!" the man called.

Paris waved again and ran faster.

At the next intersection, she waved at Mrs. Porter, who'd run the Post Office from the front of her grocery store for as long as Paris could remember. A couple of blocks later, she greeted Lotte and Logan, the Bittner twins, who were a class behind her in school and who still ran together in the mornings. By the time she turned toward home, she'd seen three more people she knew, or might know. One of them, a slim man wearing a gray hoodie, reminded her of the person she'd seen earlier.

I need to mention that kid to Greg. Paris focused on the road ahead and finished her run in slightly over an hour, refreshed and invigorated. She checked on Gran, who sat at the dining table with a hearty meal of eggs and toast. "You doing okay, Gran?"

"I'm fine, dear. Don't worry about me."

"Okay," Paris answered, and went upstairs to shower and dress for the day.

"GREG? You've got to see this." Mrs. Bailey, who checked all the emails addressed to the school, lit up with excitement.

"What is it?" Greg came out of his office, worried the computer was down again.

"Oh, don't worry. It's good news. Great, really." She pointed to the screen.

He stepped up and scanned through the email. "You're right, it's great news!" he said. "Can you get hold of Paris? She needs to see this, too."

"I'll forward it to her." She reached toward her keyboard.

Greg stopped her in mid-reach. "Can you call her instead?"

"Oh yes. You bet." Mrs. Bailey picked up her phone.

PARIS WASHED the last of the breakfast dishes and set them in the rack to dry. As she stepped away from the sink, her phone rang. Minutes later, her grandmother found her gathering her things. "I've been called to the school office. Mrs. Bailey says it's something to do with the grant proposal."

"That reminds me," Gran said. "I had a call while you were out. The orthopedist who saw me in the hospital wants me to come to his office this afternoon."

"Oh." Paris looked at her watch. "What time do I have to be back?"

"You don't." Gran smiled. "Jess said she can take me in this time."

"Jess? Won't she be in school?"

"There's some kind of assembly later today, which means she can get away early."

"That's great." Paris breathed a relieved sigh. "Then I'm on my way to the school. Guess I'll see you later." She started for the kitchen door. "Do you want me to lock it on my way out?"

"Sure," Gran said. "I doubt it's necessary, but it helps Jess feel secure."

"I'll lock it." Paris locked up as she left, wondering why she'd been called to the school. If the grant results were in, would the news be good or bad? The party atmosphere in the school office assured her it was good news indeed. Several teachers had gathered along with members of the school board, and someone had brought cookies and two-liter bottles of soda.

"Here, look what we got," Mrs. Bailey handed her a printed sheet.

Paris eagerly read the email. It announced that the proposal submitted by their school had passed initial review and would move on to the funding committee.

"It's that easy?" Paris still couldn't believe it. "I thought grant competitions were difficult."

"I expect they usually are," Greg said. "In this case, the Bates Foundation already allocated funds to several different priorities. Any proposal they consider responsive passes the initial review. That means we will be funded. The only question is how fully."

"That's great. Wonderful!"

"Thanks to you," Mrs. Bailey said.

One of the people she didn't recognize said, "Hear, hear!" and raised a cup of soda.

"To Paris!" another said.

"To Paris!" other voices echoed as people toasted her with cups of soda.

Paris's voice thickened as she answered, "Happy to help."

Half an hour later, she left with Greg's promise that he would call after the school assembly. Leaving the parking lot, she suddenly felt at loose ends. She had done everything she could for the grant project, and it seemed to be turning out splendidly. Gran didn't need her now, and wouldn't need her this afternoon, since Jess would be there. She had done all she could to prepare for her interview the next morning, and plans were already underway for the dinner she planned to cook that evening. With time on her hands, she decided to drive to the old Children of Rah compound to see the changes there.

It was only as she turned her car downhill that she realized she had once again failed to mention the boy she'd seen at Mrs. Bailey's desk. She made a mental note to tell Greg as soon as she saw him and drove down the hill.

OUT HIS OFFICE WINDOW, Greg watched her go. He could no longer think of Paris leaving *someday*. She interviewed tomorrow for a job that seemed perfect. *Someday* was fast approaching, and there was little he could do to stop it.

He stood by the window, trying to imagine a better outcome for them than the only one he could see, finding nothing, and kicking himself for allowing this to happen.

THE CHANGES at the commune were massive and sweeping. Paris watched with amazement as the space transformed before her eyes. The construction crews had arrived, and a group of workmen dug trenches for footings in one area, while other workmen set up frames in trenches that had already been dug, preparing for concrete to be poured. She was pleased to see that, although the tree swing had been taken down, the giant oak remained, trimmed back, but healthy and well. She sat in her car, window down, admiring the work and enjoying the brisk spring breeze that smelled so richly of new-cut pine and fresh-turned earth.

"Do you have business here, ma'am?"

Paris turned to find a man in a jumpsuit and hard hat giving her a cold stare.

"Just curious, I suppose." She smiled, hoping to put him at ease.

"Then I'm afraid I'll have to ask you to move on. This is a hard hat only area. Our insurance doesn't cover onlookers."

"All right. Thank you." Paris started her engine. As she put the car in gear, she realized Greg had a point about the town's future. Wondering what, if anything, that meant for her, she turned back toward her grandmother's home.

Chapter Seventeen

Paris arrived to find Jess's car still gone and the house silent. She'd forgotten to ask about appointment times, so she didn't know whether Jess had taken Gran to see her doctor or if Gran might be resting, waiting for Jess to arrive. She chose to err on the side of quiet and tiptoed up the porch steps, careful to avoid the one that creaked. Quietly, she slipped the key into the lock and let the door swing open. Then she stepped into the kitchen…

…to find herself face-to-face with the boy in the gray hoodie. He held an open loaf of bread while he chewed on a slice. When he saw Paris, his eyes grew wide and he swiveled his head around, frantically searching for escape.

Paris blocked the door. Doing her best to stay calm, she said, "You're the boy from the school, the one I saw at Mrs. Bailey's desk."

The boy didn't answer. He swallowed hard and looked toward the front door on the other side of the living room.

"The front door unlocks with a key. You can't get out that way." Paris put her arms out, filling the kitchen doorway. "You aren't getting out here, either, so you may as well tell me who you are and what you're doing here."

The boy made a sobbing noise deep in his throat but didn't answer. His wide, red eyes and rapid breathing told her his stress matched hers.

"I'm calling the police," Paris said. She carefully lowered one hand into her pocket.

The boy made a deep, guttural sound that might have been a word. Then he ran straight at Paris and hit her side, shoving her hard against the cupboard as he dashed out the kitchen door.

Paris hit the cupboards with an impact that shuddered through her. Unable to catch herself, or even to get a breath, she slid to the floor—

ears ringing, eyes watching the world go dark. She sat that way, gasping for air, trying to clear her vision, for uncounted moments until the world righted itself. It took even longer until she could struggle to her knees, find her phone, and place her call. Minutes later, the local deputy arrived.

She met him at the kitchen door. Deputy Morales, a middle-aged Hispanic man she'd known for years, gave her a quick once-over. "You need medical help. I'm calling the EMTs."

"No," Paris said. Then seeing the his disapproval, she added, "That is, no thank you, sir. I don't believe medical help is necessary. The boy hit me hard and I'm going to have bruises, but I don't think anything's broken."

Morales studied her, dark eyes narrowed. "No concussion?"

Paris thought about the blackness, but she'd never lost consciousness. "No, no concussion."

"Okay then," the deputy said. "We'll let that go for now. Tell me what happened." Paris sat and Morales prepared to take notes.

She began with the story of arriving at her grandmother's house and finding the boy inside. She answered multiple questions about who she was and why she was staying here, and then she mentioned the earlier time when she found the boy in the school office.

The deputy's forehead wrinkled. "It wasn't reported."

Paris lifted a shoulder. "I kept forgetting to tell somebody."

"I'd call that something of an oversight." The deputy's acerbic tone censured her.

"That may not be the only time I saw him," Paris continued, and mentioned times when she thought she saw someone in a gray hoodie in people's yards or coming out a window.

"And you didn't think to mention that either?"

"I wasn't sure I'd seen anything. I didn't want to waste your time."

The deputy's tone grew sharp. "You knew we were experiencing break-ins. We could have used your insight before the problem got to this point."

Paris, her head pounding and her body beginning to feel its abuse, had taken enough. "You're right. I should have said something, but I didn't realize it at the time. Now I'm telling you. Is there anything more you need? Because I could use a dose of Ibuprofen and a hot soak."

The deputy asked a few more questions and then said, "I guess that will be all.' He reviewed his notes. "You're sure the boy you saw here is the same one you saw at Mrs. Bailey's desk?"

"Completely sure. Same jeans, same ratty gray hoodie, same shock of blond hair, same face."

Morales gave an exasperated sigh. He looked at his watch. "Too bad school's out. We could ride over there and have a look, see if we can find the kid."

"He knows I can identify him. I doubt he'll go back to school."

"That's still our best shot." The deputy hesitated.

"Tell you what." Paris fought to ignore the pounding in her head. "I'll go over there now, see if anyone is still in the office, and tell them what happened. Maybe they'll know who he is."

"Good idea." Morales brightened. "But you shouldn't drive. I'll take you there."

The arrival of Gran and Jess short-circuited that plan. Deputy Morales helped Gran get inside and calmed her fears about Paris and the break-in. "Not to worry, Mrs. Kerr, we'll catch him, thanks to your granddaughter's help." He turned to Jess and asked her to drive Paris to the school. "I'll meet you there," he added. He tipped his hat and left.

Paris gave her family an abbreviated version of the afternoon's events while she downed a couple of Ibuprofen. Then she said, "Really, Jess. I can drive myself. No need for you to come."

"And leave me to answer to Deputy Snarky? I don't think so!" Jess picked up her keys.

Paris, too weak, sore, and tired to argue, got in the car.

The deputy had arrived and was speaking with Greg and Mrs. Bailey when Paris walked in, her Aunt Jess firmly supporting her. Greg's eyes widened in worry as soon as he laid eyes on Paris, but she shook her head when he moved toward her. Paris described her assailant, Greg and Mrs. Bailey recognized her description, and Greg asked the yearbook adviser to please bring pictures of the student to the office.

Holding a color photo, Morales turned to Paris. "Is this the boy you saw?"

She nodded but couldn't help the shudder that ran through her as she remembered his body slamming her into the cupboards. "Yes."

"No doubts?"

Exasperated and in pain, Paris bit her lip to keep from blurting an angry response. "Officer," she said, amazed at how calm she sounded, "the boy was close enough to shove me. His face was inches from mine, and this is the face I saw."

"Sorry, but I had to ask."

Events quickly took shape around her in a whirlwind of activity. Mrs. Bailey identified the student as Lech Nowak, the son of Polish immigrants. Lech had been living in Destiny with his grandmother since his parents' deaths. "I know how that feels," Paris murmured.

Greg said Coach Velasquez had a good relationship with Lech and suggested the officer take the coach with him when he went to the boy's address. Mrs. Bailey sent the yearbook advisor to interrupt track practice, and the coach arrived minutes later. When Greg explained the day's events, Coach Velasquez turned to Paris and asked if she was okay.

"Sore," she answered, "but I'll be fine."

Velasquez sighed. "I knew something was wrong when Lech quit the relay team. I tried to talk with him, but... I'll see what I can do." He nodded to Morales. "Let's go find him."

The officer turned to Paris. "Young lady, I know you said you're fine, but I want you to go down the hill to the hospital. Check in at the emergency room and have them look you over. Tell them I sent you."

"I don't think that's necess—"

"Consider it an order." His gaze encompassed Greg, Mrs. Bailey, and Jess. "Will one of you take on the task of getting this reluctant patient to medical care?"

"I will, sir," Greg said immediately.

Paris, beginning to feel like flotsam on the waves, bridled. "What if I don't want to go?"

The deputy softened both his voice and his expression. "Miss Cutler, the boy we are on our way to arrest is wanted for a series of home burglaries, but most of the charges are petty crime. With you, we have an assault. That ups the burglary to a felony robbery and makes his situation much more serious. How much more may depend on how seriously injured you are. We need to have a doctor's statement that will let the prosecutors know how to file charges and will help a judge determine the outcome."

Paris sighed. All she wanted was a soak and a nap, but she saw the deputy's point. "Okay."

"I'll see she's taken care of, sir." Greg stepped close, his arm around her.

Morales gave Greg a firm nod. "Thank you, Mr. Frantz." He turned to the coach. "Mr. Velasquez, are you ready?"

"Let's go," the coach said, and the two men left.

Paris felt tears welling. "I don't want trouble..."

Greg put both arms around her. "Sweetheart, the trouble came to you. Let's see what we can do to get you out of it. Come on, let's get you to the hospital."

"I guess I have to go." Paris looked to Jess. "Tell Gran what's happening, okay?"

Jess nodded and exchanged an odd look with Greg. Paris wondered at the unspoken communication that passed between them, but she let it go, thinking it was due to the day's events. *Jess is probably worried and wants to know Greg will take care of me.*

"Keep us in the loop," Jess said. She enveloped Paris in a hug. "Greg will watch out for you."

"He always does." Paris attempted a smile.

Greg said, "I'll call when we know more."

"Good enough." Jess nodded and left.

"Okay." Greg slid an arm around Paris. "Let's get you down the hill."

"I can walk," Paris said. She took two steps before the room spun.

"I've got you," Greg said, lifting her in his arms. "This should make it easier."

"Greg..." If she hadn't been so dizzy, she would have argued, but her objection to being carried like some swooning heroine in a melodrama drained away with the last of her energy. The day's events had caught up to her and she was feeling dish towel limp, newborn weak, and barely able to stand.

"Trust me," he whispered as he swept her down the hall. "This will be easier for both of us, so stop being stubborn. Didn't I hear you saying the same thing to your grandmother?"

Paris, recognizing the parallels, breathed out a sigh. "Okay," she said, giving herself up to Greg's care. As he carried her to his car. she closed her eyes. Comfort and relief enveloped her in a cozy cloud, along with another feeling she was too exhausted to ponder. She decided she'd sort it out later, much later, when she got her bearings.

PARIS DETERMINED the evening must have concentrated all the good luck available for the day. It took less than half an hour for her to be placed in an exam room, dressed in an ill-fitting gown, and speaking to the physician on duty while Greg sat in the waiting room.

Dr. Carl Fuentes, who'd grown up in Destiny, asked Paris a series of questions, looked over her bruises, and sent her for X-rays. When she was wheeled back to the exam room, Paris knew she didn't want to be alone when the doctor returned. She asked for Greg. Moments later, he stood by her side.

"Thanks for inviting me in," he said. "That desk nurse is happy to be rid of me. I pestered her with so many questions about your status that she thanked the guy who came to fetch me."

Paris gave him a wobbly smile and reached for his hand. "I didn't want to be alone."

Dr. Fuentes arrived soon carrying X-rays, one of which he put on a light board. "As you see right here," the doctor said, pointing to the image of Paris's left side, "you have a slight fracture in this rib. It hasn't separated and I don't believe it's going to, but it will be tender for a few days. I can authorize pain meds if you need them."

Paris shook her head. "I have lots of Ibuprofen at home."

"That's good," the doctor said, "and it's always better to avoid heavier drugs, but I suggest you have a few on hand, if only to be able to sleep."

Paris considered that. "Okay, can you give me a prescription that I can fill if I need it?"

The doctor nodded. "Sure, that's fine, but I see your address is in Destiny. Let me send you home with a few tablets in any case, say maybe five. That way, if you need them tonight, you'll have them on hand. I'll give you a paper script as well, in case you need more."

"Thank you," Paris agreed.

"Your rib is not what concerns me most," Dr. Fuentes went on. "You say you never lost consciousness, but the way you blacked out suggests your brain took a pretty hard knock, and Mr. Frantz just told me about how you collapsed at the school."

Paris frowned at Greg. "I didn't actually collapse. I felt a bit woozy is all."

"Miss Cutler..." Dr. Fuentes adopted a much firmer tone, "I don't believe you have a serious condition, but you do have a mild concussion. I want you taking it easy for a week or so, three days at the least. And that means no driving."

Paris was shaking her head even before the doctor finished speaking. "I can't do that. I have a job interview in the valley tomorrow."

"I'm afraid it's out of the question," the doctor answered.

"You don't understand. I have to be there."

"Miss Cutler," the doctor began, his voice hardening.

Then Greg spoke. "I can drive her."

Paris said, "No you can't. That's silly. You have school."

"I haven't taken any personal time all year. I'll go in to make sure everything's going smoothly in the morning. Then I'll put the assistant principal in charge and pick you up. I have errands I can do while you're in your interview—errands for the school, which helps me justify the trip. Afterwards, I'll get you safely home."

"You would do that?"

"If you insist on going to that interview, I insist on driving."

"I don't recommend it," Dr. Fuentes said, "but as long as she doesn't drive... Well, you two work it out, but no driving for you." He pointed his index finger within inches of Paris's nose. "I'll notify Deputy Morales that you aren't allowed on the road for at least three days."

He left to see another patient but sent a nurse in with a list of symptoms Paris should watch for. "We'll have your meds for you before you leave," the nurse added. "I'll get your discharge paperwork ready."

As soon as she was out of earshot, Paris said, "Really, Greg. You don't have to miss school. I can drive myself."

"No, you can't, and you won't." He used his authoritative principal voice. "I wish you'd call them and reschedule. I'm sure they'd understand. You can't be at your best when you've been beaten up like this and rescheduling only makes sense. But if you insist on going, I insist on driving. Your grandma and Jess would never forgive me if you passed out at the wheel." He swallowed. "I'd never forgive myself."

Paris scoffed. "I won't pass out, and I don't need to reschedule."

"Here's the deal: I can be as stubborn as you are. If you're going, I'm driving. End of story. And if you try to get around that, I'll call the deputy and report you myself. Got it?"

Paris opened her mouth to argue but Greg held up a hand. "Look, if it had been Jess or your grandmother in your shoes, what would you tell them? Would you let them go off alone or would you give the same advice I'm giving you now?"

Paris inhaled deeply, knowing Greg was right. *Why am I so stubborn sometimes? I have such a knee-jerk reaction that I don't think things through.* Hadn't she sought Greg's presence when she needed comfort? "All right."

"Really? No more arguments?"

"No arguments," she said. "Now if you'll please step out, I can get dressed so you can take me home and I can get some rest."

"You've got it." He disappeared through the curtain.

When they were on their way home to Destiny, Paris rallied and tried again, though she couldn't help feeling guilty about it. Here she was going for a job that could take her away from Greg and he was being kind enough to drive her. "Greg? If you can't take the time, it's okay. By tomorrow, I'm sure I can drive."

He took her hand. "Don't even consider it, babe."

In a soft voice, Paris asked, "Why?"

Greg glanced her way. "Why what?"

"Why are you doing this?"

Greg took her hand. "Haven't you figured it out? I love you, Paris."

Paris gave a little gasp.

Greg sighed. "Look, I know it's not the best time for a romantic declaration, but it's true. I'm in love with you and I want to do whatever I can to make your life better and happier."

"Oh," Paris said. It was all she could say. She was so overwhelmed with emotions and thoughts swirling in her head. Too much was happening too fast, and all she could think was, *What do I do now?*

Chapter Eighteen

By midnight, Paris was grateful she had pain pills. As her shock wore off, the aches intensified, both in her ribs and her head. Other less serious injuries also made their presence known.

Groaning, Paris got up and padded to the bathroom where she found the painkillers and swallowed one. While she waited for it to take effect, she realized Greg was right; she should have called TriTech from the hospital yesterday. Try as she might, she couldn't think of a way to postpone now, on the very day the interview was to happen. It might come off as a desperate plea for sympathy. No, she had to go through with it.

She woke in the morning tired and sore but feeling better than she'd expected. Working carefully around the bump on her head, she showered and did her hair. She'd already pressed her navy suit and the crisp pink blouse that went with it, and she'd polished her no-nonsense pumps.

Her grandmother stirred and Paris went to check. "Good morning, Gran. Can I make you some breakfast?"

"That sounds good. How're you feeling?"

"Better than I have a right to."

Gran noticed Paris's preparations and a look of alarm crossed her features. "Surely you're not going through with the interview?"

Paris sighed. "I can't think of a reasonable way to postpone."

"Didn't the doctor say you can't drive?"

"Greg is taking time away from school. He'll drive me down."

A new expression lit Gran's face. "I do believe that man is in love with you."

Paris wasn't ready to dive into what it all meant or to try to untangle her own feelings. But that feeling of comfort enveloped her again as she thought about Greg. "I think maybe so."

"I hope you know what you're doing."

Her voice gentle, Paris said, "No, Gran, I don't, no more than anyone does. I'm finding my way as I go along. So far, it's worked reasonably well."

"Well..." Gran looked unsettled. "I'll pray everything works out all right." Her voice took on an edge. "Have you spoken with Jess? About Greg, I mean."

"We've talked a little, but not about Greg."

"You should, Paris. You really should."

Paris couldn't help her exasperation. "Why, Gran? What's this about?"

"Talk with Jess. You need to." And that's all Gran would say.

GREG ARRIVED EARLY, but Paris was ready. In addition to making sure she looked professional, she'd spent a couple of hours studying the company's website, learning all she could about them. If not for the pain when she moved and the incipient headache knocking at the back of her skull, she'd have thought herself as primed as possible.

"Are you sure you're up for this?" Greg opened her car door.

"You were right," Paris said with a deep sigh, "I should have postponed yesterday when I had the chance. There's no reasonable way to do it this late in the game. I have aches and pains, but I think I can manage."

"You know, there are no awards for this kind of martyrdom."

"Maybe I'll get a job out of it." Then she added, "Besides, look who's talking. Today you're not only the high school principal, you're also my chauffeur and support staff."

He smiled, gently patting her hand. "I can't think of a better thing to be. Do you have painkillers with you... in case?"

"I didn't want to be groggy before the interview, so I only took Ibuprofen this morning, but I brought the serious stuff in case I need it after."

"Good. I don't want to see you hurting."

As they drove down the mountain, he asked her questions about the company and the job. She was thrilled to be able to answer each in detail. Despite yesterday's incident, everything was coming together as she hoped.

~

FROM THE BEGINNING, her interview felt more like a first-day orientation. Adele met her in the lobby and took her through the building, showing her where people worked and introducing her to everyone from the front desk receptionist to the company's hardware specialist. Then she led her into a conference room where Paris met George Sutherland and Matthew Korda, both of whom insisted she use their first names.

They chatted over mineral water, fruit juice, and a plate of snacks. George asked how she felt about assignments that might require travel and she answered that she'd always wanted to see more of the country. Matthew asked if she felt ready to dive into the world of fund accounting and she surprised them—pleasantly, she thought—by discussing some of the clients they'd served lately and their different accounting needs. Before she left the conference room, the talk turned to when she could start and her salary expectations.

"Thank goodness I was prepared for that, too," she said as she told Greg about it minutes later. "I looked up what people with similar jobs and titles are making and I had a figure in mind. It didn't seem to shake them at all."

"When will you know for sure?"

"Adele said they'll probably call tomorrow."

"Sounds like you did well."

"I hope so." The excitement that had sustained her through the morning drained away in a rush. She groaned as she shifted in her seat. "My adrenaline and the Ibuprofen from earlier are both wearing off. I hurt all over."

Greg watched with concern. "Sounds like time for a painkiller. Shall we fill that prescription before we leave the valley?"

"I don't think so. The hospital gave me several. Even after I swallow one, I'll still have three left and I fully expect to feel better tomorrow." Then, almost as an afterthought, she added, "And they upset my stomach."

"Then maybe you should eat something. What do you think? Late lunch? Early dinner?"

She smiled. "You're feeding me again?"

"If you let me." He squeezed her hand.

She had to admit it sounded good. "Thank you. I'd enjoy that."

They stopped at a cozy Italian restaurant and Paris ordered a small pasta meal. By the time she had eaten a chunk of thick-crusted bread, she was ready to swallow a pill. Her pain eased before they left the building. "This stuff makes me groggy," she said. "You won't hate me if I sleep on the way home, will you?"

"Paris, I don't think you could possibly make me hate you." Greg's voice held a teasing tone, but his look was sincere.

She saw the love in his eyes and knew her situation had hurt him. That was one of her last thoughts before she sagged against her seat, exhausted from the strains of the past two days.

ADELE CALLED EARLY the next day, before Paris could get online to look at other jobs. "You're in," she said for a start. "Everyone thinks you're the perfect fit." She went on to offer the salary Paris had requested plus profit sharing and an attractive bonus structure as well as a raft of benefits. For the first time in her life, Paris had reason to appreciate company-paid health insurance.

Then came the surprise. "Would you mind if we didn't start you for one extra week?" Adele said. "Maybe ten days. We had a bit of a plumbing problem overnight and we need to replace the flooring. We're encouraging several of the staff to take their vacations next week and others will work from home, but we can't start you off that way. It should only be seven to ten days more. Two weeks tops. What do you think?"

"That's no problem." Paris hoped Adele didn't hear her sigh of relief. Then, casually, she asked, "You got a recommendation from my past employer?"

"It's odd," Adele answered, and Paris braced, glad whatever her former boss had said hadn't put TriTech off. "The man who responded wasn't your former supervisor. He said she left in a rush without completing some of her personnel files. All he found in your file was one line: 'Good worker. Gets the job done.'"

"I wouldn't have expected that. For her to leave, I mean." She released a tight breath. "Thank you, Adele. I'll wait to hear from you about the start date."

"We'll be in touch." Adele clicked off.

Paris put down her phone and shouted, "Gran! I got the job!"

PARIS DRESSED CAREFULLY, wanting to look her best when she told Greg her news. She didn't know what the future would bring, or even if Greg would want to continue seeing her. She felt torn about so many things, but this job meant so much to her. She had to see where it led. She had to.

"Good morning, Paris." Mrs. Bailey greeted her as she entered the front office. "We've heard again from the Bates Foundation. They're funding everything we asked for."

"Wonderful! It seems there's good news all around."

Mrs. Bailey straightened. "Oh? What's your news?"

"I really should tell Greg first. Is he in?"

"He's not right now. He's gone to the gym to talk with Coach Velasquez about that boy." Her look—like she'd just bitten into something bitter—told Paris how she felt about *that boy*.

"Lech Nowak," Paris said.

"Yes, him. Greg should be back soon. Would you care to wait in his office?"

"No. I'll speak to Aunt Jess first. Back in a few minutes."

"That will be good. Be sure to sign in before you go to see Ms. Kerr."

"Oh yes, right." Paris had become so accustomed to working in the office that she'd almost forgotten the protocol for visiting classrooms.

She peeked in the window of Jess's classroom and saw her aunt talking to the class as she wrote directions on the board. Paris waved to get her attention and Jess nodded, finished her instruction, and met Paris in the hall.

"I got the job!" Paris said in a loud whisper. "I start in about two weeks." She explained the unexpected delay.

"Good for you!" Jess dropped her voice still further. "How did Greg take it?"

"I haven't told him yet. He's talking with Coach Velasquez about the boy who robbed us. I'll go back to meet him in the office."

Jess looked uneasy, an expression that confused Paris. "I hope it all goes well."

"It will, Jess, but thanks for your concern and for being part of my cheer squad."

"Always," Jess said. "Now I'll get back to my classroom while you go break a heart."

Paris rolled her eyes. "Greg will be fine. He's been my biggest cheerleader."

Jess arched an eyebrow. "Well, that may be true, but just make sure you talk it out with him." Jess blew a kiss as she returned to her class.

Paris made her way back to the school office, taking a longer route back, knowing she was stalling. Jess was exaggerating, wasn't she? Greg's heart wouldn't be broken. Paris had been clear from the start. But this news did complicate things. She hesitated, uncertain what to say. When she found Greg in his office, she chose to lead with a question. "Did you learn something new about Lech?"

"Yep. Have a seat." Greg positioned a chair next to his own.

Paris sat, happy to postpone her own news, and anxious about the boy.

"You heard part of it already. His parents immigrated from Poland. The Nowaks were medical doctors specializing in heart valve research. They came over in the late 1990s to join in some work at the U.C.S.F. Medical School. Once they'd applied for resident status, they brought Mrs. Nowak's mother to the country. Then I guess they felt rooted enough to have a baby."

"And they named him after their national hero, Lech Walesa."

Greg smiled. "You've been doing your homework."

"I thought I remembered hearing the name, so I looked him up."

"You're right, of course. But it seems their baby's name wasn't the only thing they carried from their time in Soviet Poland."

"Oh?"

"They retained a deep suspicion of the government, any government. After the couple were killed in a smash-up in the Bay Area, Lech's grandmother brought him to Destiny to get away from government spies. She was even more worried about it than Lech's parents were."

"That's so sad. Did she believe her government killed the boy's parents?"

"It's hard to tell what she thought, but she hid out on the edge of town, the *uphill* edge. She wanted to be as inconspicuous as possible."

Paris thought of the way Greg's Uncle Herbert had hung around for years, his true identity hidden from almost everyone. "This is a good place for hiding out."

"Indeed. Whether she meant to or not, she passed her fear to Lech. Three months ago, the poor woman suffered a stroke and Lech called the paramedics. He didn't tell anyone he was living alone. His grandmother had lost her ability to speak and could only write in Polish, so she didn't tell anyone either—assuming she would have, given her fear of authority."

Greg let out a deep breath. "Lech is not quite sixteen, not old enough for an after-school job, but suddenly he had no one to provide for him. And no way of accessing his grandmother's bank account. His parents had never set up an account for him. In their will, everything had been left to him but in care of Lech's grandmother. Lech scrounged around the house, looking for cash and any spare change he could find, but that ran out after a week or so. He started doing odd jobs for anyone who would hire him, but—"

"But he's been stealing food in order to eat," Paris concluded.

"Food and occasionally, loose cash he finds lying around. He's terrified of anyone knowing he's alone. He thought the government would take him away and he'd never see his grandmother again. He did what he could to cope."

Paris remembered too well what it felt like to be orphaned at sixteen, but at least she'd had Gran and Jess. "I guess by now someone has explained that theft wasn't the best approach."

"Oh yeah." Greg smiled wryly. "He's heard that from a few of us."

Paris looked away, blinking back tears. "The poor kid. That poor, scared kid."

Greg took her hand. "You're a generous soul, you know that?"

"Not so generous." She shook her head. "I remember what it's like to be orphaned young, but I still want to see that kid disciplined."

"That's reasonable." Then Greg looked around. "How did you get here? You didn't drive, did you?"

"Just from the house," Paris answered, her tone defensive. "It isn't far, and I'm not under the influence. You saw the last dose of painkiller I took."

"I'm not sure that makes a difference. The doctor didn't want you driving because of that bump on your head." Greg looked around. "Maybe I should ask *why* you're here? You didn't come just for the visit."

Paris reminded herself to be upbeat. She smiled and said, "I got the job!"

Greg was silent a moment and Paris saw something flicker behind his eyes. Sadness? Frustration? She couldn't tell, it was so brief. A moment later he beamed and answered, "That's super. Congratulations!" He enveloped her in a warm hug.

"Thank you." Paris explained the delay in her start date. "That should give me time to recover, and also to locate an apartment and move my things."

"That's good, that you have extra time. Let me know how I can help."

"You, Principal Frantz, have more than enough on your plate."

"I can still find time to help," he said. "We'll have some time before you have to be in and settled. I can borrow a panel truck to help with your things—"

She put a finger to his lips. "Let's not get ahead of ourselves."

He kissed her finger. "Okay. This is your show. Just let me know when you're ready."

"Will do. And now I'll let you get some work done." She remembered Mrs. Bailey's announcement. "Oh! And congratulations. I hear the Bates Foundation is giving you everything you asked for."

"Everything *you* asked for," he corrected.

"You did a lot of it," she answered, "and be sure to thank Mrs. Delgado. She gave me the wording for several sections. You and Mrs. Bailey had the bulk of the information put together before I got involved."

"We just didn't know what to do with them." He stroked her hand, his eyes studying her face. "I'm worried about you, driving home. Let me give you a ride."

"Then how will I get my car? Honestly, Greg, I can drive."

"Paris—"

"Greg, this is not your call," she said, her tone steely. She immediately regretted it when she saw hurt in his eyes. *Why do I keep doing that? Snapping for no reason when people who care about me are trying to help?* She took a deep breath. "Greg, I appreciate everything you've done for me. And I promise to take it slow and easy and go straight home. I won't leave the house for the rest of the day. I have some things I want to start working on anyway."

"Okay," he said, his frown relaxing, "but I don't like it. And I'm taking you to dinner tonight to celebrate. That is assuming you feel up to it."

She gave his shoulder a playful shove. "You can be pushy, you know that?"

"And you can be stubborn." He kissed her nose. "Pick you up at six."

She wrinkled her nose at him but blew a kiss as she left.

As she drove out of the parking lot, the truth hit. *This is going to be hard.* Her heart bounced between elation at landing her dream job and sadness about leaving Destiny...Gran, Jess, Amber, and everyone else she'd grown closer to. Not to mention her mixed feelings over Lech's circumstances. She hoped things worked out for the boy.

And then there's Greg. She sighed. Leaving Greg would be hardest of all. Her coming departure would be more difficult than she'd ever imagined.

Chapter Nineteen

Greg took her to dinner that evening. They ate together every evening for the rest of the week, either at a restaurant or at Greg's. On Saturday, Greg came to Gran's to help Paris assess what she needed to move. He checked the boxes she'd stored in Gran's garage and declared he could move it all in the school's panel truck. Then, with him hovering and worrying about her health, they climbed the trail to Herbert's cabin for a farewell picnic in the meadow.

Some of the trees had blossomed and wildflowers carpeted the meadow in a profusion of colors—yellow, orange, red, pink, and purple, especially the deep purple of the wild lupine. "It's so beautiful here." Paris leaned back against the half-log perch, her shoulder snuggled against Greg's side. "It's always so peaceful. I'll miss this."

"Paris?" His voice was tentative. "You can always come back to visit—or even to stay."

"Oh, Greg. We've had this talk—"

"I know, but I wonder whether you've given the idea a chance. Destiny is changing and growing. It isn't the tiny mountain town you remember."

"That's true, but what would I do here? Even if I applied for every grant the school might want and took a cut of every one that came through, it wouldn't add up to a decent salary."

"You know I could—"

She held up her hand. "Don't even go there. I'm an independent woman and I mean to stay that way." Realizing her tone had been sharper than she intended, she added in a softer voice, "It's who I am, Greg. It's the way I've needed to live since I saw how my mother's life collapsed when Daddy died. Please don't ask me to be otherwise."

"I understand." He didn't look happy, but he didn't argue.

Feeling her own inner conflict, Paris leaned her head on Greg's shoulder and snuggled deeper into his side. She inhaled deeply and tried to get a grip on her own mixed-up feelings. Part of her wondered if she was doing the right thing, if Amber and Gran were right. *Am I making a decision that I might regret?* What would happen if she found it was a mistake? Would Greg still be there? She was trying to sort out her feelings for Greg and her feelings about her job and her financial independence. She could not, would not, end up in a situation like her mother. "Let's enjoy this time together."

"Yes, let's," he said, but she heard the sadness in his voice.

"Kiss me?" She turned her face to his.

"Like you have to ask?" His kiss was thorough, deep, and extended far beyond the physical connection. It touched her deep in her soul, communicating his love more than his words ever could.

"Thank you," she whispered.

"Don't thank me," he said, and kissed her again, this one even more intense than the last, a claiming, possessive kiss.

She let it happen, abandoning for the moment her intention to keep things light. Only after several more kisses did she put her hand against his chest. "I think we'd better stop."

He nodded, but didn't speak, and took a few deep breaths. When he finally spoke, his words were barely a whisper: "I love you, you know."

Paris felt her own voice quaver as she answered, "I love you too." There. She'd said it. She had finally voiced the words that had been in her heart. "I love you, but I have to go."

LATE THAT NIGHT, Greg lay sleepless in his lonely bed, her words cycling in his mind: "I love you too, but I have to go." How was it possible Paris felt the same way he did, but still planned to leave?

He tried to put the shoe on the other foot. What if he was in her position, being asked to prove his love by staying where he couldn't work in school administration, or even as a teacher? It didn't help that he couldn't imagine a place that wouldn't need educators. Nor did it help that he'd been raised in a traditional family where his father supported the family and his mother raised the children and cared for the household. Her eventual part-time job was more of a hobby than a career.

That way of life is practically extinct, he reminded himself, although he couldn't really see why something that had worked so well should become outdated. At the same time, when he was honest with himself, he knew that much of what he admired about Paris was her mind and the way she used it, together with the ability she'd developed as a writer. *An ability I encouraged when she was in high school, and I was a student teacher.* The irony amused him even as it frustrated. *What am I going to do?* He groaned, unable to see any outcome that didn't end in heartbreak.

MORE DAYS PASSED before Paris got a text from Adele, postponing her start date for one more week. That gave her two more weekends in Destiny which relieved one of Gran's worries. Having committed to volunteer at the Arts Fair but unable to get there or fulfill her responsibilities without help, Gran had feared she might have to back out, leaving Lucy Grimes and the others short-handed. With Paris still in town, Gran had a chance to follow through—if Paris agreed.

Though she'd hesitated to get involved, Paris discovered she liked the excuse to dawdle in town, saying goodbye to the people she knew and the community in general. Besides, she wouldn't have to worry about Lucy committing her to any other committees with her move now on the horizon.

Gran was assigned to the entry table where artists and crafters checked in and paid their booth rental fees. Paris helped Gran settle in and stayed through the busiest morning hours. When the sign-ups slowed, she wandered the aisles. One booth charmed her, run by an amateur jeweler who created lovely things from semi-precious gems. She purchased a pendant, wire-wrapped onyx on a silver chain, and a pair of onyx-and-silver earrings. They'd make a perfect gift for Jess's birthday next month.

On her way back to Gran, Paris stopped at a booth that sold "boho" attire. She bought a tie-dye skirt that would serve nicely for casual Fridays at work and enjoyed a fun chat with the pink-haired artisan. Taking over the check-in desk to give Gran a break, Paris reflected that she'd enjoyed her time at the Arts Fair. In fact, she'd enjoyed her time in Destiny, a benefit she had not expected. Her extended visit had caused her to her revise her opinion of the town; she would miss this place and the people in it.

Saturday arrived and Adele texted, confirming that TriTech wanted Paris to start on Monday. Paris packed the last of her things, ready to leave her grandmother's home, she hoped for the final time—visits excepted. She closed her suitcase and carried it to the truck where Greg waited.

"Is that it?" he asked.

"Yep, that's the last. I just have to say my goodbyes to Gran and Aunt Jess."

"Okay. I'll wait here."

Paris offered an encouraging smile as she went back in. She hugged her grandmother and thanked her again for the soft place to land when life tossed her into the void. She thought briefly of Lech, who'd resorted to stealing food when his soft place was pulled out from under him. She'd remember to ask about Lech and hoped things worked out for him. She kissed Gran's cheek and hugged Aunt Jess.

"Thank you both so much," she said as she drew away. "I'll try not to impose on you again."

"You know we loved having you," Jess said.

Gran added, "You're always welcome. Any time, whether to stay or just for a visit."

"I appreciate that." Paris stepped back, eyes misting.

"Well," Gran said. "Your young man is waiting."

Paris considered responding again to *your young man* but thought better of it. She had no idea what Greg would be to her after she settled into her new place, new job, new life. The irony of her situation wasn't lost on her. When she returned to Destiny, her life had been in limbo because of her work situation, and now it was in limbo because of her relationship with Greg. *But does it have to be?* She pushed her conflicting thoughts away and smiled at the two most important women in her life. "I'll call this evening when I get settled."

Jess answered, "Please do. Mama worries."

"And you don't?" Gran gave Jess a hard look. Jess chuckled in response.

Paris slipped out the door, waving goodbye as Gran began to sniffle.

She found Greg leaning against the van, looking pensive.

"I guess I'm ready," she said.

"Good. It looks like we'll have a clear day for the drive."

Paris didn't trust herself to do much talking, or she might just burst into tears. The evening before, as they ate a casserole prepared by Mrs. Winthrop, Greg had brought out a calendar and tried to schedule weekends when they could see each other.

"Can we postpone this until I get a better sense of the job?" she'd asked.

"I thought you already understood the job."

"Yes, in general, but I'll be traveling out of town sometimes, and it may be a while before I know when I'll be gone."

"I see. I didn't realize." Greg paused a moment. "Can we at least plan for me to come to your place? I can be there two weeks from today."

"That sounds good. Please understand I may have to change that."

His jaw stiffened but he said, "Okay." They made it through the rest of the evening without obvious tension. A lingering stiffness hung between them now. Paris didn't know how to break through, so she chose silence instead.

As they passed the former Children of Rah compound, she commented on the progress of the work crews. Three different buildings had metal frames up and one had most of its exterior walls. "This place is really changing," she said, hoping to encourage a light conversation.

Greg answered, "Yes, it is."

And that was that. They made most of the ninety-minute trip in silence, Paris watching the changes along the road while Greg drove. Each of them commented from time to time on something they passed, but they couldn't seem to manage a sustained conversation.

Finally, they reached the studio apartment Paris had rented near her new office. Greg had arranged for his college buddy and a few other friends to help them unload. Paris's furniture was moved into her new place within an hour, placed where it needed to be—her bed and her small entertainment center put together and her TV hooked up, even her modem installed and working.

"This is wonderful, guys. Thank you so much."

They assured her it was no problem. The pizza and soda she'd ordered arrived and she made sure she had plenty of food to fill a small army, letting them know how much she appreciated their help. They inhaled the food and then, almost as a body, they disappeared, wishing her well. She and Greg were once more alone.

"Anything else I can do to help?" he asked.

"I think I'm there." She smiled, hands on her hips.

"I can help you unpack some of these boxes. This one says kitchen. Shall I start putting plates and cups in the cupboards?"

"No." Paris took both his hands. "Greg, it's okay. You've done so much for me. I'll take my time with the rest."

"But I can—"

"Really." She squeezed his hands. "I have these two boxes for the kitchen, one each for the living room and the bedroom, and a small one for the bath. I can do that myself in three or four hours tops. I think Greg's Moving Company is done for the day."

His voice was husky as he said, "I don't want to leave you."

She heard her own voice thickening. "I know. I feel the same way, but it's time. I need to get established here and you need to get back to your life in Destiny."

"I..." He stopped.

"It'll be all right," she soothed. "You'll see. If all goes smoothly, we'll be able to spend Saturday together, two weeks from today."

"I'll look forward to that." He looked around. "Nothing I can do before I go?"

She scanned the room. "Nothing I can think of."

"Then I'll see you in a couple of weeks. Expect texts and phone calls in between."

"I'll count on them."

He turned, heading for the door, but turned back and swept her in his arms, holding her so tightly, she could barely breathe. He kissed her—a hard, claiming kiss. Then he turned and walked out the door. He went straight to his truck and left without looking back.

"Goodbye, Greg," Paris whispered as she watched the truck pull away. "I hope this is not the end, but—" She stopped, leaving both the sentence and the thought unfinished.

Chapter Twenty

The job was everything Paris had hoped for. It challenged and stretched her but also showed her what she could do. She quickly caught on to the concepts embodied in her firm's software. Although she would never be an accountant, she understood what accountants would need in the software she brought to them and how to write the instructions they'd need.

Her first project was for a charity that helped kids from poor, inner-city neighborhoods go to summer camp in the high Sierras. Paris loved learning about the charity and the camps with their fishing, climbing, hiking, swimming, archery, crafts, and other activities. These camps were often a teen's first experience outside the city.

"They're a great organization, Greg. I think you'd love working with them," she said in a phone call late that first week.

"Trying to set me up with another job?" he teased. "I'm busy enough."

She played along. "In case you ever want to pile on…"

He chuckled. "I'll remember that. Now tell me about your work."

Paris tried describing what she did, but words made it sound dull —and it wasn't, not to her. "I don't know what to say," she explained. "Talk will be easier when we're face-to-face."

"I expect so," he agreed. "How do things look for a week from Saturday?"

"So far, so good. See you then?"

"Plan on it." They made tentative arrangements, and she promised to look into a couple of the activities he suggested.

It seemed they weren't designed to communicate well at a distance. Greg texted often, and she responded. But their conversations were stilted. They wanted to try video chats after hours but neither of them had the time or energy to talk in the evening after work. So far chatting over their lunch breaks was all they'd been able to do. Even when she called him, they always seemed to end with an uneasy goodbye. The elephant in the room was always in the background: She'd made her choice, and her choice was to leave.

On the Thursday before Greg planned to visit, Paris was asked to dinner by Jake Stone, an attractive blond software developer with a dimpled grin and a cheery approach to his work. "I'm afraid I have plans, but thanks for thinking of me," she answered.

"Maybe next week?"

"I'm not sure. I guess we'll see." Paris smiled before she turned away, mentally kicking herself. She almost went back to tell Jake she was seeing someone, but at this point she wasn't sure where she and Greg stood. She promised herself she'd tell Jake about Greg if he asked again, but the conversation left her uneasy, almost as if she'd deliberately deceived both Jake and Greg.

That emotion felt familiar. Had she deceived Greg, leading him on when she had no intention of staying? She shrugged off the pang of guilt, reminding herself that she'd always been honest about her plans. That didn't change her other truth—that she'd let herself fall for him. Hard and deep. She still loved Greg but how were they going to make this work? She calmed herself with the thought that maybe this was just a rough patch. Maybe things would be better after a fun and leisurely weekend together—unless Greg's feelings toward her were beginning to cool.

On the Friday evening before Greg's scheduled visit, Paris got back to her place late, stressed, and exhausted. She'd promised Greg she'd research activities but had found little time to pursue that. Paris grimaced as the irony hit her: In tiny Destiny, they'd never been short of things to do. If all else failed, they'd always had the mountain with Herbert's cabin and meadow. Here, in the metro area surrounding the state capitol, they had a world of activities, and Paris felt stuck for something to do.

Disturbed that what should have been fun was now a bothersome chore, she hopped online, made several phone calls, found some attractions closed, chose possible others, and decided on one good activity. When Greg arrived around ten the next morning, Paris greeted him with a hug and kiss. "I thought we might go to the zoo. Good?"

"Sure. Sounds fun."

She grabbed a tote she'd packed with sunscreen, a light sweater, and some snacks. Minutes later, they were in Greg's car, following his GPS and the highway signs to William Land Park and the Sacramento Zoo.

"It's been some time since I've been here," Greg said as they found a parking spot. "The last time I was chaperoning a school class. I'd guess it's been...well, years."

"I think it's been longer for me." Paris tucked her arm through his, her tote swinging at her side. "I read up a little on their website, though. They're proud of their meerkat colony."

"Fun! What else besides meerkats?"

Paris explained some of the exhibits she recalled from her reading. Soon they were wandering through, enjoying the turtles and the newly hatched flamingos in the central pond. They appreciated the zoo's justifiable pride in the babies born there, including an endangered snow leopard. They were both intrigued by the rarer animals, charmed by the infants, and pleased by the giraffe encounter, where they watched little children—as well as some moms and dads—feed the giants from a high mezzanine. Greg bought feed and Paris thrilled at the touch of a gentle giant as a reticulated giraffe took food from her hand.

They ate lunch in the park and took a slow stroll through Old Town Sacramento, passing the railroad museum and the statue at the western end of the Pony Express trail. They ended their day with an early dinner at a cute, trendy place on the boardwalk. Then, as they walked toward his car, Greg noticed an old-time photo shop, the kind where guests dressed in Old West costumes and posed in front of backdrops from the late 1800s. "Let's get a souvenir."

Paris looked at the photos in the window. "I don't know about those saloon-girl costumes."

"We can find something you'll like. Come on." Greg tugged her through the door.

The man behind the counter greeted them in a put-on western

drawl. "Y'all lookin' t' have yer picture took?"

Greg slipped into character. "Sign us up, pardner."

Paris was not so certain. "Um, do you have...uh—"

Greg squeezed her hand. "My lady friend ain't no saloon girl. What else ya got?"

The proprietor hee-hawed, enjoying the game, and pulled out a rack of women's costumes, dress fronts and sides with ties to connect in the back. "That way, they all fit no matter," he said, giving Paris an appreciative once-over and a flirty wink. He moved through the rack, showing off each costume. "This'n come from the mayor's wife, and this here one got wore once by the pastor's lady." He had a story for every dress and a hat or bonnet to go with each.

Paris focused on one. Made to look like a tan skirt with a blue satin blouse, it had long, leg-of-mutton sleeves and a modest neckline that showed her collar bones. "That one!" she said.

"You got it, lady. Ye'll look a respectable farm wife in that'n." He handed her the costume and an over-sized t-shirt and directed her to a changing booth barely as large as an old-style phone booth where she dressed with little trouble. When she looked at the back of the costume, she realized why the t-shirt was important: without it, her goal of modesty would have been shattered.

Greg was waiting when she came out, outfitted as the local sheriff with a hat, badge, and a prop that looked like a gun, but reminded Paris of Amber's story about the kindergartener with the show-and-tell toy. They took a moment to admire each other's costumes. Then they picked their favorite backdrop, one that looked like an old-style living room.

They posed and the man took several shots. By the end of the photo shoot, they were both giggling like teenagers. After they changed back into their own clothes, they perused the digital images to pick out their favourites.

"That one," she said, choosing the image that showed them holding hands and smiling at each other.

"That's my favorite too." Greg ordered two copies.

"Ya got it, friend." The proprietor disappeared behind a partition but soon returned with two copies of the photo, framed in cardboard. "Thank y'all fer yer bizness," he said. "Tell yer friends!"

They walked back to the car, laughing about the photographer's full-bore approach to the Old West. Destiny High's baseball team was playing in the district quarterfinals and Greg wanted to be there, so he took Paris home and kissed her at the door. "I had fun today. The zoo was a great idea."

"I think so too," she said wrapping her arms around his waist, enjoying the easy camaraderie they'd reclaimed. A part of her wished they could spend the rest of the evening together, but she didn't feel right about asking Greg to change his plans. It would have been fun to go to the game with him if she'd still been staying in Destiny, but she couldn't manage the time for that now. Again they confronted the barriers that separated them.

"I won't be able to get back for a couple of weeks," Greg said. "Are you thinking of coming up?"

"I'm not sure about next weekend," she answered, "but the following Saturday, Amber's mother is turning fifty and the family's having a party. I promised I'd come for that. Would you like to join me?"

"Count on it." He kissed her again. "See you soon!" He waved as he left.

The rest of the evening, Paris kept picking up the photo and gazing at it. Although they were playing roles, they looked very much like a married couple. She could still hear Greg's voice, slipping into character with a western movie accent and calling her "my lady" and she felt a tightness in her heart as her eyes blurred with tears.

THE DESTINY HIGH Prospectors won their game in the bottom of the ninth. When the opposing team had already begun celebrating with a two-run lead, and the Prospectors looked like they were going down with two outs and a full count, their batter connected for a homer that knocked in not only his own run, but the runners waiting on first and second. Enjoying the town's excitement, Greg tackled the next week with renewed energy.

Maybe the tension in his phone conversations with Paris came from the stress of her new job. Spending Saturday together had been wonderful. Their relationship had slipped back into the same warmth it had when she was in Destiny. He kept the picture shot in Old Town in his briefcase. Every time he glanced at the image, he warmed with renewed hope that everything could work out, if only they were living in the same place.

In the time since he'd helped her move, Greg had done some serious thinking. He'd moved to Destiny hoping it would be his destiny too. He'd bought the family car and home planning to stay forever, and he still wanted that. But falling in love with Paris had caused him to rethink it all.

That led him to a conclusion he'd been dodging for a while: Paris was right about one thing: They weren't going to work long distance. Aloud, he murmured, "I'd better start looking for a job in the valley."

~

PARIS WOKE EARLY SUNDAY, happier and less stressed than on any morning since moving back to the city. Her relaxing weekend had served her well. She had a few small chores to do around the house, but she spent most of the day taking it easy and pampering herself, getting ready for the busy work week ahead. She carved out some time to immerse herself in her surroundings with a walk through her neighborhood. In the afternoon, she even managed a nap.

Greg called that evening and announced that the team had won their quarterfinal game and would be going into the semi-final the next weekend. "I hope you can come up for it. As long as they keep winning, they're playing on our diamond, so the game will be right here in Destiny."

"It sounds like fun, but I already promised I'd be there for Olivia Reyes' birthday party, and I don't know if I can manage two weekends in a row."

"Can you check to make sure?" Greg ended the call early, not giving them time to start stumbling over one another's words.

Before she went to bed, Paris got out the picture she and Greg had taken and put it into a pretty frame. Studying the image, she had another thought: Maybe it wasn't the down time that made her feel so good yesterday. Maybe her peace came from being with Greg. She thought of his voice calling her "my lady" and of the gentle way he had treated her all day. She traced Greg's image with her finger and promised herself she'd find a way to get to the game the next weekend.

Paris's bosses had a surprise for her next morning: her first out-of-town assignment. The client with the high Sierras camp had requested a personal representative from the company to talk their people through the new accounting software and Paris was tapped for the job. That meant a company-paid flight to L.A., accommodations near the client's downtown office, and an expense account to cover meals and incidentals.

It also meant leaving on Wednesday and not returning until the following Tuesday. Unless she wanted to cover her own costs to fly back to Sacramento and then to L.A. again, she would miss the game.

"I'm sorry I can't be there," she told Greg on the phone that evening. "Please cheer the team on for me."

"I'll miss you," Greg said, "but I'll let the team know they have a fan in L.A."

"You bet they do," she answered.

Two days later, Sheryl, a co-worker, drove her to the airport. "I have your flight schedule for next week," Sheryl said as she left her at the curb check-in. "Let me know of any changes."

"I promise you'll be the second person to hear," Paris said, waving Sheryl on.

That first trip taught her a great deal about business travel. Because she was "on" all day, she fell into bed early and exhausted each evening, missing opportunities for sight-seeing. She also learned that wearing loose clothing to the airport meant the scanning machines found too many places to conceal a possible weapon. She was frisked on both the outbound and return flights. She liked the expense account, though, and ate some interesting ethnic meals that she hadn't tried before. The Thai food smelled of ginger and lime and made her miss Greg and all their restaurant excursions.

Although she and Greg spoke at least every other night, she frequently felt too tired to enjoy their conversations and often had to say goodnight early. When he called on Saturday evening to say the boys had lost their semi-final, she had to work up the energy to stay on the phone.

"It was quite an effort," Greg said, obviously still revved from the experience. "It was just the opposite of the last game. Our boys led until the final inning. Then their team won three-to-two in the final moments."

"Sounds exciting." Paris moved the phone away while she stifled a yawn.

"It was. Sad, but exciting." Greg shifted gears. "I'm eager for your trip next week."

She held the phone away so he wouldn't hear her yawn again. "S-so am I."

"Paris? Are you okay?"

"Um-hm. Just tired. They're working me hard."

"Even on Saturday?"

"Yep. I went in for a quick meeting this morning and ended up spending hours showing one of their accountants the same part of the software over and over."

Greg's voice changed. "You were safe, weren't you? I mean, you weren't in there alone with just one or two guys?"

She almost laughed. "Stop worrying! They're working me hard, but they're taking good care of me. Any time I'm in the building, there are at least four people from their company, and there are always at least two other women. I think they're more afraid of setting themselves up for a sexual harassment complaint than they are of me being troubled."

"That's a relief. But do be careful. I hear they have some mean streets down there."

"No meaner than in parts of Sacramento. Honest, Greg, I'm fine."

Later, as she clicked off, she was happy that he cared enough about her welfare to be worried about her, and sorry that she was always too worn out to be good company.

Chapter Twenty-One

By the time Sheryl picked her up the next Tuesday, Paris had decided that business travel was markedly different from tourist travel, and she didn't like it much. She gave herself a pep talk about how she'd get used to it in time, learn to pace herself so she wasn't so exhausted, and enjoy it more. Even as she thought it, she struggled with doubts. But didn't every job have a downside?

Because she had worked through the weekend, her bosses gave her Friday off. Thursday evening, she was packing to leave for Destiny when she got a call from Matthew Korda. "I know we gave you tomorrow, but we have a client who wants an upgrade to his software, and we need changes to the user manual. Can we trade you Monday and have you come in tomorrow?"

"Sure. I can do that." Paris hoped she sounded more excited than she felt. "But doesn't the software need to be finished before it's time for me to walk the client through it?"

"I started a couple of the software guys on it yesterday and they're finishing sooner than we thought. If you come in a little later tomorrow—say, by ten o'clock—they'll be ready to show you how the upgrades work. You can take it from there."

Paris wanted to be sure she knew where she stood. "And you're trading me all day Monday in exchange for tomorrow from ten a.m.?"

"Well, yes," Korda said, "plus maybe a little time on Saturday if we need you."

Paris hesitated. She had promises to keep on Saturday—the birthday party for Olivia Reyes, who had filled some of the parent role for her after her own mother died, and the date she'd planned with Greg. But how could she say no when she'd just started? "I have plans for Saturday," she began, "so I'll need to finish the work tomorrow—if at all possible."

"That's the spirit! We'll see you tomorrow."

As soon as she clicked off, Paris knew she had to call Greg, but she put it off, first calling Gran to tell her she wouldn't be there until Friday night, or possibly as late as midday Saturday. She explained why and Gran said, "I'll tell Jess. Are you going to call Amber?"

"I don't think I need to. I should make it on time for the party."

"Okay," Gran said, but she didn't sound happy. "Take it easy when you drive up."

"Thanks, Gran. I will."

Paris clicked off, took a deep breath, and called Greg. As soon as he said hello, she blurted out that the company needed her, and she'd be coming up later than expected. That led to their first real argument.

"You're backing out on the party?"

"I didn't say that. I said I have to work tomorrow, and I may also need to put in a little time on Saturday morning. The party doesn't start until three, so I can make it with time to spare."

"Honestly, Paris, I thought the Reyes family meant something to you. I should think their party for Olivia would be worth more effort on your part."

Paris's temper flared like a rocket on the Fourth of July. "Don't start. Just don't."

"Paris—"

Fighting back tears, Paris said, "You have no right to criticize or judge me. I said I was still going to the party. This has to do with me not driving up tomorrow and spending time with *you*, before the party. I'll be staying overnight Sunday and driving home Monday instead, so the time we spend together would still be the same, but I guess that's not good enough for you."

"Paris, you're being ridicu—"

"I have to go. Bye Greg." Paris clicked off before he could speak again.

When the phone rang almost immediately and she saw his number, she ignored it. He texted her a few minutes later but feeling more frustrated than she had in some time, she blocked his number.

She went to bed angry, frustrated, and in tears, and had disturbing dreams. The next morning, she woke up exhausted as if she hadn't slept at all. When she got to the office, the software designers had the new product ready, and she sat with them to work on the changes. When Jake Stone again asked her to dinner, she answered that she'd be driving up to a family event in the foothills, but she neglected to mention Greg.

The changes were less complicated than she expected, and Paris had the user manual revised before she left around five-thirty. Matthew came in to say how pleased he was with the team's work and to tell her not to come in before Tuesday. As he prepared to leave, she said, "Matthew? Can I see you for a moment?"

He frowned, but said, "Is there a problem?"

"Not at all. Just something to mention."

He nodded in the direction of the hallway, and she followed. When they were out of the team's hearing, she said, "An interesting thing happened while I was in L.A. One of the supervisors came in complaining they'd just lost their grant writer. He asked if our firm ever did grant writing."

Matthew stroked his chin. "We've had similar requests over the years, but we've never looked at it seriously. Then again, we've never had anyone who listed grant writing on her resume. Is that something you'd consider?"

"I...uh, I have a little experience, but—"

Matthew said, "I'll discuss it with George. Good thought, Paris. Thanks."

She gave herself a mental pat on the back about her boss's response but had to wonder why he frowned when she first asked to speak to him. What was it about her that made people think she was about to lay into them or get upset or complain? Was it some vibe she gave off? She was getting along great with everyone at work, but sometimes she got the feeling people were wary of her. Maybe she hadn't noticed it at her previous job because of all the work drama? Everyone at her last job was on edge, and that had become the norm.

Or maybe she was overthinking things after her fight with Greg. She exhaled a deep sigh. *Why did I explode like that at Greg?* She realized part of it was her own guilt about feeling like she was letting everyone down. In the end, they'd argued over nothing because she was able to drive up Friday evening after all. But there was more to it. It wasn't the first time she'd asked herself that question, and she doubted it would be the last. She'd been accused of overreacting before. Why did other people always seem to handle these situations better than she did?

She reached her apartment, picked up the light bag she'd packed the day before, and headed toward Destiny. A few miles out of town, she pulled off at a scenic view area and unblocked Greg's number, but the phone didn't ring again for the rest of the evening.

AT HOME IN DESTINY, Greg picked up his phone and brought up Paris's number but stopped short of making the call. What point was there in trying again? It wouldn't go through. He felt lost, and lonelier than he could remember, at least since his last break-up, and the comparison to that didn't help his mood. Paris didn't just refuse his calls. She'd blocked his number. It was a severe overreaction and not the first flash of temper he'd seen in her—although he thought she'd have outgrown such tantrums by now. What was going on with her? Was he maybe in over his head? Had he been so caught up in his attraction that he couldn't read the signs that maybe they weren't well suited? *You've been down this road before, buddy.* Maybe it was time for him to rethink that list of traits he wanted in a partner.

Determined to work through the emotion, he started a project he'd put off until summer: He took the doors off his kitchen cabinets, moved them into his garage, and began sanding them down. Redoing the kitchen had been in his plans for some time. Someday, a woman who loved him enough to stay would want an updated kitchen. He pushed the idea away, choosing instead to update it for himself—just in case. He threw himself into sanding with more energy than he thought possible.

GRAN MET Paris at the door. "Welcome back, love. It's been too long."

Paris hugged her tightly. "No more walker?"

Gran held up a walking stick. "I still have this ugly thing, but the walker has found a new home in the cellar."

"That's wonderful, Gran! I'm glad you're doing better."

"Hey, stranger!" Jess called to her from the stairs. "Good to have you back!"

"Thanks, Aunt Jess."

Paris enjoyed the meal they'd prepared. Then she told her aunt and grandmother about her job and listened while they caught her up on changes in Destiny. She wasn't surprised to learn that Lucy Grimes was organizing a party to honor the Prospectors baseball team for their successful season. What surprised her was how interested she was in the team, the party, and even Lucy Grimes' event planning. In fact, she enjoyed getting caught up on all things Destiny-related, and that surprised her most.

It was still early when Paris declared she was done for the week, said goodnight to Gran and Jess, and took her things to her room. She started her bedtime routine, but she couldn't help but think about Greg and how she'd treated him. She sent out a quick text: "Do you still want to come to the party with me? Starts at 3."

She lingered over her usual rituals, but when she felt her eyes drooping, she crawled under the covers. She checked her phone but found no response.

HAVING WORKED HIMSELF TO EXHAUSTION, Greg went to bed early, but he also woke early on Saturday. The gloom of the night before still hung about him but vanished the instant he checked his phone. He didn't know what was going on with Paris, but it was worth finding out. He replied to her text and said he'd pick her up at 2:45.

She responded almost immediately with a thumbs-up emoji.

He smiled and went into the garage to look at the project awaiting his next steps. "You can wait," he said aloud, addressing the partially sanded doors. Then he went back inside and started getting ready for a birthday party.

He arrived at the Kerr home at precisely 2:45 to find Paris not yet ready. "She says she'll be down soon," her grandmother announced as she and Jessica left the house, but Greg could hear a hair dryer running upstairs and knew they'd be cutting it close. When Paris came rushing down the stairs, he guessed they'd likely be late. What was it about Paris and being on time? Several times when they'd gone out, she'd been late. It wasn't a big deal, but a few times she also neglected to let him or Mrs. Bailey know about her schedule when she was working on the proposal. He hoped that whatever was going on with her had to do with stress from her previous job and a lack of a work routine. Maybe now that she was settling in at TriTech, she wouldn't have those issues anymore. "You look great," he told her, meaning it. The day before, he'd wondered if he'd ever see her again.

"Thanks. You clean up well yourself." Greg led her to his car. As Paris slid into the passenger seat, she noticed the wrapped package on the seat behind them. "You brought a gift?"

"Isn't that what one does at a birthday party?"

"I thought the invitation said no gifts." Then she gave him a startled look. "Oh. I didn't tell you that, did I? And I'll bet I didn't mention it's a surprise party, either."

He laid his hand over hers. "It's okay. Everything's okay." For the first time in days, he almost believed it. Worries niggled at the back of his mind, but he ignored them for now, as he drove toward the Reyes home.

OLIVIA'S PARTY didn't start well for Paris. She and Greg arrived several minutes late. Almost immediately, Greg was drawn into the family room where a group of men had gathered. Paris recognized many of the other guests, but she knew few of them well, and she felt a bit at loose ends trying to join in until Amber came out of the kitchen. "You've done a beautiful job here," she said, greeting her friend with a hug.

"Where were you?" Amber stage whispered. "We counted on you to help decorate."

Paris's knees went weak as memory rushed in. "Amber, I'm so sor—"

Amber waved away Paris' apology. "It's all right, we got it done. Tyler and his wife helped me get started yesterday and Sunny helped this morning."

A slim, light-haired woman approached. "Did I hear my name?"

Amber brightened as she drew the newcomer into their conversation. "Paris, you remember Sunny, don't you?"

"Of course." Paris and Sunny acknowledged each other with a smile.

"What're you doing back in Destiny?" Sunny asked, and lowered her voice, "And did I hear you're dating Mr. Frantz?"

"He's here with me today," Paris murmured back. Then, "What are you up to now?"

Sunny said, "You first. Catch me up."

Over the next few minutes, Paris told them about her new job and Sunny talked about her decision to go to college. "It started with that museum job, so I decided to give it a shot. Then I took a history course my first term and fell in love with it. Anyway, I'll graduate with a history degree in a couple of weeks."

"Congratulations! What then?"

Sunny shrugged. "Graduate school, I hope."

"Good for you!" Paris looked around. "Is Skye here? Is she coming?"

Amber interrupted. "We don't know. I invited her and she said yes, but—"

"—but we never know about Skye," Sunny finished.

Paris touched her hand. "I'm sorry, hon. I know you've always worried about her." Then she looked around the room, "Where's the guest of honor?"

"Dad took her to Berman's for a late birthday lunch," Amber answered. A chime from her phone got her attention and she read her screen. "I just got a text that they'll be here in about two minutes." She turned to the group. "They're on their way, everybody! Quiet! Please."

The group hushed and turned expectantly toward the door. Anticipation got the better of some and the murmurs began again until they heard a car pull up and the room fell silent. Moments later, the door opened, and as Olivia Reyes entered, guests shouted, "Surprise!"

A candle-laden cake appeared and everyone sang as a happy yet surprised Gloria blew out the candles and friends offered congratulations. Greg was not the only guest who had missed or ignored the no-gifts request, but Olivia opened his last. Paris oohed along with everyone when Olivia opened her new home tortilla iron, gushed with pleasure, read the card, and thanked both Greg and Paris.

"You didn't need to do that," she murmured to Greg, who stood beside her, his arm about her waist. "I wasn't even in on it."

"You invited me," he murmured, adding a quick kiss on her ear, and she felt a rush of unexpected tenderness.

With Greg at her side, Paris mingled with the other guests, catching up with old acquaintances and meeting new ones. She couldn't help feeling more at home than she usually did in social situations and realized it was easier to socialize when Greg was with her. He was calm, funny, charming, and genuinely interested in people and what they had to say. An hour later, guests began to leave. Paris turned to Amber, "I think it's time for us to say our good—"

The front door slammed open. A petite, oddly dressed woman with a mass of raven-black curls burst in, bringing the strong scent of alcohol with her. "Hall-o, everybody," she drawled, and stumbled into the room.

Chapter Twenty-Two

"Skye was always the one we worried about," Paris said as she and Greg drove away. "Still, I never imagined she'd create that kind of scene at her aunt's birthday. I know how much the Reyes family gave up taking in those girls. And when I see what they saved them from…" She paused. "How could she do this?"

"She was pretty far gone into the alcohol even when I was a student teacher here." He turned down the highway. "Berman's Mesa sound good for dinner?"

Paris balked. "No. I don't feel like eating. Didn't you see what happened back there?"

Greg gave her a starch look. "Yes, I saw what happened. Did you? The family obviously expected this or something like it. I'm sure they've seen it before."

"She looked like a bag lady and smelled like a brewery. She was practically falling-down drunk. And you're acting like it's normal."

"For Skye, it probably is."

"Greg—"

"If you were surprised by what happened back there, you're the only one. Skye was well on her way to becoming the town drunk even when she was a teenager. How old was she when I did my student teaching here? Fourteen? Fifteen?"

"She was a sophomore that year, so about that." Paris's throat tightened. "I still don't see how you can say—"

"Because I saw it, Paris. I saw her giggling and stupid, out-of-her-mind drunk at least twice that school year. At school, during the day."

Paris sat back hard. "I don't believe it."

"It's true. The first time was Halloween day. She was in the after-lunch English class, and she was already unsteady on her feet and giggling about nothing when she stumbled in. I overheard her whispering to Jaxon Rollins about whether he could get 'more' for her. She said she had cash. He looked around, told her sharply that she was speaking too loudly and was going to get him in trouble. Then I heard him say he could get her a twelve-pack later that evening."

"Really? But—"

"I guess he didn't know I was right behind him. When he saw me walk up the aisle, he looked panicked for about half a second. Then his eyes narrowed, and he looked like he wanted my head on a platter."

Paris felt her words pour out like acid. "And you let him intimidate you into staying quiet?"

"It wasn't like that. I was a *student teacher*, Paris, the lowest of the low. Naturally I mentioned it to Mrs. Elam and later to Principal Ross, but it wasn't up to me to *do* anything. They said they'd take care of it, and I left it at that."

Sadness welled up in Paris, mixed with frustration, and anger. "You could have done something. You should have."

"Paris, you can't save people from themselves."

"She was a kid! A child! She needed help!"

"Paris—"

"Take me home, Greg." Tears were forming. "I need to go home."

"Can't we talk about this?"

Sudden, hysterical tears flowed freely. "I want to go home."

Greg sighed, but he turned the car toward Gran's. Neither spoke as they made the short trip. She didn't trust herself to say anything more. Paris jumped out of the car as soon as Greg pulled into the driveway and ran up the back stairs. Greg sat, watching until the door slammed behind her. Then he pulled onto the road.

GREG TOOK the long way home, driving slowly through back streets, even stopping at the gas station to top up the tank. He bought a protein bar and a bottle of water and sat in his car wondering what to do, not wanting to be home alone and uncertain which emotion ranked highest. Frustration? Disgust? Worry? No, confusion was at the top of the list. He smacked his hand against the steering wheel. *What in*

the heck was all that about? Paris's hair-trigger temper concerned him more than Skye's drunken scene. Some forty minutes after leaving Paris, he returned home, changed into work clothes, and started sanding again.

∽

GRAN AND JESS were shelling the last of the spring peas at the kitchen table when Paris ran in. They both looked up.

"Paris?" Gran asked. "Is everything all right?"

"No," she said, "not really."

Jess asked, "What happened?"

Paris shook her head. "I can't really talk about it. I need to be alone for a while." She looked to the other women with a kind of sad desperation.

Gran nodded. "You want us to call you for dinner?"

Paris hesitated. "Sure. I may not feel like eating but tell me when it's time." She scurried up the stairs.

When Jess knocked to tell her dinner was ready, she'd worked through much of the emotional turmoil. "I'll be down in five," she answered.

Gran had gone to some effort, Jess had helped, and the dinner was lovely. Paris discovered she was ready to enjoy a good meal despite her bust-up with Greg over Skye's scene at the party. Though neither Jess nor Gran pressed, they both glanced at her as they ate, and slowly, her story came out.

"It was ugly," she said as she finished. "Skye stumbled in looking terrible, smelling worse, and obviously drunk. She embarrassed her aunt and hurt her feelings and gave the rest of this town something to gossip about for weeks. I was ashamed for her!" She paused, and then added, "And worried too. I know Sunny is scared. Amber seems more...resigned, I guess. It's like she's given up—like everybody's given up."

"I'm sorry," Gran said, leaning toward her.

"Me too," said Jess. "I always loved that family, and what they did taking in their nieces was a true act of compassion." She paused and looked at Paris. "You know I taught Skye as a senior. I knew she was in trouble then."

"I don't understand!" Paris swallowed emotion. "If everybody knew she was in trouble, why didn't someone *do* something?"

"Paris—" Gran began.

"We all tried," Jess said. "But there's only so much the law will allow a teacher or other non-guardian to do. We all spoke with Olivia and Enrique—at least, I know I did, and Mrs. Elam did too. I also think they were doing their best. They took her to therapy while she was still living with them, and I hear they paid for expensive rehab hospitals a few times. Skye just walks out."

Jess paused, as if considering how to go on. "I think everyone who knew or suspected Skye's problems tried to help, but she seemed so broken inside, damaged by her life in the commune before she came to live with her aunt and uncle. It was like, no matter what they did, it wasn't enough. Skye needed to want to change. And that kind of change takes a lot of work and daily commitment. Maybe Skye is still not ready." Jess looked Paris steadily in the eyes. "You can't save people from themselves."

Paris nodded, her voice soft as she answered, "That's what Greg said."

Jess exchanged a quick look with Gran, who said, "How did Greg feel about this… this scene you described?"

"He'd seen it before, and he thought most of the people at the party had."

Jess nodded. "He's probably right."

"Why didn't I know?" Angry tears threatened. "I know I've been away, but Amber—"

"I can't know for sure," Gran said, and then she glanced at Jess, her expression communicating something Paris couldn't read. "But Paris, honey, you aren't always the most perceptive person. You probably overlooked the clues in high school, and you told us that you and Amber fell out of touch. Besides, Amber likely intended to protect Skye by not sharing details."

Paris nodded. "I suppose."

They finished dinner. Paris took care of the dishes and excused herself. In the privacy of her old room, she sent Amber a text: "Can we meet tomorrow? I'd like to talk about what happened."

Amber didn't reply immediately, but some twenty minutes later, Paris received an answering text: "Does 11:00 sound good? Come for brunch, then we'll go somewhere and talk."

Paris confirmed the meeting. Then, before she could talk herself out of it, she sent a text to Greg: "Sorry about today. Shock, I guess. I'll be busy until mid-afternoon tomorrow. After that, can we hike to the cabin?"

The response came back quickly: "Let me know when you're ready. I'll pick you up."

Paris liked having a plan, but she couldn't let go of her distress. She'd felt off-kilter all day, bothered by everything from spacing on a promise to help Amber with decorating, to feeling out of place at the party, to her angst about Skye. And of course, her fight with Greg. She knew what happened today wasn't entirely about Skye. Under today's harsh feelings lay the big issues—and the distance—that kept her and Greg apart, that kept them from being a couple.

Gran and Jess had made some good points. Destiny never felt like home to her back in high school, and she couldn't wait to leave for college. But was it Destiny's fault or hers? What was that Gran said about how she wasn't always the most perceptive person? Why wasn't she? As she brushed her teeth, she wondered again, why when it came to relationships, she overreacted sometimes, overlooked things other times, and as Gran said, lacked perceptiveness? Looking into the mirror, she murmured, "What's wrong with me?"

PARIS AWOKE the next morning eager for the day to unfold, but her tidy plans began unraveling early. Within minutes, she received a text from Amber: "Brunch off. Skye here and fur flying. Will call when free but could be tomorrow. Work for you?"

She quickly replied: "Works for me. I have the day off. Don't you have school?"

The answer came quickly: "Teacher prep day. Specialist doing workshops. I'll have to stay at school, but I can spare a couple of hours in a.m."

Paris started to reply, but another text from Amber came almost immediately: "Things crazy here. Let's plan for tomorrow, my office, ten-ish. K?"

She sent back: "K....ten" and got a thumbs-up in reply.

Disappointed, but in a way relieved, Paris attended church with Gran and Jess. She was thrilled to find Greg there, waiting to help Gran up the stairs. "This is good of you," she said as they easily reached the top.

Gran gave him a grateful smile and a grandmotherly pat on his cheek. "I appreciate it, handsome."

Greg grinned. "Always happy to help a beautiful lady."

Gran poked Paris. "He helps every week. Even picks me up for church if Jess can't make it."

"Thank you, Greg." Paris smiled her appreciation. "That really is kind."

"Happy to help," he answered. He eased Gran into a pew and scooted in next to Paris. He reached for Paris's hand. "Is this okay?"

"Sure," she said, and she squeezed his hand in turn.

When the meeting ended and Greg had helped Gran back to her car, he told Paris he had a picnic packed. "Pick you up in half an hour?"

"I'd love that." Paris hoped for a peaceful afternoon on the mountain. Despite their differences, she loved Greg. She couldn't help loving him, and she knew now that she didn't want to lose him. So why did she keep pushing him away?

"THE WEATHER'S BEEN WARMING," Greg said as they began their hike. "We could have some slithery company."

Paris shuddered. "I'll trust you to clear the way."

They were most of the way up the trail and Paris was admiring the bright white blossoms in a nearby dogwood when Greg whispered, "Shhhh."

Paris stepped close behind him, whispering, "What?"

He pointed and Paris peeked over his shoulder. Maybe eighty yards above them, a black bear and two cubs crossed the trail—the mother a magnificent creature, her coat shimmering in the sun, the babies tussling and tumbling over one another as they followed Mama Bear. Paris and Greg stood motionless until the bears were out of sight.

"Beautiful," Paris whispered, "but scary. Should we go back?"

"I don't think so," Greg whispered. "They have places to go and they're off our path now. By the time we get where they were, they'll be well away from us. Besides, feel which way the wind is blowing?"

"Well, yes, but—"

"The wind will carry our scent away from them. I think we're good to go."

Paris hesitated. "Are you sure?"

"I've seen that sow before. We each give each other space and we get along fine."

"Even when she has cubs?"

"She doesn't want trouble. If we keep a respectful distance—" Then he looked into Paris's face. "Hey Babe, if you're frightened, we can turn around."

She swallowed, gathering her wits. "No, I'm okay. I guess I'm just not used to seeing bears outside a zoo."

"Then consider yourself privileged. This Mama shared a moment with us."

Paris doubted the encounter was deliberate. "Did she know we were here?"

"Oh yeah." Greg spoke with assurance. "A black bear's sense of smell is thousands of times better than ours. She knows we're here, but she doesn't see us as a threat. Shall we keep going?"

Paris nodded and fell into step behind him.

They reached Herbert's cabin and the clearing beside it. Paris helped set out Greg's picnic and was touched that he had remembered her favorites. They chatted as they enjoyed the simple meal. Then, as the afternoon warmed, they settled against the cut tree stump to watch the lovely tableau in the meadow, changing now as the earth turned toward summer. Paris looked at Greg and felt again that rush of tenderness. "Greg?"

"Yes, love."

"I'm sorry for the tension between us. I know it's my fault." She paused, making sure he was listening. "I was so afraid of getting stuck in Destiny that I haven't given us—you and me—a fair chance. And yes, I know I'm the one who left, but I want us to have time together. I want to try for the long haul, to see if we have staying power, like you said."

"Thinking long-term, are we?" He scooted closer, his tone teasing. "You're proposing to me, right?"

"You idiot," she said, giving his shoulder a playful shove. "You should be so lucky."

He settled against her. "Tell me about your life in the valley."

She told him how she loved her job, but it had its downside. "The travel isn't what I thought it would be and the work is exhausting. I keep telling myself it will get easier as I get used to it, but there's no way of knowing for sure."

"I expect it will get easier." He stroked her arm. "How has it been to be back in the big city where your neighbors don't know your whole family and everything you've ever done since kindergarten?"

Paris sighed. "It's odd. I thought I wanted that, but I haven't even met my next-door neighbors, or anyone outside of work. I see people in the elevator and at the mailboxes and I have a general sense of who lives around me. We have a couple of divorced moms with teenagers, two middle-aged men who are probably divorced and alone—or maybe together..." She shrugged. "And a few young singles like me, almost no older people or couples with kids."

"Doesn't feel like a neighborhood, huh?"

"Not at all. And I'm surprised to realize I miss that. I'm friendly with some of the people at work, but there's no one I'd consider a friend. Not yet anyway. And I can't imagine any of them putting on a birthday party like the one yesterday."

He nodded. "Even with the drama, that was quite a party. Have you talked with Amber?"

"We texted this morning. We were supposed to meet, but Skye is there. Amber said things were 'crazy.'"

Greg twirled a lock of her hair. "I imagine things are often crazy around Skye."

"I'll ask Amber when I see her. We're supposed to meet in her office tomorrow morning. She said she'd be free because of workshops with some...specialist."

Greg nodded knowingly. "We're getting the same specialist next week. She's teaching us about people who are differently abled when it comes to learning."

"Differently..." Paris felt her forehead wrinkle. "Can you skip the politically correct language and tell me what you're talking about?"

Greg offered a reassuring smile. "You aren't the only one who's confused. We're talking about kids with ADHD or mild degrees of autism, or dyslexia or disorders in auditory processing. Dr. Sayyid will teach us ways of identifying learning differences and helping the affected kids use the skills they have to compensate for weak spots in another area. We want to help all the kids stay on pace with their age peers."

"I imagine Skye could have used that kind of help."

"Yes. If she'd had that when she first started in the school system, it may have helped her avoid some of the problems that came later. Of course, it wouldn't have dealt with all her emotional issues."

They talked about Skye then, what they both knew of her background in the Children of Rah and how she arrived in the Destiny schools well behind other kids academically. They discussed her struggles with fitting in and anything else they could remember that might help them understand why she'd become an alcoholic and how she might still be helped.

They went on to talk about how completely the Children of Rah grounds had been renovated and what a difference the new spa would make in Destiny. That's when Greg said, "There's one other change I'd like you to know about. Are you up for a little walk?"

"Sure."

He led her behind Herbert's cabin and a few hundred yards on the path around the mountain. When they arrived at the spot he had shown her before, she could easily see the changes. Mining operations were underway. "They found diamonds?"

He nodded. "It's still mostly industrial quality, but their test bore came out with two small gem-quality stones. And they have hints of other minerals worth mining. I've been negotiating with the company, and—drum roll, please—we signed a contract last week."

"Wonderful! Greg Frantz, the millionaire. And to think I knew you when."

He chuckled. "You still know me when. If they don't find anything, nobody earns anything."

"But they will find good stuff, won't they?"

"I believe they will. Otherwise, I wouldn't have pursued this the way I have."

She drew her brows together. "Greg? When you become a wealthy mine-owner, will you still want to be a high school principal?"

He straightened. "Yes. At least, for a while. I suppose I could get so busy with mining that I can't do both. Or someday things could get bad enough in the schools that I'll be happy to take the easy way out and quit. I've certainly seen that happen to colleagues. But for now..."

He turned her toward him. "Most people probably wouldn't believe this, Paris, and it's possible you won't either, but I swear it's the truth." He took a deep breath. "This business with the mine? It has much less to do with possible wealth than it does with following through on Herbert's belief in the place. He trusted me with his dream. I want to give this claim every possible chance. For his sake more than mine. You understand?"

"Yes, I think I do. And the school kids?"

"I see problems with the way we're bringing up the next generation —what we're feeding them, both literally and figuratively, and how we're preparing them for adulthood. I think I can make a difference. I want to help. That's why I got into education in the first place."

"I believe that too, and it's honorable and good of you. But I'm guessing you won't run from riches if the mine becomes profitable."

He hesitated before speaking. "I've never been one of those guys who has to prove his worth with all the stuff he has. I live comfortably and I have enough, but no, I wouldn't run from money. If the mine earns piles of cash, I'm not above spending some of it. I've often thought that experiences are more important to kids than things, so when I someday have children, I might take my family on vacations in interesting parts of the world, maybe let them keep horses or take them SCUBA diving or up to Bedford Falls to ski. You know, experiences and hobbies that cost. Other than that..." He paused long enough that Paris wondered if he had more to say. "Other than that, I expect there would be scholarships for deserving high school kids, better places for our elderly poor to retire, and grants to those non-profits you're working for."

She took several seconds before answering. "That's amazing. You have a good heart, Greg. You're a kind man. An unusual one, too."

"Not all that unusual," he said. "I just know what I value." He smiled into her eyes as he took her hand, kissed her fingers, and led her back toward the meadow.

"Greg? About those non-profits I work for? One of them asked my bosses if they'd thought of expanding their services to include grant writing. Because they saw the proposal I wrote for you listed on my resume, they want to talk with me when I go in next week."

"Great! Glad to hear it."

"I have you to thank for that. Thank you."

"You're welcome." Then he gave her a quick kiss. "I love you, you know."

"I know." She smiled. "I love you too. And Greg? That stuff you were saying about giving your children experiences?"

"Yeah?"

"I think that's the kind of life I want for my children too."

He rewarded that with a big grin and a bigger kiss.

They spent a long time in the meadow, chatting and sharing more cuddles and kisses. The sun had begun its descent behind the trees when they made their way back to the trailhead.

Chapter Twenty-Three

P aris was on her way to Amber's office when her phone chirped the ring tone for Adele Rich. Had there been some confusion? Did Adele expect her to be there on her day off? She calmed herself with a breath before picking up. "Hello, Adele."

"Listen, Paris, I know you're off today, but Matthew spoke with George about the idea of adding grant writing to our services and the two of them have been investigating all weekend. Turns out George's sister does grant writing for a firm that specializes in finding RFPs for non-profits and writing those that fit their clients' needs. She's been cutting back on the number of clients she serves because she wants to retire, but that also gives her some available time.

"Anyway..." Adele took a deep breath. "She told George if he pays her enough, she'll come in for a while to help us get a similar process going. She said the fact that we have an experienced grant writer makes it easier."

Paris's heart rate kicked up at hearing Adele call her an experienced grand writer. "Hold on. I told George and Matthew that I wrote *one* proposal for one successful, very small grant. I'm not sure that qualifies me as—"

"You know a whole lot more than anyone else here."

"But—"

"Don't worry! The bosses know you're new. If they decide to do this, you'll have time to learn. We just don't want you to be blind-sided when you come in tomorrow."

"Oh. Okay. I appreciate that."

Adele chuckled merrily—or perhaps nervously. "We underlings have to watch each other's backs. See you in the morning."

"Bright and early." Paris clicked off, wondering what she was getting into.

She found her way to the elementary school office only to be told, "Ms. Reyes isn't in."

"Oh? We had an appointment—"

"I remember, Ms. Cutler." The secretary's tone was crisp. "Ms. Reyes had something that required her care. You may wait in her office if you wish."

"Thanks. I will." Under her breath, she added, "And maybe I'll talk with her about her assistant's attitude." Paris entered Amber's office and began looking around, rediscovering the old friend she knew in the pictures on the shelves. She saw the expected mementos, such as plaques awarded to the school for excellence or for high scores on standardized tests. There were also personal items which Paris examined more closely.

A large, framed picture showed the Reyes family, including Sunny and Skye. It must have been taken around the time Amber and Paris graduated high school. Paris remembered the Amber's asymmetrical haircut. She took a long look at the image of Skye. With the clarity of hindsight, she had no trouble spotting clues about the problems Skye was developing then. She wished she'd noticed when they were younger.

Paris wandered from that photo to another, and another. On the top of one cabinet, she found a picture of her with Amber. They stood with their arms around each other, grinning at the camera and holding up a sign saying, "Go, Prospectors!" A flood of memories returned of the friendship they once shared, and regret rippled through her. Had 'out of sight, out of mind' always been a pattern in her life?

Holding the photo, Paris sat beside the desk, thinking of what Destiny had meant in the years after losing her dad and then her mom. She thought of her relationship with Greg, and how rocky things had been since she moved away. In that moment, she recognized another pattern. Except for Gran and Jess, and even sometimes with them, she often distanced herself, letting too many days pass without checking in, or in the case of friends like Amber, letting time slip away.

"Hey, sorry I—" Amber entered the room, smiling softly as her eyes met Paris's. "I see you found that old photo."

"I'd forgotten all about this day." Paris stood, set the photo on the desk, and gave Amber a huge hug.

"What was that for? I mean, I love hugs, but—"

"That's for being my friend, not just in high school, but again. Thanks."

Amber shrugged. "I'm glad to have you back."

Paris dropped into her chair. "Talk to me. Catch me up on what's going on with you—and all that business with Skye."

For most of an hour, Paris listened as Amber unreeled the story from the time her mother recognized her nieces needed rescue. Paris interrupted only to ask a question or seek clarification. When Amber finished, she said, "I felt so angry when I saw Skye stumble in. I was furious! Then I wondered why no one tried to help her. I see now that you've all been trying to help." Her voice softened. "Do you know why she won't accept it?"

Amber bit her lip. "We don't really know, but Sunny has given us some clues." She folded her hands. "I guess things got pretty rough out there. At the Children of Rah camp, I mean."

Paris nodded. "Go on."

"Their mom was often drunk or drugged and not keeping an eye on the girls. Sunny said some of the men were trying to touch and handle her even when she was little. She learned to talk her way out of those situations, but she isn't sure Skye did."

The words struck Paris like a slap. "Oh, the poor kid. She was... mistreated?"

"As I said, we don't know, but we suspect it. There may even have been a pattern."

"And there wasn't anyone to help until your mom took them away." Paris glanced at the Reyes family picture.

"We think Skye was afraid to tell, even after she came to live with us. She seemed to think that if she told anyone, her mom would get in trouble. She didn't want that."

Paris saw the picture coming together. "So instead of getting her mother into trouble, she absorbed the trouble herself."

Amber tapped a pencil on her desk. "We think that's what happened."

"Poor Skye. Is there anything I can do to help her? Or help you? Or your family? I'm sorry I haven't been a better friend."

Amber's voice was gentle. "Sweetie, we didn't expect you or anyone to fix this. Nobody can fix Skye but Skye, and we're beginning to realize there may be underlying causes—like a family propensity toward ADHD."

Paris wrinkled her brow in confusion. "What does that have to do with… I don't get it."

"I'm not sure I do either, but I'm trying to learn." Amber swiveled in her chair. "It's possible her mom was self-medicating. Maybe Skye is too. We're all trying to find answers. That's part of the reason I'm excited about today's workshops." She glanced at the wall clock. "Can you believe we've talked for nearly two hours?" She stood. "I need to go keep the peace in the cafeteria. After that, I'm scheduled for the afternoon session with Dr. Sayyid. Maybe I can get some insight into Skye's addiction issues."

"I'd like to hear about what you learn. Maybe we can do a late lunch?"

"Sounds great." Amber moved to the door. "I love Joe's rosemary turkey sandwich."

Paris followed. "Make it Berman's Mesa, my treat."

"Ooh, rich living! Okay, Berman's it is. See you around four?"

"You've got it, lady." Paris left, turning her sights toward the high school. Maybe she could see Greg again before she drove back to the valley.

In his office, Greg listened to his football/track coach. People had been maneuvering behind the scenes, working to decide the fate of young Lech Nowak. With the help of Coach Velasquez, a plan was coming together, one that seemed fair to everyone. Greg hoped it worked, but that largely depended on Paris.

The prosecutor's office had agreed with the public defender regarding special circumstances. This was a first offense with the future of a scared kid hanging in the balance. Lech's grandmother wasn't doing well, and reports suggested she may not last long. That made today's announcement from Coach Velasquez even more amazing. With their youngest child graduating and going into the Marine Corps, the coach and his wife had already applied to be foster parents. As of this week, they had their final approvals. And they wanted to give Lech the stability he needed.

This morning a deal had been reached: If Lech pleaded guilty to a lesser charge, the prosecutor would ask for time served plus probation and the boy would be placed in the coach's custody. He'd return to Destiny High the following year, and, if he kept his nose clean, his record would eventually be expunged.

"Has the D.A. spoken with Ms. Cutler about this?" Greg asked Coach Velasquez. "The prosecutors will want to make sure Paris agrees, since she was the target of the assault."

"I don't know if they have," the coach said, "but I hope she agrees."

"I'll call her," Greg said as he ushered the coach from his office.

Greg had more to discuss when he spoke with Paris. That morning he'd received the first nibble on the applications he sent to schools in the valley. If he couldn't talk Paris into coming to him, maybe he'd go to her. He picked up his phone but set it down again as Paris walked through his door.

"Hey, guy," she said, giving him a flirty smile and a quick kiss.

"Hey yourself." Greg closed the door to keep Mrs. Bailey from seeing the more serious kiss he returned. "What's behind that big smile?"

"It's been an interesting day." Paris told Greg about her talk with Amber. He told her about the plan for Lech Nowak and asked if she'd be willing to drop the assault charges. Then he explained why he liked the idea. Paris hesitated but was glad the boy wasn't falling through the cracks. Her own situation had been eerily like Lech's, and she couldn't imagine how she'd have coped without Gran and Jess. "If the D.A. wants to drop the charges, I'll approve it."

"Great!" he said. "I'll call the prosecutor's office and let them know. They'll want you to formalize things—"

"They have my number. I'm sure they'll call when they need me."

A bell rang and Greg glanced at the clock. "I need to go. Can I take you out for another late lunch?"

She told him about her plans with Amber, but added, "I'd like to see you again before I leave."

"I'll call you," he said as he hurried away.

Paris left with her thoughts and emotions in a tumble. The day so far had been filled with revelations large and small—some rewarding, some disturbing, and some causing deep self-reflection. She had the sense that a gem of self-discovery lay buried in that wealth of ideas. She only hoped she'd have the wisdom to uncover it.

At Berman's Mesa, Paris returned from taking her phone into the hall. While she was gone, their orders had been served. Amber asked, "Everything okay?"

"I think so. That was the D.A. making sure I'm dropping formal charges against the boy who did the break-ins."

"Ah, the one who gave you that nasty bump on the head and the bruised ribs."

"Right, that one," Paris answered, her tone wry. She explained the legal arrangement.

Amber looked hesitant. "And you're okay with that?"

"Yeah, I am. I was angry when it first happened but I've had time to think. The kid was alone and hungry and scared half out of his mind. Not that breaking into people's homes and stealing was a good choice, but he's a kid, you know? Maybe I wouldn't have made a better choice when I was fifteen."

She saw Amber's look. "Maybe Skye didn't see better choices when she was fifteen either."

Paris nodded thoughtfully. "Maybe she didn't. I expect she was frightened too."

A look of understanding passed between them as they began their meal. It wasn't long before Paris asked, "Do you want to tell me about you and Chad?"

Amber shrugged. "Not much to tell. I thought we had something.

When I took the job here in Destiny, we agreed to keep seeing each other, but it never seemed to work, you know?"

"I'm afraid I do." Paris took a bite of salad. This story sounded way too familiar.

"Sometimes he'd have to cancel, sometimes I would. Sometimes we went for three or four weeks with little more than emails or texts and maybe a call or two. After a while, we knew it wasn't working." She shrugged.

Paris saw herself and Greg in that description and a shudder ran through her. "Do you still miss him?"

Amber sighed. "I try not to. I tell myself it's just the way things are and someday soon, I'll find a great guy, but honestly? I haven't even been out with a man since Chad and I split. Some of that is the lack of available men in Destiny—"

"There aren't many," Paris agreed, wondering why Greg and Amber hadn't clicked.

"And part of it is… I guess I'm not over him."

Paris nodded. "I get that. When I wondered if things were over with Greg…once, when I was furious with him, I didn't want to date anybody else. There's a nice guy at work who asked me out, but I made excuses."

Amber gave her a searching look. "Did you tell him you were seeing somebody?"

"No. I thought maybe I should, but I wasn't sure I was still seeing someone."

Amber seemed to chew on that idea even as she took another bite of her salad. "So, you don't want to be with anyone else, but you haven't committed to being with Greg either?"

Paris pushed the plate away. "Sounds fickle when you put it that way."

Amber set her fork down. "Is this still about your fear of being stuck in Destiny? Because if that's the only problem—"

"I haven't really figured it out." Paris drew in a deep breath and let it out slowly. "I know. I need to think it through."

Their server took their plates and offered dessert, which both women declined.

Amber said, "Maybe I know some of why you feel the way you do about our lovely little town."

"Oh yeah? Fill me in."

"I think part of it is tied up with your dad's death."

Paris considered that. "Maybe. I've always equated his lonely, unnecessary death with small town living. Had someone else been with him—"

"But he wasn't living in Destiny when that happened," Amber said. "Your folks were living in Sacramento then."

"Good point." Paris let that thought sink in.

Amber went on, "Your dad died because he was sent into a dangerous situation alone. The company didn't realize how dangerous, but after your father, they knew their workers should always have back-up. The point remains that your dad was living in a big city at the time of his accident. Destiny had nothing to do with it.."

"I know that, but I don't feel it, you know? And there was Mom—"

"…who was also living in the city when she was diagnosed with cancer. Yes, she came up here—and moved you to Destiny—when she was going through treatment, but it's not like she was isolated here. I remember all the trips your grandmother or your Aunt Jess took driving down the mountain to take your mom to appointments. Sometimes you went with them."

"I know, but—"

"She got the best care available from the best doctors in the state capital. Small town living had nothing to do with that, either."

Paris held up both hands. "Okay, you win! I've been holding grudges against the town that aren't the town's fault. I get that. In fact, I've been coming to that conclusion on my own. It's just been hard to see through all those old emotions, you know?"

Amber played with the saltshaker. "I guess we're all trapped in the emotions we develop as kids, at least until we think our way through them." She caught Paris's eye. "We agree that Skye needs to work through hers. Maybe both of us have stuff we need to work through too. I hope you're getting there, hon. We could use you up here."

"I'll give it some thought."

Paris considered their conversation as they left the restaurant.

When they were back in Amber's car, she said, "I've wondered what would change if I got over my grudge against Destiny so I felt free to come to Greg. The issue is work. What could I do for work here?"

Amber turned to the main highway and began the climb toward the school where Paris had left her car. "I don't know either, but several Destiny residents have found ways. I'll bet you could figure out something."

"Maybe. I'll have to think about that too."

Amber flashed a smile. "I hope you can. It would be good for Greg. I haven't seen him this happy in a long time, probably not since he broke up with your Aunt Jess."

Paris trembled as if a wave of ice water had swept the car. "What?" Her throat constricted, and she swallowed. "What did you just say?"

"I said I haven't seen Greg this happy since he broke up with Jess. You know, back when everyone in town thought they'd get mar—" Amber looked at Paris again and her jaw went slack. "Oh no! You didn't know? How could you not know? Oh Paris, I'm so sorry!"

"Take me home," Paris said, choking out the words. "Please, Amber. Take me home now."

Chapter Twenty-Four

P aris threw things into her small suitcase, grateful she hadn't brought much. Tears ran freely as images jumped into mind, pictures of Greg and Jess together. She found it easy to see Jess in her place in a variety of warm moments she and Greg had shared. Greg and Jess had come close to marrying? Just how close had they been? And why had no one told her?

She closed her mind to the possibilities, but other images began popping in. This time they were memories…her first day in Destiny when her grandmother had started to say something about Mr. Frantz and Jess, but Jess cut her off with an explanation about misunderstandings between teachers and administrators. As if *that* was the problem!

"She *lied* to me!" Paris couldn't remember ever feeling this hurt or angry—this *betrayed*—in her life. "Jess lied and Gran went along with it." Her knees weakened and she sank to her bed. She thought of all the times Gran had told her to talk with Jess, and her anger toward her grandmother eased. It hadn't been Gran's story to tell. *Jess should have told me.*

Or Greg. He'd been in on the deception as well. When he told her of the feud between his grandfather and Herbert, she'd answered, *Secrets and betrayal should never happen in a family,* and yet he'd never said a word. Both Greg and Jess had dodged multiple opportunities to tell her the truth, and both claimed to care about her. Greg even professed to love her. She swiped at her tears but they continued to flow, and she hugged herself tightly, trying to regain control. *I've got to get out of here.*

If Amber knew, the whole town knew. Had they all been talking about it, laughing behind her back? She wouldn't put it past this town. One thing was certain—she needed to confront Greg, and she needed to do it in person. Her mind made up, Paris felt calmer as she washed her face and carried her bag to the car. Briefly, she wondered how the car got here from the school. She'd been too much of a mess to drive, hadn't she? She certainly didn't remember the trip.

A part of her wished Gran was here so she could talk to someone, but what could Gran tell her that Amber hadn't already revealed? In any case, Gran wasn't home; a friend had driven her to physical therapy. Paris paced in indecision and then wrote a note for her grandmother.

> 'Bye, Gran. I'm going home earlier than expected.
> I doubt if I'll be back for some time. Take care of yourself. Paris.

She ought to add the words, *I love you*, but her sense of betrayal cut too deeply. She left the note, put the pen away, and went to her car. Now it was time to give Greg Frantz a piece of her mind—the only piece of her he'd ever see again.

GREG HUNG up the office phone and spoke to Mrs. Bailey. "The deal is done. Lech will stop here at the end of next week to pick up books and assignments. Coach and Mrs. Velasquez will catch him up over the summer, and he'll be back by next fall."

"Oh, I hope that's a good idea." Mrs. Bailey twitched nervously. "Remember Paris saw him going through my desk."

"He was hungry, Miranda. He hoped you had extra lunch tickets."

"Still—"

"Let's throw him a line. He can either use it to crawl out of the hole he's dug for himself, or he'll tangle himself up in even more trouble."

Mrs. Bailey still frowned. "We don't usually welcome criminals."

"He's a kid, Miranda, not a hardened criminal. If he's committed to a life of crime, I expect we'll know that before the fall term can—"

Greg turned as Jess strode in. "Mr. Frantz, do you have a minute?"

The look on Jessica's face told Greg he needed to make time whether he had a minute or not. "Come in, Ms. Kerr," he said, and ushered her into his office.

It had barely closed when Jess asked, "Did you tell Paris about us? I mean about you and me dating."

Greg stared, his expression dazed. "I thought she knew. Everyone in Destiny knew."

Jess's voice hardened. "She hasn't been living in Destiny, Greg."

"But she's been living in your house for weeks. Surely you've told her."

Jess dropped hard into a chair. "It wasn't my business to tell her *your* dating history. I left that to you."

Greg sat down slowly as cold reality spread through him. "What's going on?"

"I just had a call from Amber Reyes. She and Paris were together this afternoon—"

"Yes. Paris said they had a late lunch, but—"

"But apparently Amber said something about how we dated, and Paris fell apart." Jess sat forward, her voice sharp. "Greg, how could you not tell her?"

"She lived with you for weeks. How could you not—"

Greg's door slammed open and Paris barreled in. "Greg Frantz, I need to see you. Now." She looked from Greg to Jess and venom filled her voice. "Well, isn't this cozy?"

Greg said, "Paris, please—"

At the same time, Jess said, "Honestly, sweetie. I didn't know you didn't know."

Talking over both of them, Paris growled, "Get out, Jess. This is between Greg and me."

Jess stood. "Paris—"

"Out. Now."

Greg watched with a growing sense of panic as Jessica slunk from his office.

LATER, Greg couldn't have told anyone much about that conversation, just that he'd known something terrible was happening. He remembered the woman he loved looking at him with pain and fury in her eyes as she accused, "How could you lie to me like that?"

Even before he understood what she considered a lie, he struggled for excuses, trying to understand it himself. "I thought you knew. Surely Jess said something—"

"Was it her job to tell me your dating history? What were you doing, Greg? Settling for the younger model when the older one wouldn't have you?"

His own anger flared then, but he immediately realized this was not the time, not if he ever wanted to see Paris again. "I didn't realize you didn't know—"

"You must have realized! How could you not know?"

"How could *you* not know?"

"Don't try to shift the blame on me, *Mr. Frantz*. How was I supposed to know if no one told me?"

Minutes passed, filled with white-hot anger and icy heartbreak. He'd hardly had a chance to speak when Paris announced, "I'm leaving, and I don't know when I'll ever be back. I may someday have to forgive Gran and Jess since they're the only family I have, but *you*—" She turned on Greg with a full load of righteous wrath. "I never want to see you again. I don't want to hear your voice or your name or anything about you. Don't ever try to call or text me. I'm blocking your number." She stood, her face a mask of pain and anger. "Leave. Me. Alone," she said and stormed from his office.

Greg slid into his chair, his mind in a spin cycle, his thoughts torn between wanting to run after Paris and wishing he could simply erase the actions—and inactions—that had brought them to this precipice. Looking back, he realized he'd been remiss—stupid even. Yes, Paris tended to fly off the handle over little or nothing, but he couldn't write this off as little or nothing. She had a right to be furious, and there might not be a way to fix this. Maybe this was the end.

Chapter Twenty-Five

P aris rehashed the argument as she drove back to Sacramento. Greg hadn't shouldered any responsibility, hadn't even apologized. He'd tried instead to make excuses, even blaming her for not knowing! The nerve! And Jess had done the same. Jessica should have said something; after all, they were family. But her anger toward Jessica was already cooling.

Maybe Jess had been waiting to talk with her, expecting Greg to tell the story. Paris tried to remember if she might have visited when Greg and Jess were dating, but she hadn't made the drive often during that last all-consuming job. Visits had been infrequent, sometimes weeks apart, and they'd always been short. Usually she'd drive up on a Saturday morning and back by Sunday evening, sometimes before church.

Then too, Jess was right that it wasn't her job to rehash Greg's dating life. Greg should have done that. He'd had more than enough opportunity, so why hadn't he? She could only conclude that he'd deliberately hidden this salient detail, and he must have had a reason. That realization fueled the tempest brewing inside her.

Her rage toward Greg burned hotter the more she thought of their moments together and how he'd betrayed her trust. She didn't recall much of the argument, but she clearly remembered her last speech as she slammed his door. Reaching the old Children of Rah compound, she pulled to the roadside and blocked him from her phone. He'd already left two voicemails and three text messages, all of which she deleted. She blocked his number and slipped her phone back in her purse.

Her mind shuffled through memories and fixed on the day when they had discussed their past romantic relationships. She'd asked him point-blank if he'd ever been in love and he had never once mentioned

Jessica. "If that isn't lying by omission, I don't know what is." She fumed all the way to the valley.

AT HOME THAT EVENING, Greg tried calling Paris again, only to discover his phone had been blocked as she promised. Unwilling to believe he'd lost her forever, he considered ways he could make things right and kept coming up empty. Why hadn't he said something about Jess? He pondered that through the evening as he worked on the kitchen cabinets, throwing his emotional turmoil into sanding and scraping and polishing hardware.

From the beginning, he'd assumed Paris knew. He still wondered how she could have missed knowing when their dating relationship was common knowledge. Of course, Jess was right that Paris hadn't been living in Destiny then, but hadn't she visited family during that time? Maybe she hadn't, and then when she did come to town, the gossip mill had moved on. Still, wouldn't someone have said something? Then he realized Amber Reyes *had* said something, which is how Paris knew. Unfortunately, Paris had found out too late and from the wrong person.

He had an obligation to share all his past relationships, but he thought he had. Hadn't he? That day in the meadow when Paris asked him if he'd ever been in love, he clearly recalled telling her about dating a woman in Destiny and thinking the relationship had potential, but in the end, they'd both known it wouldn't work. He'd added something like, "but you know about that."

He'd been sure Paris knew he spoke of Jess. If she didn't understand, wouldn't she have said something? Or was it possible that he'd deliberately danced around the issue, afraid of Paris's reaction? Uncertain of his own thoughts and mentally kicking himself, he worked until the early hours of the morning, until he finally collapsed, exhausted, into bed.

PARIS SLEPT little and tossed much. Memories kept returning of the many times it would have been easy for Greg or Jess or Gran to drop a mention into the conversation: "You know Jessica and I dated for a while, right?" or "I suppose you've heard that Greg and I dated" or "Don't shush me, Jess. Anyone can see our Paris is interested in Greg. She deserves to know that you two went out..." Why hadn't anyone ever said it? The fact that Jess had shushed Gran several times spoke volumes. She didn't want Paris to know, or to find out from her anyway. She'd most likely been waiting for Greg to tell her.

Jess had always been closed-mouthed when it came to her dating life. She'd never confided in Paris about romantic relationships. In fact, one of Jess's quirks was how little she confided in Paris about anything, except in the most general terms. Maybe it had to do with how Jess thought of Paris as a kid sister. But that was no excuse! Maybe Jess remembered Paris's high school crush on Greg and thought she'd be upset if she knew. But a high school crush was just a high school crush.

Paris only came up with more questions as she tossed and turned. She got up before her alarm, determined she would arrive at TriTech early, throw herself into her work, and refuse to think about Greg. She'd make herself indispensable to TriTech and build a new life. Even as she thought it, she knew her conception of what constituted a full life had grown and rounded since she'd dated Greg. She thought of the children she'd begun to imagine, the ones with Greg's brown hair and chocolate eyes, and she knew she'd never be happy living the single life forever.

Although she arrived early Tuesday as planned, Matthew and George were waiting, eager to draw her into discussions about the new service TriTech might provide. "It only makes sense," Matthew said as they entered the conference room. "Our clients are all non-profits, so virtually all of them need to have someone researching what grants are available and applying for the ones that fit. Most of them have someone in-house, but a few have been outsourcing. If we can offer that here at TriTech, we not only get more of their business, but we're also in at the beginning of any new initiatives that might affect our fund accounting programs."

"That's right," George said. "My sister, Helen, worked for a company that did exactly that. She can come in later this week if you're willing to meet with her."

"Yes. Certainly." Paris did her best to look confident. "I want to understand just what we're talking about, though. Will I be changing jobs? Trying to do part of one and part of the other? How do you see this working?"

George and Matthew looked at one another, a look that said they hadn't thought that far. Matthew cleared his throat. "I don't think we know that yet. After we get Helen's take, we'll make more decisions."

"But we expect you to be part of the decision," George added. "We'll want your full input before we make changes."

Sometime later, as she went to work on an updated user manual for a non-profit in Florida, Paris glowed with that understanding. On the job only a short time, she had already become a valued member of the team. The realization filled her with pride and gave her hope for building a meaningful career, but it did nothing to fill the hole in her heart.

Paris put in ten hours that first day back, trying to complete as much of the current project as possible before George's sister came in on Wednesday. The next two days were even longer as she worked with Helen. She found George's sister to be a kindred soul—funny, driven to succeed, genial and easy to talk to.

By the end of the week, George and Matthew decided the concept was feasible. They divided their client list and contacted everyone they thought might be interested, asking whether this service might fit their needs.

Paris spent Friday morning in conference with Matthew, George, and Helen as they discussed what they'd need to make it work. Helen gave her opinion that Paris understood the work well enough to spearhead the new project. Matthew thanked her for her advice and declared a lunch break, ending with, "When we come back after lunch, we'll need to hear from you, Paris. You'll need to let us know where you stand."

Confident about where she stood, Paris went into the staff room to get her lunch from the fridge. She found Jake Stone already seated and starting his own meal, and she to eat with him. When he invited her to dinner that evening, she smiled and accepted.

⌒

THAT SAME AFTERNOON, Greg walked into his office and plopped down, exhausted. He'd been meeting with the committee planning for the graduation ceremony that was just around the corner. It appeared all sixty-eight in the senior class would earn their diplomas.

He thought back over the days since Paris left. His house looked better since the kitchen cupboards were refinished. Parents and school board members alike seemed pleased with his work. His school had received recognition for good scores on standardized tests. With the help of over-the-counter medications, he was even sleeping again, most of the time. Everything seemed to be pointed in the right direction.

Except he was miserable.

In the past few weeks, he'd also learned about ADHD, and the recent workshops with Dr. Sayyid had taught him more. He'd even had a few moments alone with the expert to ask whether the condition extended into adulthood.

"Yes, of course," Dr. Sayyid had replied. "When the brain is wired differently, it doesn't rewire itself just because the person grows older. The condition can have a huge impact on an individual both in childhood and adulthood." They'd talked a little, and Dr. Sayyid had been clear about hoe ADHD influenced relationships. Greg's eyes had been opened.

Since that day, Greg had spent hours reading about adult ADHD, and he recognized many of the symptoms in Paris. He'd even read a few articles about how the condition impacted romantic relationships. Much of what he'd read sounded way too familiar. He could only imagine what Paris would say if he approached her with these ideas. Then again, shouldn't someone tell her? She could then get a doctor's diagnosis and find out if medication and therapy were good options, as well as learning coping strategies.

He'd twisted his brain into a pretzel, trying to think of a way to approach her, to apologize for his mistakes, and to make things right. Short of accosting her at work and refusing to leave until she heard him out, what other choice did he have? That prompted images of Paris reporting him as a stalker, and Greg being hauled into custody, and that brought a wry smile as he considered what an arrest would do to his career. Besides, what could he say to her besides admitting she was right and begging for a second chance? He hadn't exactly been apologetic that day Paris had stormed into his office. He'd offered excuses instead. He'd tried to apologize in his voicemails and texts but she'd blocked him.

He knew where she lived. Maybe he could show up at her place? He sighed. What would prevent the stalker scenario there? Frustrated, he scrubbed his hands through his hair and watched several strands fall onto his desk. "Great," he mumbled. "Now I'm going bald."

"Miranda," he announced. "I'm going out for a while." He grabbed his keys. "I'll be on the playing fields, but I'll have my phone. You can call me, but please, only for an emergency."

"Got it," she said. Then, "Greg, are you okay?"

"No, not really," he answered. Seeing her worry, he added, "But I will be," and flashed a less-than-convincing smile.

"If you say so." He rushed out, aware Mrs. Bailey hadn't bought his assurances. Well, could he blame her? He didn't believe them either.

Chapter Twenty-Six

The following week, TriTech hired a recent graduate with a master's in communications who'd just completed a six-month internship. Ethan Coombs would replace Paris in writing manuals while she moved full-time into the company's new enterprise. Helen worked nearly full-time, helping Paris kick-start the new undertaking. They were already working with two of their best clients. The work looked promising, and her supervisors were pleased

Paris's social life had also picked up. She'd been out once with Jake and once with Ethan. They were both nice men who treated her well and she enjoyed her time with them. At least she tried to. With regret, she acknowledged the men weren't the problem. Her heart had taken a beating, and she needed to heal.

Days later, as she ate a lonely lunch in the staff room, she realized she had everything she thought she'd ever wanted—a job she loved, an apartment in the city, and a pleasant social life. She'd once believed reaching this pinnacle would bring happiness.

She was miserable.

Though she hesitated to admit it, these emotional doldrums were about Greg. She sighed and bit into her tomato-on-wheat. She saw nothing to be done other than hoping time would heal her. She resolved to put away thoughts of Greg and focus on making herself indispensable at TriTech. Returning to her office, she found Helen packing up.

Her stomach plummeted. "You're leaving?"

"Um-hm." Helen didn't look up, but busily stuffed things into a bag. "I'm still working for a few of the clients from my old job and one has an emergent situation I need to deal with. You'll see that occasionally in this work. An RFP comes open that you didn't expect, or your client finds one and tells you about it just before the deadline—"

"But you'll still be around, right? In case I need to ask you something?" Paris only now realized how much she didn't know. Her stomach tightened as she imagined trying to handle the work alone.

"Sure. You have my cell." Helen held up a pencil sharpener. "Yours or mine?"

"Ours," Paris said.

Helen set it down and loaded a couple of pens instead. "Ring me any time you get stuck," she said. "Try it on your own first, though. That's one of the best ways to learn."

"I will." Paris tried to calm her nerves. "You've been amazing. I can't thank you enough." She hoped she didn't sound too pathetic when she added, "Will you drop in sometimes?"

Helen's soft chuckle did little to reassure her. "You're that nervous?"

"Well, yeah, I guess I am."

"Don't worry. George has already asked me to check in occasionally. Since he's promised to pay me, I promised I would." Helen smiled at her own small joke.

Paris took a deep breath. "It seems a long way for you to come, but I'm grateful for your help and guidance."

Helen's forehead wrinkled. "What do you mean, a long way to come?"

Paris raised a shoulder. "I know the firm you work for and they're in Palo Alto, right? That's a long commute from here."

"I don't know where you got that idea. I drive down from my home in Rancho."

"Your company has a branch in Rancho Cordova?"

Helen snorted. "A branch? Not unless I constitute a branch."

"I don't underst—"

"Come on, Paris. You've seen the work I do. My clients are all over the country. I stay in touch with them via phone, teleconference, fax, email… There's no reason to go to them, and little reason to see my bosses in person either. I drive to Palo Alto if the need arises, but mostly, I work from home. It's one of those telecommuting jobs you hear about, working remotely. More and more people are doing it and companies are realizing it boosts productivity and reduces overhead."

"Work from home. I hadn't considered..."

"It's a win-win," Helen continued. "I can work my hours around my home life, or when my clients in other time zones are available. If you're a self-motivated person who can work on your own, and meet all your deadlines, it works great. My bosses are happy with the arrangement, so are the clients, and so am I."

"That never occurred to me," Paris said, though she couldn't guess why it hadn't. It now seemed obvious.

"It's a good plan," Helen assured her. "When you get comfortable with the work, you can probably do the same. In fact, if you want, I can mention it to George."

"Thanks, that would be wonderful."

She could work from home. She turned it over in her mind as she helped Helen with the last of her things. She could live anywhere, work from anywhere. Images of Destiny and Greg popped into mind, bringing only pain. Like a farm wife with a broom, she chased them out, determinedly replacing each with her dream of a small house near the seashore. She didn't need Destiny. She could go anywhere, anywhere at all.

For a moment, the freedom—the vast potential of it—made her a little dizzy, as if the floor had just tipped beneath her, and Paris shook her head. She tried again to conjure her bungalow by the sea, but images of tall pines and Douglas fir intruded and stubbornly refused to leave, so she let them come forward. Hm. Maybe she did need to go home, at least for a quick trip. She missed Gran, and what had happened wasn't Gran's fault, not with Jess warding her off. It wasn't Gran's responsibility to tell her anyway. She decided to call Gran as soon as her workday ended.

"I think that's about it," Helen said. "I'll have one last quick meeting with George and then I'm out of here."

"I'll be in the conference room. Stop in and say goodbye before you leave, okay?"

Helen pursed her lips. Paris could almost hear her thinking they'd done their goodbyes, but maybe Helen saw her fear. "Okay," she agreed, and started down the hall.

Paris hurried to the conference room and began organizing materials she wanted to ask about when she saw Helen again. Ethan found her there.

"Hey, I'm glad I caught you." He took the chair beside her. "The Sacramento Music Festival is in Old Town this weekend. I thought you might like to go with me. We could wander around, listen for a while, have some dinner—"

Paris cut him off. "Thanks for thinking of me, Ethan, but I don't think so. Perhaps I should have said something sooner, but I only recently ended a serious relationship and—"

"I thought we had fun together." Ethan looked crestfallen.

"We did. I had a great time, but I realized that I'm just not ready to get back into dating."

He flashed her a suspicious look. "Is that what you're going to tell Jake Stone, too?"

"Actually, yes, it is."

"Tell me what?" Jake, who was passing in the hall, stepped into the room.

Paris took a deep breath and tried to smile. "You may as well both hear it together. I was just explaining to Ethan that I'm not ready for dating. I've gone out with both of you, and I've tried to be good company, but—"

"I thought you were great company," Jake said.

Ethan mumbled, "Me too."

"Then I'm glad I didn't ruin the experience for you. The fact is, I just recently ended a relationship that seemed to be leading toward marriage. I thought I could put it behind me, but I still have healing to do. It's no reflection on either of you. You're both wonderful company—"

"But your heart isn't in it," Jake finished.

"I'm afraid not." Paris found it easier to smile, realizing that Jake, at least, wasn't taking her decision personally. She added, "If and when I decide I'm ready to get out there again, I'll be sure to let you know. Both of you. Thanks for understanding."

Recognizing his cue to leave, Jake gave Ethan a playful slug on his shoulder. "Come on, dude. Let's go drown our sorrows in some hard work."

"Yeah. Okay." Ethan started from the room. Then he turned, looking at Paris over his shoulder, and stage-whispered. "I'm sorry about... whatever happened. But when you feel like dating again, call me first, okay?" He grinned and winked.

Paris chuckled. "I'll think about it. Thanks for asking." She turned her attention to her work, eager for Helen to come in, and dreading for her to leave.

Chapter Twenty-Seven

I t was time to stop waffling and Paris knew it. She needed to make the drive to Destiny, and she needed to talk with Gran. The many times her grandmother had encouraged her to speak with Jess helped Paris believe that Gran had always had her best interests at heart but felt obligated to let Jess share the truth. Thinking of Jess and the many times she might have told her brought another surge of anger, but Paris chose not to stay angry. Gran and Jess were the only family she had. She'd leave first thing in the morning. It was time to make peace —with them, anyway.

As she left her office, another idea arose. As much as she wished to think otherwise, she might need to see Greg too, if only to give her closure and the peace she needed to date again. At first, the thought of such a confrontation burned through her like wildfire, but she had loved Greg, truly loved him. She could never trust him again, and she'd lost any hope of a future relationship, but she didn't need to see him as an enemy either. Deciding she'd reconsider after talking with Jess, she began to prep for a trip to Destiny.

GREG LEFT the school conference room, pleased with all he'd heard. Various committees of the school's Parent-Teacher Organization had rolled out their plans for graduation, now just two weeks away. Funds raised by the prep committee ensured that Prospector Stadium would reflect the usual party atmosphere festooned with balloons, confetti, glitter, and a banner honoring this year's class. A sub-committee worked busily on printed program bulletins. The clean-up squad planned to arrive the morning after the ceremony, a gift Greg greatly appreciated. But the most impressive plans were for the "Strictly Sober All-Night Grad Blow-Out."

The risk of a grad night tragedy had dropped significantly since parents began staging this event complete with fancy *hors d'oeuvres*, soft drinks and mocktails, photographers on site to shoot portraits of individuals and groups, and a variety of games. Activities included everything from kids dressing in Velcro suits, jumping and sticking to Velcro walls, to pairs wearing Sumo wrestler body suits, bouncing off one another in a makeshift ring.

The PTO's well-drafted plans showed off the best of Destiny. Neighbors came together in good times and bad. They sometimes got too nosy, but they took care of one another. He wondered if Paris missed that sense of community. He knew he would—if he ever moved away.

An offer had come that morning from a high school in the valley. Their hiring committee liked his resume and wanted him to interview. The pay was good, better than what he was earning now, and the job came with nice perks and benefits. It would have appealed if he'd still been thinking of following Paris.

I'll come in tomorrow and send them a thanks-but-no-thanks. That decision made, Greg locked up the office and left the school on his way to spend another long evening alone. Driving by the Destiny Animal Rescue, he wondered if he should get a dog.

PARIS ARRIVED at her apartment building to find Amber on the second-floor landing, knocking on her apartment door. "Hey, lady," she called from the parking lot. "To what do I owe this visit?"

"Come up and I'll tell you," Amber called back.

Paris hurried up the stairs. While she unlocked the door, Amber answered. "I came to see Skye, but I hoped I could catch you too." She followed Paris inside. "I only just made up my mind on the drive down or I'd have called to let you know."

Paris was stuck on the first sentence. "You came to see Skye? She has a place down here?"

"Not exactly." Amber set down her mug. "She's in the county jail. I thought I told you."

"No. I'd remember that."

"I expect you would." Amber sighed. "It's a long story, but you know what direction Skye has been heading."

Paris sat and patted the sofa beside her. "Yep. I'm afraid we all do."

Amber joined her. "The day after Mom's party, Skye showed up and wanted Mom and Dad to give her money for some strange scheme. They refused. She took off angry, got drunk, jumped in her car, and sped down the hill."

Paris feared she knew what came next. "There was an accident?"

Amber nodded. "It wasn't severe, thank heaven. Minor injuries, but both cars were totaled along with property damage to two of the houses on the street. Not to mention Skye was driving on a suspended license, with no insurance, and had two priors."

"Ohhhh." Paris blew out a breath. "She's going to get jail time, isn't she?"

"Her trial date has been set. It's a few weeks away. She wants my mom and dad to bail her out before then, but they don't believe they can trust her not to run."

"And if she ran, they'd lose whatever they put up for the bond."

"Exactly."

"I can't blame them for not risking it."

Amber sighed. "I can't either. They've sacrificed a lot to help Skye, and nothing has worked. One good thing is the jail commander runs a tight ship. Skye won't be drinking there. Maybe, if she can go for a long time without access to the booze, she can kick the habit."

"I hope that's not wishful thinking."

"Yeah. Me too." Amber looked at her watch. "Visiting hours will start soon. While I'm still here, can we talk about Greg?"

Paris opened her mouth to say no, but what could it hurt to let Amber talk? "Okay, but I retain the right to change my mind if this conversation gets uncomfortable."

Amber nodded. "Fair enough." She paused, collecting her thoughts. "Look, hon, I was there. I know how hurt you were. I'm just wondering if maybe your reaction was a bit extreme."

"Wha—"

"And I'm thinking that maybe you're hurting yourself as much as you're hurting Greg and Jess." She leaned forward. "You're still in love with him, aren't you?"

Paris's throat tightened. "I tell myself I'm not, but I am. I'm so hurt, and I'm not over being angry. But I can't date anyone else. I've tried, but I'm not over Greg."

"When you think about it, what is it that bothers you most? That he dated your Aunt Jess? Or that he didn't tell you about it?"

"Both!" Paris worked to calm herself. "I keep seeing images of them together and I... I can't help wondering if he was still in love with her and looking for a substitute in me."

"Ohhhhh." This time Amber blew out a breath. "I'm beginning to get it now. Do you think you could say that to Greg?"

"So, he can deny it? You know that's what he'll do, but how would I know if he's telling the truth? It's not like he was honest before." Angry tears threatened.

"You don't know for sure what he'll say or how you'll feel until you give it a try." Amber was using her calm teacher voice. "At the very least, talking to Greg could give you closure."

"Closure." The word escaped on a sigh. "I've been thinking a lot about that lately, and I'd almost talked myself into seeing Greg—even before you came." She reached across to pat Amber's hand. "Maybe you've persuaded me. I plan to drive up to Destiny tomorrow. I want to see Gran and I was already planning to talk with Jess. They're family."

"Um-hm." Amber raised a brow. "Same reason I'm going to the jail."

Paris nodded. "I guess you understand."

"And Greg?" Amber asked. "Are you going to see him too?"

Paris bit her lip. "I'm not sure. I may have to try. But please. Don't say anything—in case I wimp out."

"My friend, you are many things, but you are *not* a wimp."

Paris laughed. "Maybe you don't know me as well as you think you do, but it's *possible* I'm ready to see him."

Amber stood. "Then my work here is done. Will I see you in Destiny?"

"It's possible. Good luck with Skye."

"Good luck with Greg."

The two women hugged, and Amber turned to go.

"Amber?" Paris called after her.

"Yes?"

"Tell Skye I hope things work out for her."

Amber's eyes filled with tears. "I'll tell her," she said, her voice thick with emotion.

As Paris watched Amber leave, her spirits lifted. Skye's situation reminded her there were worse problems than the one she faced. She prepared to make peace with Gran and Jess, and maybe even find closure with Greg. Despite her remaining anger, she missed him terribly and she couldn't help wondering if he missed her too.

Chapter Twenty-Eight

Paris turned onto Gold Pan Road as Jess pulled into the driveway. Paris pulled to the side and watched from a distance as Jess got out. As Jess went around the car, Greg got out of the back seat and then he and Jess helped Gran. His car was across the street. Had Gran fallen again? Why was Greg helping? Confused and not ready to see Greg, she pulled out and cruised past as Greg helped Gran up the back steps. She drove around the neighborhood waiting to make sure the coast was clear before she went back to Gran's. When she returned, Greg's car was gone, and Paris felt ready for the first conversation.

The door was still unlocked, so she opened it and walked in to find Jess and Gran sitting at the kitchen table. Both women looked up, clearly surprised to see her. "Paris!" her grandmother said. Jess gasped but said nothing.

"I thought it was time to check in." Paris had a small day bag she set near the door.

Jess stood, pulling out a chair. "We're planning lunch. You're welcome to join us."

"I've eaten, thank you." Paris kept her voice cool, formal. "I'm more interested in catching up." She looked from one woman to the other.

Gran started to get up from her chair but a groan escaped her, and her face twisted in a grimace as she sat back down.

Paris's heart wrenched. "Did you fall again, Gran?"

"No," Gran said. "But the physical therapy can be as bad." She sat back, breathing slowly.

"We'd be certain to tell you if something major happened," Jess said.

"Really?" Paris couldn't help the censure. "As I recall, you haven't always been forthcoming in matters that concern me."

Gran spoke quickly. "I wanted to tell you, Paris. You had a right to know—"

"It's all right, Gran. I don't blame you for anything." Paris walked over to her grandmother, leaned down to hug her, and placed a kiss on her cheek. She whispered, "I've missed you, Gran. I love you." As she spoke, a wave of tenderness came over her. She added, "It wasn't your fault."

Paris turned to Jess. "We need to talk."

"You're right." Jess looked toward the stairs and Paris nodded. Jess asked her mother, "Can I get your lunch? We may be a while."

"I'm fine," Gran said. "I can never eat right after a session anyway. You two go ahead."

"Call if you need us." Jess started up the stairs.

Paris followed, filled with questions, but no longer burdened with indignation. The warmth she felt at being home again had sneaked in under the foundations of her anger, undermining its footings and weakening the walls.

She entered the room she had always considered hers to find Jess sitting at the foot of the bed. She sat near the head. Jess waited, so Paris spoke first. "It's good to be home again. I've missed this." Until she said it, she hadn't realized its truth.

"We missed you," Jess said. "I'm so sorry for everything. I thought Greg should have been the one to tell you—"

"Why didn't you tell me when I first got here? That first day, Gran started to tell me that you and Greg had dated, and you cut her off. Why?"

Jess lifted a shoulder. "Convoluted thinking, I guess, but I'd always seen you as a kid, you know? Kind of like the little sister I never had."

Paris nodded. "I wondered about that. Go on."

"That day, I saw you all grown up. In the instant Gran started to speak, I realized you were of an age to be interested in Greg. I wanted you to be able to meet him and shape your own opinion without input from me."

"I find that a weak explanation," Paris said, some of the pique still simmering, "but okay. I accept that. What about later? What about when you saw me falling for him?"

"Another weak excuse, I guess." Jess glanced away and back again. "At first, I didn't see how close you two were becoming. I knew you were at the school every day, but you were working on that grant, and I was gone so much that I didn't see how much time you were spending together away from school." She let that drift. "By the time I knew you were getting serious, I assumed you had already talked. You should have by then."

"You're right. We should have." Paris felt even more of her anger toward Jess diffuse. "But you could have said something."

"I could have. I realize now that I should have, and I'm so sorry I didn't."

They sat looking at each other, letting the memories and emotions fall into place.

Jess broke the silence. "I told Greg I was sorry I hadn't told you. You can't imagine how broken up he's been since you left."

Paris saw red. Or was it green? "You went to see Greg? You two gossiped about me?"

"Stop, Paris. It wasn't like that. We both work at the high school. One day last week, I had some papers to take to the office, so I went there during my prep period and ran into Greg. I guess we both realized we needed to clear the air. He invited me into his office."

"And you had a cozy chat about poor little Paris." Anger surged.

Jess let out a sigh. "If it helps, he left the door open the whole time. I'm sure Mrs. Bailey heard everything." She huffed in exasperation. "Paris, there was nothing intimate or sneaky or wrong about our chat. We were talking about a situation that involved both of us and ended up inadvertently hurting someone we both love."

The word 'love' stopped Paris cold. "Tell me what happened."

"Greg said it wasn't until you left that he knew what he was losing. He's a wreck, Paris, barely holding it together to get the seniors to graduation. I don't think he's sleeping, and I know he's not eating. People keep commenting on his weight loss. I promise you—he's miserable."

Paris knew that if she were over Greg, the idea of him wallowing in misery might give her satisfaction, fair punishment for how he hurt her. But her first reaction was worry and concern for his welfare, and she knew how much she still loved him. "Why didn't he tell me?"

"I asked him that, and I've been thinking about what he said ever since. You know how men are different from women?"

Paris rolled her eyes. "Your point, please?"

"We think differently, too. He told me that when you two discussed past relationships, you talked about men you had dated, no names mentioned, and so he did the same. He really thought nothing of it."

"I didn't date his uncle!"

"I know, but he doesn't see a difference."

Paris snorted. "I can't believe that!"

"It's what he said, and he certainly seemed to mean it. I've never seen a man any more desperate or dismal."

Tears welled as Paris's anger grew. "Whenever I pictured the two of you—"

"Wait. Hold it right there." Jess put some steel behind her tone. "If you're thinking of us *together*..." She raised an eyebrow. "...think again. It was never like that between us."

"Oh, come on! Greg said he was serious about someone recently—the timing for you fits perfectly—and Amber said the whole town thought you'd marry."

"The *town* thought it. You know how Destiny gossips. And for a little while, we both thought maybe. After all, here we were, two adults of the same age, working in the same place with the same passion for education, practically the only singles our age in the whole town. It seemed like it should be good, you know?"

Paris glared. "So, why wasn't it?"

"Early on, we began noticing differences, some of them irreconcilable. We'd only gone out a couple of weeks when we realized it wouldn't work, certainly not long term. I'm not right for him, Paris, but I think maybe you are."

Calmer now, Paris asked, "You said you had differences. Like what?"

"I'll tell you the biggest one. Greg wants a family."

"I know. He told me he wants at least four kids. Four!"

"I don't want children."

Paris stared, sure her aunt was exaggerating. "Not at all?"

"I'm giving my life to raising other people's kids, helping them grow up the best way I know. I'm around kids all day, and I enjoy them when they're teens. But the little rug-rats? I wouldn't know what to do with one."

"You're serious."

"Absolutely, and that was the death knell for anything between Greg and me. I mean, we had lots of differences. That thing I told you the first day, about A.P. classes and such? That was just one of the small clashes. There were others. When we got to the question of children, we already knew anything between us was a long shot. After that, there was no point in trying."

"And you were never…"

"No, we weren't. Do you feel better now?"

Paris considered that. "Oddly, yes. I do."

"And to be honest, the way Greg is around you? He was never like that with me."

"Really?"

"Definitely. He lights up like a Christmas tree when he's with you. You know how sometimes even if you have everything in common, there's still something missing? That extra spark is there with you and Greg."

Paris felt the anger toward Jess drain out of her and the hurt faded with it.

Jess stood and held out her arms. "Hug?"

"Please?" Paris answered.

The embrace, long and tender, left them both in tears.

Paris said, "I'm sorry I missed your birthday."

"I know why you did." Jess's tender look backed her words.

"I bought you a gift I think you'll like." Paris brought out the onyx-and-silver jewelry she'd purchased at the Arts Fair.

"I love it!" Jess put on the earrings and lifted the necklace from the box. Paris fastened it for her.

"It's beautiful, Paris. Thank you so much." They shared another hug. "Now," Jess said, wiping at her cheeks. "Are you going to see Greg this weekend?"

"I'm not sure. I still have a few things to work through."

"Do you want me to tell him when I see him?" Jess grabbed a few tissues from the bedside table and handed one to Paris.

"I'd rather you didn't." Paris dried her eyes. "I prefer talking to him myself, when I'm ready."

"I understand." Jess said. "I want you to be happy, sweetie. And I could see how happy you were with Greg."

"I don't know if we can get back there."

"Maybe you just need healing time. And a good talk with Greg. Look at how we cleared the air."

"Maybe," Paris said. "But I still have some thinking to do."

"All right." Jess kissed Paris's cheek. "I think I'll go check on Mama and make a grocery run for lunch."

"I'll be down soon." Paris took a few minutes to wash the tears from her face and tidy her hair. Jess was right. She should talk to Greg, even if she didn't feel ready. Gran was in her recliner, her eyes closed, when Paris approached and dropped a light kiss on her cheek.

Gran's eyes opened. "Everything okay?"

"Things between Jess and me are working out. I'd like to stay for lunch, but I have another visit to make."

Gran brightened. "I hope you're on your way to see that nice young man of yours. He's a keeper."

Paris considered contradicting her but decided that skirmish wasn't worth fighting. "I'm hoping this is a good day to catch him. Catch him at home, I mean."

Gran chuckled. "I expect it will be. Go make your peace. Then come tell us about it."

"Maybe I will," she said, "and maybe I won't."

"Fair enough." Gran chuckled, waving her fingers at Paris as she went out the door.

Paris drove the streets of Destiny, thinking how familiar and homey it felt being here. Maybe Amber had a point about how she related to this town. Virtually everything she passed stood as a landmark connected to memories—most of them good. Her car seemed to know its way to Greg's house. As she drove, she wondered what she would do and say when she got there. What she knew was she needed to do this.

~

GREG GOT out sandwich makings and started putting lunch together. He didn't feel like eating, but too many people lately had commented about him looking gaunt. Just a few hours ago, Annette Kerr had said something when he took her and Jess to the PT appointment.

When he heard a car pull up in front of his house, he thought it odd. Living as he did at the end of a mostly empty street, he rarely saw anyone near. He'd made it clear from his early days as principal that he only conducted school business at school, so unless he invited someone, his only visitors were couriers, the kid with the newspaper, or people soliciting for donations. That's what he expected when he answered his door, but what he found was...

"Paris? You look... wonderful!"

Straight-faced and somber, she asked, "May I come in?"

"Yes. Please." He stepped back, swinging the door open. "May I take your jacket?"

"I'm not sure," she said. "I don't know how long I'll be staying."

Did his heart really drop into his gut? Or did it just feel that way? "All right." He looked around, unsure of his next step. "Would you like to sit?"

"Yes." She frowned. "Or no. I'm not sure."

"Paris, what—?"

"Greg, we need to talk."

"I know. I mean I agree. I'm just grateful you're giving me this chance. Paris, I never meant to hurt you. I didn't even understand what I'd done wrong until your Aunt Jess explained—"

"I know. She told me. Greg, I... I thought you and Jess..." She paused, unable to go on.

"You thought we were more... involved than we were."

"Yes, and I feared I came along just in time to be the weak substitute for the woman you really wanted."

"You must know that's not true—"

She shook her head, her eyes filled with tears. "How do I know what's true? You kept an awful lot of the truth to yourself."

"I never intended—"

"Don't tell me that!" She stepped away. "Tell me what you were thinking when I asked you straight out about your dating history and you chose not to mention my aunt."

"I told you I thought—"

"Don't tell me that either!" She took deep breaths, calming herself. "That's a lame excuse and you know it—or you must realize it by now. Tell me why you thought it would be okay to gloss over that relationship."

He squirmed. What could he tell her that he hadn't already said? He considered carefully and began. "You remember we were talking in the meadow, and I mentioned I'd dated someone I thought had long-term potential, but we both decided it wasn't working. I recall saying something like, 'you know about that.'"

She narrowed her eyes. "Greg…"

"Please," he said. "Hear me out."

"All right. Go on," she said, her voice flat.

"I remember thinking that if you *didn't* know about it, this was your chance to ask."

Paris blew out an exasperated breath.

"That's what I was thinking *consciously*, but I've wondered since if maybe—you know, subconsciously—maybe I hoped that would be the end of it and we wouldn't need to say more."

Her eyes narrowed. "What are you trying to say?"

"I've wondered if maybe I was afraid to tell you—not consciously, you understand—"

"Right. I heard that part." Paris looked down, tracing a pattern in the rug with her toe. Then she looked Greg in the eye. "I don't know how to feel about this. I can't say that I'll ever fully trust you again, so I don't know that we have a future, but Greg?"

He swallowed. "Yeah?"

"I don't want to be your enemy."

He licked his lips. "You know I want more than that, but if all you'll ever let me be is your friend, I'll be grateful to have that much."

"Friends? I'm not even sure about that, but at least we can be cordial."

He lifted his arms. "How about a hug?"

"Greg—"

"I promise that's all, just a hug. You know, like between friends."

"Well…" She licked her lips. "Okay." She stood waiting.

Greg stepped forward and took her in his arms—gently, cautiously, not too close. He'd meant what he said. He loved Paris, but if her friendship was all he could have, certainly that was better than nothing. "There," he said, stepping away long before he wanted. "Friends again?"

"Well," she said, "friendly, at least." She stepped toward the door.

"Can I take you to the meadow after church tomorrow? I'll pack a picnic—"

"No." She paused. "No, thank you. I have a lot to think about. More than you realize. I'm going to unblock your phone, but I need you to give me space, and I won't be in church tomorrow. I'm driving back to the valley this afternoon."

"Oh." He swallowed his disappointment. "Okay."

Her eyes narrowed again. "You'll give me time? If you don't, I may block you again—"

"Got it," he said, not wishing to hear whatever came next. He held the door for her and watched her walk to her car. She gave a small half-wave as she got in.

He waved back, wondering how he could feel both elated and devastated at the same time.

Chapter Twenty-Nine

Back at Gran's, Paris ate lunch with her aunt and grandmother. Later, on her drive down the mountain, she couldn't recall what they'd eaten. Her attention had been on the discoveries she was making about herself, about Destiny and her closest relationships.

The rest of the weekend passed in a blur. On autopilot, she did basic household chores and prepped for the coming week, but her mind wandered its own twisted path. Were relationships this difficult for everyone? She thought of times with friends and classmates, times when people accused her of overreacting, of being aloof or unapproachable, silly and childish, undependable or even irrational. Why? Was she really all that different from anybody else?

She arrived at TriTech at her usual time on Monday, only to discover she'd missed an early morning meeting. "How is that even possible?" she asked Adele after both George and Matthew told her they were disappointed she'd missed their brainstorming session. "I don't remember hearing anything about it."

Adele reminded her of a conversation in the conference room shortly before closing the previous Friday. "You were there with Helen. She was all packed up and ready to go, and Matthew popped in to say he and George had a couple of new RFPs you could start on right away. He told you they wanted you in early today—"

"I'm sorry." Paris shook her head, part denial and part bewilderment. "I believe you, I'm sure it must have happened, but I don't remember anything. I didn't know—" She stopped, aware she rambled. "I don't remember. I guess that's all there is to say."

"Well…" Frowning, Adele looked down the hallway. "How soon can you meet?"

"Now." Paris grabbed her laptop. "Or as soon as George and Matthew are ready."

"I'll check." Adele disappeared down the hall and returned in minutes. "They're ready. Just make sure you let us know if you can't make a meeting."

Paris hurried toward her bosses, promising herself she'd be poised and professional. People sometimes missed meetings. It wasn't the end of the world. She'd play catch-up and all would be well. At least, she hoped so.

She left the meeting an hour later, more stressed than she'd been in some time. George had two clients who were ready with RFPs and Matthew had a third. All three were counting on the grants they could land through this process, and all three deadlines were around the corner—much sooner than Paris felt she could manage. "I'll do my best," she promised as she left.

"We're counting on it." George's voice sounded stiff, stilted. As Paris returned to her cubicle, she wondered if he had any idea what went into writing a proposal, or any clue of how much more complex these projects were than the only one she'd ever done. Maybe listing grant writing on her resume hadn't been such a great idea after all.

The rest of Monday found her absorbed in reading and rereading the RFPs, making phone calls, and sending emails asking for background information. She'd been so hard at work that she didn't even notice the time until she had to go to the washroom and saw it was almost nine p.m. She'd worked almost seven hours straight without anything to eat since lunch. On the drive home she stopped off for a salad from a drive-through, but she only managed a few bites before falling into bed exhausted.

Tuesday found her in early, even earlier than the meeting she'd missed on Monday, and working just as late. By Wednesday morning, she knew she could not make the earliest deadline the next week, not even with all the overtime. If by some miracle she did make it, she'd have no time to finish the other two, both due within days of the first.

When Adele invited her to lunch, she hesitated, aware of the workload. Then she decided to accept, hoping to pick her colleague's brain about how to approach their bosses. "I can't get it done," she explained. "The deadlines are too close and there's still too much to do."

"You can't tell them that." Adele listened to Paris's explanation with growing unease. "You simply can't. These first grants will set the stage for everything they want you to do. You have to find a way. That's all there is to it."

Back in the office, Paris looked again at the workload, increasingly discouraged. Hearing a knock, she turned to find… "Helen! I'm so glad to see you." Relief poured out with her words as Paris described the three proposals and their deadlines. "Can you give me a hand?"

"Probably not." Helen eyed one RFP as she spoke. "But I can stay this afternoon. I'll look over these three to see how to expedite the process."

Aware that even a few hours of Helen's time could be well worthwhile, Paris buried her hope for more. "I'll be grateful for anything you can do," she answered. Knowing they'd need more room than available in Paris's small cubicle, they carried the materials to the conference room. That's where Matthew found them.

He offered Helen a quick greeting and then spoke to Paris. "Look," he said, "I know you're busy. We want to make sure you get those proposals in—early if possible, so we don't miss the deadlines. But we've also had a call from Wings of Hope about the manual you wrote for them. They've got a new guy on their staff, and they've asked specifically for you to train him. We can fly you out there this weekend—"

Paris flashed a worried look at Helen but tried to keep her voice even. "I can't do both, Matthew. That's why you brought Ethan on. Please talk with him about this weekend in Florida."

"That won't do. The client is asking for you—"

A reaction verging on panic weakened her knees and brought tears to her eyes. Paris choked out, "Excuse me," and bolted for the ladies' room, where she locked herself in a stall and wished she could disappear into the floor. She wanted—needed—to scream. Instead, she bit her knuckles until they almost bled, moaning to herself while tears ran freely. When the worst of the storm had passed, she left the stall, planning to wash her face, touch up her make-up, and try to salvage her job.

She found Helen waiting. "How are you feeling?" Helen asked as Paris stepped to the sink.

Paris saw no reason to lie. "Stressed. Over-burdened and under-appreciated. Honestly, I don't know how to move forward. I can't do everything—"

"I know," Helen said. "George and Matthew know it too."

Paris flashed a look toward their offices. "I doubt it."

"Let me put it this way." Helen smiled amiably. "They know it *now* since I took them both to the woodshed."

"Oh no." Paris's hand went to her throat. "Tell me you didn't."

"You bet I did. George has been getting my sister lectures since he was a kid. He and Matthew have been buddies since junior high, so Matthew has heard his share as well." She paused, thoughtfully twisting a paper towel. "The thing is, they both know I don't say anything until I'm right, so when I light into them, they take it seriously."

Paris swallowed down panic. "But when it's on my behalf—"

"Don't worry." Helen's easy smile helped calm Paris's panic. "They know you didn't put me up to it. I told them I've looked at all three RFPs and there's no way I, with many years of experience, could finish them all in the time they've allotted, let alone do the weekend in Florida. For them to expect that when you're new? They now know they shouldn't have overpromised to the clients. I also told them that as HR manager, Adele should be making sure the company has an organized planning system with an up-to-date calendar that lists all deadlines and meetings so that everyone can stay on track.

"As someone who works remotely, I find an electronic planning system is a lifesaver. I told my brother to sign up for the same one I use. At the end, I told them they've been insensitive jerks—yes, I used those words—and if they don't get it together, they could lose one of the best employees they've ever hired along with their best chance for growing their business. You'll find them easier to deal with when you see them again."

"Oh, Helen, I don't know what to say. Thank you so much!"

"You're welcome."

Paris glanced at her phone. "I've been gone too long. I need—"

"No, you don't." Helen laid her hand over Paris's. "I told the guys I'm going to need some time to clean up the mess they've made and I'll need your help. I said they shouldn't expect to see either of us again for most of the afternoon."

Paris blinked and blinked again. "Seriously?"

"Seriously." Helen threw away the twisted paper towel. "Come on. Get your purse. I'm taking you out for an ice cream or a smoothie or whatever will help you unwind."

Paris took the first relieved breath she'd had in days. "That sounds amazing."

Half an hour later, she sat across from Helen, sipping on a piña colada smoothie.

Casually, Helen said, "I hear you missed a meeting last Monday."

Caught off-guard, Paris jumped into defensive mode. "I had no idea, honest. Adele said they mentioned it on Friday in our meeting, but I guess I wasn't paying attention."

"Hmm...that's where a calendar software helps." Helen took a sip of her berry smoothie. "Tell me, does that sort of thing happen often?"

Paris hesitated but chose to answer honestly. "More often than I'd like."

Helen asked a few more questions—gently probing queries about procrastination, decision-making, temperament. Though Paris grew increasingly uneasy, she gave honest answers. Then she said, "Why are you asking these questions?"

Helen leaned in closer. "Have you ever been diagnosed with ADHD?"

Taken aback, Paris froze. She wanted to argue, but as she tried to form an answer, puzzle pieces started falling into place. "I...No, but I had some problems in the early grades. My teachers wanted to have me tested, but Mom resisted having me labeled. I found out later that the principal put a note in my file explaining my trouble concentrating was due to my father's recent death."

"Um-hm." Helen took another sip of her berry smoothie. "Anything else?"

"In high school, my history teacher caught me daydreaming and suggested ADD, but that's when Mom was going through chemo.

My grandmother waved off the testing. Do you think I have ADHD?"

"Actually, yes. I do." Helen used her straw to make patterns in the top of her drink. "I recognize some of the symptoms."

Paris bit down hard on her straw as she thought of the work she'd done for Destiny High. "It can't be true. It's Attention *Deficit*, right? As in not enough attention? When I get involved in a work project or something I'm passionate about, I get so absorbed I can forget to eat or drink."

"Um-hm," Helen said again. "That's called hyperfocus, and it's one of the symptoms. Those of us with ADHD can focus like crazy on projects we enjoy, but simply space out when we don't care about the subject."

"But—" Paris paused. "Did you just say, 'those of us'? Do you have ADHD?"

"Yep." Helen sucked hard on her straw. "In school, I always got As in classes I loved. Other classes, I didn't do so well." She quirked a smile at the shared confidence.

Paris identified quickly. "One report card, I had three As, a B+, a D, and an F."

"Let me guess. The F was in a class you hated?"

"Figure drawing. I dropped it as soon as I could."

"I get it." Helen finished her smoothie and pushed the glass away. "It takes a professional to diagnose ADHD, but—"

Paris interrupted. "One other thing. The H is for hyperactivity, right? I've never been accused of being hyperactive. So maybe I don't have ADHD, maybe I have ADD?"

"Do you tap your toe or wiggle your foot or doodle in the margins of your notebook when you have to sit still for a while?"

"Well, yeah, but—"

"That's part of it. So is daydreaming or staring out the window, both of which are more common in girls than boys." She wiped the corners of her mouth with her napkin. "Doctors used to draw a distinction between ADD and ADHD. Now they say it's all the same, with people falling somewhere along the spectrum."

"Even the daydreaming part makes sense," Paris said as more puzzle pieces fell into place. "What you've told me explains a lot."

"As I started to say, it takes a professional to make a diagnosis, but you can do some self-analysis online. I'll send you some links, or you can search adult ADHD. The quizzes you'll find can help you figure out if you have it or not, and the websites can lead you to local professionals for a definitive check-up. You'll also find info on how ADHD impacts relationships—"

"Whoa!" Paris pushed her cup away. "ADHD affects relationships?"

"Definitely." Helen nodded with sympathy. "Just ask either of my ex-husbands."

"Oh." Paris sat back heavily. "I'm sorry."

"It's all right. But imagine being involved with someone who makes promises but forgets to follow through," Helen said. "Someone who acts impulsively and is given to emotional outbursts, or who sometimes interrupts when you're sharing something meaningful, only to talk about the bird that just passed the window."

Paris flinched. "That sounds familiar."

"People with ADHD are often considered undependable or flighty. They sometimes miss social cues and don't always understand what's going on around them. They—or we—can be impulsive, sometimes doing things we can't explain later. They just seemed like good ideas when we did them."

Paris saw more puzzle pieces fitting in. "I used to think the kids around me all read some social etiquette book I'd never seen. They understood things that zipped right past me."

"I know what you mean. I've often felt that way."

The two women sat silently for a few moments, locked in mutual understanding.

Her drink finished, Paris stood. "Is there any upside to this ADHD stuff?"

"Definitely. People who see the world differently are positioned to change the world. Look at Beethoven, Einstein, Jobs, Zuckerberg, and odds are you're seeing great minds with ADHD." Helen also stood and picked up her purse.

"You've giving me a lot to think about."

"I know. It's a lot to take in. I wasn't diagnosed until a few years ago. Hearing the list of symptoms was like looking in a mirror, a rather dark one—at first, anyway."

"Yeah. I get that." Paris saw the full image her puzzle formed. A dark mirror indeed!

"Come on," Helen said. "Let's get back to the office. Maybe we can find a way to get *some* of that work done."

By the time she left work, at a reasonable hour this time, her bosses had arranged for Ethan to make the trip to Florida. They'd hired Helen as a freelancer to finish the proposal with the earliest due date, and they'd brought in temporary clerical help to gather the information Paris needed for the other two. George and Matthew had also promised to include Paris in their planning sessions whenever they discussed future proposals with other clients. And they'd ordered the calendaring software Helen suggested.

As she drove toward her apartment, Paris thought of what she'd learned about ADHD and relationships. She knew she had homework to do, this time having nothing to do with TriTech, RFPs, or grant proposals.

GREG LEFT the school early that Friday. With graduation just a week away, he'd put in plenty of overtime. He could afford to take one afternoon off early. He went home to scramble a couple of eggs and make some toast, thinking wistfully of the late lunches he'd eaten with Paris.

An hour later, he sat at his laptop, poring over the websites he'd found that described the symptoms of adult ADHD and reading up on how to navigate a relationship with a loved one who had the disorder. He wasn't surprised to learn that some of the greatest inventors, composers, and other creators in history exhibited the symptoms. As more than one source emphasized, people with ADHD excelled at not only drawing outside the lines but thinking outside the box. The more he read, the more he recognized Paris.

He saw that loving a person who excelled at divergent thinking would present challenges. He asked himself if he was prepared for that with Paris, given everything he now understood. He saw both her weaknesses and her brilliance. If they could talk with each other, deal openly with the issues and questions, be partners in coping with the problems, then...

His ringing cell phone startled him out of his reverie. He was even more startled to see who was calling. "Paris?"

"A funny thing happened at work this week," she said without preamble. "Can I come over and tell you about it?"

"Come over? Are you here? In Destiny?"

He heard the smile in her voice when she said, "Actually, I'm outside your front door."

He rushed to the door and flung it open. "What are you doing out there?" he called.

"Waiting for an invitation?" Moments later, she stood on his front step, threw both arms around his neck, and greeted him with a kiss.

"Uh... That was some kiss, but can you tell me what's going on?"

"Invite me in and I'll tell you."

An hour later, they'd shared their mutual discoveries about ADHD with both its upside and its down. After mentioning problems such as impulsiveness and overreaction, Paris said, "That probably influenced the way I responded to hearing about you and Jess. My reaction was over the top, but I was responding out of hurt pride and overreacting because...well, because that's what creative people like me do." She offered a tentative smile. "Forgive me for getting a little crazy?"

He wrapped her in his arms. "Oh sweetheart! There's nothing to forgive. Can you forgive me for messing up the communications? Even if I didn't fully understand, I certainly could have been more sensitive. There's so much I should have done differently. I—"

She interrupted him with a kiss, adding "I love you" as she cuddled nearer.

They talked then—about *all* their past relationships, names included, and about how miserable they both were over the past weeks.

"The distance had something to do with it," Greg said. "You were right about how difficult long-distance relationships can be, and that brings up something I've been hoping to tell you. I've been investigating administrative jobs in the valley—"

She put her finger to his lips. "You'd do that for me? Leave Destiny and the school and the mine and... everything?"

Emotion thickened his next words. "When I thought I lost you, I realized I'd be willing to give up almost anything to have you back in my life."

"And you actually considered moving." Her eyes filled with wonder, with love.

"Full disclosure, I stopped looking after you blocked my phone number."

"Another overreaction," Paris admitted.

"Well, it got through to me. I thought I'd blown my chances. Being principal at Destiny High and the owner of a productive mine meant nothing compared to being with you. After you left, they still meant little compared to losing you, but they gave me a reason to look forward."

She touched his face. "I'm so sorry I put you through that. As it turns out, I may have found a way to come back to Destiny." She explained the changes at TriTech and the possibility of full-time work from wherever she wanted to be, so long as they had regular video conferences and her presence at some meetings.

"It isn't anything firm," she added. "We don't know for sure that this new initiative with proposal writing will work, but it looks good. And even if it doesn't work with TriTech, I'm beginning to understand this business. With more experience, I could even work on my own. I never believed it could happen, but I've found a way to have the career I want and live anywhere I like."

"Even in Destiny?"

"Even in Destiny." She kissed him again.

Her statement filled Greg with doubts. "But would you want to live here? You could hardly wait to leave."

"Yes, I said that, and I meant it at the time, but you aren't the only one who's been doing some thinking. I've held this town responsible for the tragedies in my life without ever realizing that the town and the tragedies weren't connected. I also thought I'd have to leave here to have the kind of career I wanted."

She took a deep breath. "I know now that Destiny has always been *home*. I didn't realize it, but I've been orbiting this little burg my whole life. It's the only place I know where I can go for a half-hour walk and wave to a dozen people I've known since childhood. Now that I've found a way I could work here, I like the idea of coming home. Maybe even raising my own children here."

"You're serious?"

"Absolutely, although I've always dreamed of living on the coast— somewhere with a view of the ocean."

"My uncle Jake has a cabin in Ft. Bragg, and principals get vacations too, you know."

She grinned. "You're speaking my language." She took another deep breath. "I'm beginning to learn about the problems that come with ADHD. You may have noticed that I can be skeptical about some things, and it can take a lot to convince me. Other times, I can jump at a new idea without thinking. Did you notice?"

A wry smile accompanied his answer. "Yes, I think I noticed that."

"And you may have noticed that if something upsets me, I have a tendency to react emotionally first—even overact—and maybe think about it later, or not at all." She winced as she said it. "Have you noticed that?"

"Yes, I believe I noticed that too."

"And I sometimes have a terrible temper."

He answered dryly, "I do believe I noticed that as well."

"And I sometimes talk with my mouth full and tend to make decisions more from my gut than my head and interrupt people and have a myriad of other faults that are too many to count."

"Not that I've—"

"Shh," she said, her finger on his lips again. "Please don't argue. I'm on a roll here."

The corners of his mouth lifted. "Okay."

"In spite of all that, and especially in spite of the temper, do you still want me?"

The wry smile was replaced with a loving one. "With everything I am and have. But Paris? I do have one condition."

She sucked in a quick breath. "What kind of condition?"

"If we're going to be together, I have to know you're in it, really in it. I can't be constantly standing on one foot expecting you to have an outburst and leave. If you'll commit to giving this relationship a serious shot and not backing out over bumps along the way, then I'm all in too."

"Are you sure? I can be pretty awful—"

"...and creative, and brilliant, and kind, and loving, and funny, and oh so beautiful!" He lifted her hand, kissing each of her fingers. Then he added, "Yes, I'm sure."

"Then I'm yours. Now and always."

He gathered her into his arms, kissing her thoroughly. A pleasant minute passed while they kissed and held each other. Then Greg said, "Wait a minute. You said, 'now and always.' Did you just propose to me?"

Paris heard the words again, surprised they didn't scare her. "Oh my. I believe I did."

"So," he said. "You're ready to become Paris Frantz?"

She winced. "Ooh, we may have to negotiate the name thing. Maybe Paris Cutler-Frantz. But there's time for that. None of this will happen overnight."

"No, we'll need time to work on the details, but..." He grinned. "But you're the one who proposed. How about that?"

"That is not the official tale we'll tell our children," she said. "The public version will be a beautiful story of how you got down on one knee—"

He dropped to one knee to make it true. "Paris Cutler, will you be my wife?"

She beamed at him. "You dear, wonderful man! How sweet of you to ask."

A Message to YOU from the town of Destiny

Thank you for reading *Paris in the Springtime*, the revised and refreshed first book in the Seasons of Destiny Series. If you enjoyed it, please take a moment to give it a review. Help our lovely little town attract more readers for future stories.

If you want to find out how YOU can become a member of "Susan's Sweet Team" and get free books and other fun perks, you can email Susan at **susan@susanaylworthauthor.com**. In the meantime, enjoy each season.

Paris and Greg would love to have you join them at their wedding where you'll meet
Sunny Ray and Deputy Sheriff Evan Millet
our heroine and hero of the second book in the Seasons of Destiny Series.
Read on for a Sneak Peek of Book 2, *Sunny's Summer*.

Sneak Peek

🌹

Sunny's Summer
Seasons of Destiny Series Book 2

Signs of the fire were everywhere. As Sunny drove north toward Chico along Highway 99, she passed hundreds of acres of grassland and pasture burned in the blaze. While the flames had ignored century-old stone fences marking boundaries, new grass and blackened fence posts were the last reminders of the catastrophe that had devastated this beautiful part of the Sacramento Valley. Arriving in Chico, she turned east, taking the Skyway upward into the Sierra foothills toward the town of Paradise and shocked at the extent of the destruction around her—mile after mile of scorched earth topped by dead and dying trees.

She had read of the fire, seen pictures, interviewed survivors who came to the insurance office where she worked. Nothing prepared her for the emotional impact of seeing it all first-hand. She blinked back sudden tears, moved by the enormity of the tragedy.

How did this happen? And how were people able to survive? Many had been asking the same questions since the dramatic events last November. The local congressman came, followed by the governor, the U.S. president, and countless other officials. All were seeking answers to the same unanswerable questions.

The Camp Fire, named for Camp Creek Road where it started, was the deadliest wildfire in California history with eighty-five lives lost. It was also the first time, entire communities had simply vanished.

Sunny remembered the "Paradise Lost!" headlines, but Paradise was not the only town to go up in smoke. Concow was gone, as was more than half of Magalia. Pulga and other small Sierra foothill communities were damaged or destroyed, leaving some fifty thousand people displaced.

Butte County will have a tough time recovering from this, Sunny thought. *In fact, this was a big enough disaster to have a ripple effect across the entire state. All of California may have a difficult recovery.*

Sunny, who had spent her childhood in the Gold Rush towns of the Sierra Nevada, knew the mindset of the survivors, the tens of thousands whose homes, belongings, businesses, or workplaces were now nothing but ash and rubble. Many had lost everything they knew—all they had ever known. Some had also lost loved ones—people who either did not receive word of their impending doom or who chose not to evacuate until it was too late.

I can identify with some of this, Sunny reflected, *maybe more than people realize... maybe just a little too much.*

"Are you sure you can handle this?" her Aunt Olivia had asked.

Sunny had answered that she could—that she *wanted* to do it. Now she wondered.

As a jane-come-lately student in the schools of Destiny, California, Sunny knew the pain of being behind all her classmates and struggling to catch up. She knew what it meant to rely on the kindness and community spirit of a small town to bring her through trauma and loss. She even knew how it felt to lose someone, although her losses were not the same as the losses of those who had lived through the fire. She thought of her mother, taken by a heroin overdose, and of her sister, Skye, in jail on her third DUI. *Where there's life, there's hope. I'm trying not to give up on you, Skye, but you've got to try, too.*

Thinking like this wasn't helping at all. Sunny deliberately turned her thoughts to her current project. In less than a month, she would graduate with a degree in U.S. history, something her high-school history teacher would find hard to believe. *Things changed as I grew up. I'm so glad they did!*

She had applied to the California State University system for grad school. With luck, she'd be accepted at Chico State, her first choice, or Sacramento State, her second. Truth was, she'd go anywhere in the system if it allowed her to work toward graduate degrees and a possible future in teaching, maybe at the college level or maybe in high school. *My high-school history classes always made history seem like a bunch of boring names and dates. If I could teach it the way I know it now, as real people living their lives and making the best choices they could, what a difference!*

She thought of last night's conversation with her roommate. Libby started by asking a question similar to the one Aunt Olivia had posed: "Will you be okay with this? It's going to be hard."

"I'll be okay. I need to be. This paper will finish out my degree and get me started on my thesis as well, assuming my eventual graduate committee accepts my proposal for it. The real question is, are you sure your folks are okay with this? They run a bed-and-breakfast for a living. Doesn't seem fair for me to impose."

"You're not imposing," Libby assured her. "Mom and Dad are looking forward to having you there. As long as you leave before the rental crush during Chico State's graduation, they'll love it. No worries."

"That's very generous. I couldn't afford to make this trip without their help."

"They're happy to help. They may want a copy of your paper, though."

Sunny laughed. "I doubt that. The dry, academic style Professor Liu requires isn't particularly readable."

"They'll probably want to read it anyway. They've been affected by the fires, too."

Of course, they have. We all have. But maybe I can make something good come of it, and not just for me. If we see how this happened, maybe we can keep it from happening again. Sunny could almost hear her cousin Amber's voice asking, "Are you sure you're up to this, Sunny? This project would be tough for anybody." *And especially tough for someone like me. Is that what you mean, Amber?* But she couldn't fault Amber for caring. *I'm grateful I have family and friends who care.*

Most of her conversations lately had taken the same direction. No one seemed to understand her drive to do this—to see the devastation for herself and record everything she could of all that had been written and said about it. She was especially interested in people's first-hand experiences. *Documenting the Camp Fire, the way a true historian does will make for a great master's thesis. I probably already have enough for Dr. Liu's class, but to do the job right for a thesis, I'll need another sixty or seventy interviews—and I have to be back to school and work in just two weeks. Better get busy.* Sunny pressed the accelerator and picked up her speed.

She passed the entrance to the Tuscan Ridge Golf Course—or, more accurately, what had *been* a golf course. It had become the staging arena for the utility company crews working in the burned-over areas: assessing property damage, removing dead and dying timber, clearing toxic materials, doing all the clean-up work no one ever realized needed to be done until something like this happened. The service camp had once covered acres, though little remained of it now. *Maybe this will be a golf course again someday. Maybe there will even be people to play here.*

Farther up the road, she could see into the canyons on both sides of the Skyway and witness the way the fire had swept over the ridges and into the canyons. Fueled by gale-force winds, the flames had funneled down those canyons toward the valley, becoming a voracious monster that devoured everything in its path for miles. She shuddered. *Hell, on earth. It was a literal hell on earth. It's a wonder so many got out.*

As the elevation increased nearer to Paradise, the burned growth grew heavier. Soon she was entering pine forest, what little remained of it. *This must have been a beautiful town, thick with trees and shrubs, much like Destiny.* She stopped herself short of realizing that her hometown of Destiny in the foothills above Sacramento could burn just like this. Just then she passed the place that once held the town's welcome sign: "May you find Paradise to be all its name implies." She remembered the "before" pictures of the beautiful sign for a lovely community. Little remained of either now.

The surreal experience of driving into the burned-out town came as a second emotional jolt. *It's like entering a cemetery.* Fire-seared chimneys stood like headstones and seemed to announce *Here lies the Smith home* or *Here lived the Jacksons.* They stood in rows, one after another, block after block, a graveyard for families' former lives that stretched as far as she could see, clear to the edge of the charred forest.

Some lots had been cleared, dying trees logged for their timber, rubble hauled away, ashes removed, even the scorched topsoil taken, its brew of toxic chemicals carefully disposed of elsewhere. A few spaces even had new construction underway, but most of the plots of land looked just as they must have since the flames were finally cooled by the quenching rains. Those lots were littered with the remnants of heating and cooling systems, kitchen sinks, melted windows, and even a sporadic burned-out vehicle. Each scorched vehicle that remained was marked with a large, spray-painted X indicating to search crews that it contained no bodies.

It's hard to believe… difficult to imagine. But Sunny didn't have to imagine what that first ghastly morning had been like. She had seen the videos shot by panicked people, fathers and mothers, sons and daughters, friends and neighbors who recorded their flight as they scrambled to outrun a racing wildfire. Some prayed as they drove. Others sobbed as they recorded what they believed to be their last words, hoping their cell phones and the record found there would outlive them. The terror reflected in every video was poignant and raw.

In several videos, Sunny watched homes burning on both sides of the road, burned-out shells of vehicles still on fire, trees exploding into flame all around. One video showed fire blocking the road as a shaky voice announced, "There's no way out of this but through it. I hope we can get past this. If we don't, remember we love you." A baby screamed in the background while a young child's voice quavered, "Mommy, are we gonna die?" Sunny's throat tightened every time she thought of it. *What must it have been like?*

She drove through several neighborhoods, simply staring at the devastation. At some point, she realized that all she was doing was driving and gaping *I suppose some shock is natural. Destruction on this scale is hard to fathom. Still, I came here for a purpose, and it's time I remember that.*

Sunny got out her camera and began to document all she saw.

On the two-acre lot that had once been his own small piece of Paradise, Evan Millett worked steadily, stacking most of what remained of his home and belongings into piles: one for trash removal, one for toxic waste and potentially hazardous materials, and a third small stack for items that might be worth keeping. There was very little in the third stack. *Everything I dreamed of, all I wanted, gone. Just gone.* It was almost too much to face.

He hadn't faced it at first. Throwing himself into work, he avoided even driving past this place. Later, when he finally made the pilgrimage, he was horrified to find all the trees being removed, even those the fire had missed. Finally, a state-certified botanist explained that the heavy rains that followed the fire, leaving flash flooding and debris flows in their wake, had washed the smoke and toxic gases from the air back into the soil, poisoning the hardy plants that survived the initial disaster. *It will be a hundred years before this forest recovers.* He hated even thinking about it.

Almost as much as I hate the vultures who've swept in since. Evan knew not everyone felt as he did. Some were grateful for any intervention and saw all outsiders as sources of help. But the attorneys and insurance investigators who set up shop in the area before the fires were extinguished, struck him as scavengers, feeding on the remains of all that had been here, looking for someone to sue to recoup their own losses or make a profit. Evan bristled when he recalled their quick and slick promises to sue on the survivors' behalf well before fire investigators had any clear idea of how the fire started or who might be responsible. Some of his neighbors had been grateful and open to hearing more, but Evan turned them all away—rudely when he could.

I have to find a way to get past all this, Evan thought as he worked, but the pain of loss was like a cold, hard stone in his gut. The guilt was even worse.

Sunny found frequent opportunities to stop. Sometimes she snapped pictures from her car window; occasionally she got out to walk up to the remains of someone's home. She stopped short of actually walking inside, brought to a halt by her reluctance to intrude as well as the odd mix of rubble, ash, and what looked like gooey paste—the fire's version of mud.

Sunny had been taking pictures for half an hour when she turned a corner and saw someone dressed entirely in camo sifting through the debris of a small home. Though it was May and the weather warming, the worker was outfitted for HAZMAT conditions in a white hazard mask, heavy boots, and thick gloves. Man? Large, short-haired woman? At this distance, she couldn't guess.

The building's footprint stood a little apart from others around it, telling Sunny it had once occupied a large lot covered with tall trees. Only stumps remained. The lot looked as if it had been clear-cut. Other nearby lots looked the same. *I'll bet this person has a story to tell.* She got out of her car.

"Hello!" she called. "Mind if I shoot some pictures?"

"Why?" A deep bass voice responded.

Definitely a man. "I'm documenting the Camp Fire for a master's thesis in history."

"You're sure? You're not from one of the insurance companies or the people who want to sue the utility company?"

"No. I do work for an insurance company, but this project is a personal one, and I don't intend to share it with my bosses."

"Likely story." He turned his back. "Yes, I mind if you take pictures."

Sunny bit her lip in frustration. *That's what total honesty gets me.* "Okay, then, no pictures," she said, still shouting across the wide space. She put the camera back into her car. "Can I just come over and talk with you? I'd like to get your fire story—you know, what happened here."

"Why?" he asked again.

"I told you.... Never mind. May I just watch for a while?"

He shrugged. "Suit yourself."

She drew nearer, looked the man full in the face, and caught her breath.

"Something wrong?"

"No, no. You're just not what I expected." *No way was I expecting you.* She'd imagined a much older man. This one was close to her own age, solidly built, and very attractive, his eyes a startling blue. "May I ask your name?"

He actually curled his lip. "Maxwell Smart."

"Very funny. I've seen the movie." She stepped forward and held out her hand. "I'll tell you mine if you tell me yours."

He took her hand, but the look in his eye hadn't changed. "Very well, Miss Not-from-the-insurance-company-but-yes-I-do-happen-to-work-there. My name is Evan Millett."

She offered her most winning smile. "I'm Sunny Ray."

He didn't just drop her hand. He threw it back at her. "Sunny Ray? Like I'm supposed to buy that? I think you need to leave now, Miss Whatever-your-name-is."

She took a deep breath followed by an exasperated sigh. "It's actually Golden Sunny Ray, but I only use Sunny. If you'd ever known my neo-hippie mother, you'd understand."

Steel glinted in his eyes and venom laced his voice. "I asked you to leave."

"All right, all right. I'm going. But I have a business card. It has my name—my real name, Sunny Ray—along with my phone and email. If you decide you want to talk, give me a call. People tell me it can be very therapeutic to share their story."

"Off. My. Land." He seemed angrier by the moment.

"I'm going!" As she turned, she spotted a large stump near the edge of Evan's property. *That tree must have shaded the front door of that home for decades.* "I'll leave my card right here, just in case."

He opened his mouth to speak again, but she didn't need any more warnings. "I'm gone!" she said. As quickly as she could manage across the rough ground, she made it back to her car and jumped inside. Then, before anything else could happen, she drove down the street, not even stopping to shoot pictures of other properties until she was well out of the man's sight.

So much for making progress.

A few minutes later, she came across a couple, probably in their fifties, who were working on a smaller lot with a bigger home footprint. She spent the next hour recording their detailed and harrowing story. When she thanked them for sharing it, they thanked her for giving them the chance. It had been that way with everyone she talked to so far—everyone but Evan Millett. *I wonder what's up with him?*

During the rest of the day, she spoke to five more people who were happy to share their stories. She didn't leave Paradise until the sun was down and a brilliant, fiery sunset tinted the western sky.

I hope you enjoyed this little sneak peek of *Sunny's Summer*. Please visit www.susanaylworthauthor.com for more information.

A Note from
Susan Aylworth

The tiny, unincorporated town of Cherokee, California is the model for my town of Destiny. What's left of Cherokee lies about twelve miles northeast of Oroville in the Sierra foothills. Many times smaller than Destiny (it doesn't have its own schools), it still has some of the flavor I wanted for my struggling Gold Rush town.

The story of "Destiny Diamonds" is true; it happened in Cherokee. At the height of the Gold Rush, the Cherokee Mine produced about ten million dollars in gold. In 1866, a miner spotted a diamond in his sluice box. Within a few years, more than 400 ice clear stones were discovered, the only true diamonds ever found in California. One weighed more than six carats.

According to an article by Ben T. Traywick in *The Tombstone News* of February 14, 2019, "a stranger appeared and the mine was closed." Newspaper records of the time credit or blame the world's largest diamond cartel. According to their records, the cartel felt threatened by the "flood" of perfect stones coming from the western U.S., made the owners a huge offer, bought the mine, and closed it. Speculation about what may still lie beneath the closed mine entrance helped to fuel this story.

Books by
Susan Aylworth

Visit **susanaylworthauthor.com** to get any of the books listed here.

The Rainbow Rock Romance Series

Welcome to Rainbow Rock, Arizona, a quaint small town nestled in the striped hills of the Painted Desert region, where every rainstorm brings a rainbow and every heart is filled with hope and love. Meet the McAllister family—brothers Jim, Kurt, Chris, sister Joan, and their beloved widowed mom, Kate. Follow each of their stories as they find love under the high desert stars. Get to know the McAllisters' friends and neighbors in Rainbow Rock and enjoy more heartwarming romances in this wonderful and memorable close-knit community.

Each story may be read separately but there is great enjoyment in reading them in order.

Over the Rainbow: **Prequel**

Joan McAllister never imagined a world without her larger-than-life father. After his sudden death, she is overwhelmed with sorrow, harrowed up by guilt, and coping with her father's dying wish: helping her mother run the family farm and care for her three younger brothers. To complicate matters, Joan is attracted to a man she met at her father's funeral. How can she be thinking of romance when her life is in turmoil?

Bob Riley sees in Joan the woman he has always wanted. Even though they met under somber circumstances, there's nothing somber about his feelings. Bob knows he and Joan have much in common, and he's pretty sure she's attracted to him, so why does she keep pulling away? Come to Rainbow Rock, Arizona, and learn what awaits Bob, Joan, and the rest of the McAllister clan in *Over the Rainbow*.

Ride the Rainbow Home: **Book 1**

In time for her ten-year class reunion, Meg Taylor is lured back to the tiny town in northeastern Arizona where she suffered through high school. Overweight, step-daughter to the principal, she was anything but popular. Now she's slim, attractive, and accomplished—and still wary of all she knew then.

Except for Jim. "Little Jimmy" McAllister was one of her two best friends. Ten years have changed him, too. (No one calls him "little" anymore!) He always cared about Meg and seeing her again only enhances those feelings. He wants her to stay, permanently, but Meg, the daughter of a serial-marrying mom, can't imagine herself in "happily ever after." What will it take to change her mind and bind her heart to his?

At the Rainbow's End: **Book 2**

Alexa Babbidge is about to hit it big as a Hollywood scriptwriter—if only her car will cooperate. Stranded near Rainbow Rock, Arizona, she is rescued by Mr. Could-Be-Right. Too bad she isn't looking for romance! But she is looking for a job, at least until she can reschedule her meeting in movieland.

Kurt McAllister is looking for a scriptwriter, not a wife. But Alexa fits easily into his video production company, and almost as easily into his life. As they work together, taping a documentary about Navajo weaving, he longs to persuade her to stay.

Gold beckons at the end of the rainbow, and Alexa, who has seen too much of poverty, can't resist its pull. Kurt longs to hold her, but at what price? As their time together draws to a close, each must decide whether it is wealth and fame or love and family that await them *At the Rainbow's End.*

Don't Promise Me Rainbows: **Book 3**

When faced with a birthing emergency in his prized breeding stock, pig farmer Chris McAllister calls the local veterinarian for help. He expects the wiry, middle-aged man his family has long trusted, not a petite but tough young woman whose edgy personality could qualify her as an Amazon queen from Greek mythology. Even so, he can't avoid a magnetic attraction to the pretty, red-haired vet.

Beneath her composure and stiff professional demeanor, Sarah McGill hides deeply painful secrets. She's only returned to Rainbow Rock for a short time, filling in for her dad while he recovers from a nasty knee injury. The last thing she needs is some cute cowboy stirring up trouble, digging for answers, making her feel emotions she hoped never to feel again.

When a project for the Navajo Nation throws them together, Chris and Sarah must decide whether they can risk their hearts to promises that come without guarantees.

A Little Night Rainbow: Book 4

Max Carmody was married once. It wasn't pretty. Now he finds himself stuck for the summer with a thirteen-year-old daughter he barely knows and a sister who will take her in, but not unless he comes with her. Marcie tells her dad she wants him to marry again, but the last thing this Mozart-loving-car-parts manufacturer needs is romance. In fact, his ever marrying again is about as likely as finding a rainbow in the night sky.

Cretia Sherwood was married too, and it definitely wasn't pretty. She is finally healing and regaining some independence after years of struggling to raise her kids on her own. Now that her daughter Lydia is thirteen and her son Danny is eleven, Cretia can take a breath and focus on making sure she can give her kids everything she didn't have growing up. The last thing this Mozart-loving mom needs is to lose her new-found independence to a man. When her daughter asks her if she would ever consider remarrying, Cretia replies—when she sees a night rainbow in the sky.

When love brings them a rainbow, both Max and Cretia have to choose between the security and safe routines of their present lives or a leap of faith, betting on the future.

Note: This book introduces thirteen-year-old Lydia Sherwood whom you'll meet again in *Always a Rainbow* (Book 7); thirteen-year-old Marcie Carmody whom you will meet again in *The Promise of Rainbows (Book 8)*, and eleven-year-old Danny Sherwood whom you will meet again in *Once in a Rainbow (Book 9)*.

A Rainbow in Paradise: Book 5

Eden Grant vowed never to go back home. A painful childhood growing up in Rainbow Rock made Eden swear off marriage and a family of her own. With a successful childcare business in Phoenix, Eden can lavish all the love she has on the children of others. But when her best friend, Sarah McGill, asks her to be her maid of honor, Eden makes the trip home to Rainbow Rock for Sarah's wedding. What Eden doesn't count on is her immediate attraction to the best man.

Logan Redhorse might be the best man at his friend Chris's fairy-tale wedding but holding Eden in his arms feels like his very own paradise. How can Logan reconcile his immediate attraction to Eden with the promise he made? An attorney for the Navajo Nation, Logan vowed to his ancestors and descendants that he will marry a desert child, a daughter of *Dinehtah*.

How can Eden and Logan reconcile their differences to embrace a future that could bring them both a love beyond paradise?

The Trouble with Rainbows: **Book 6**

Joe Vanetti was deeply in love with his late wife, Roberta. Even thinking of another woman feels disloyal. Although his romantic life ended with Roberta's death, he still has their children to raise. He's returned to Rainbow Rock so they can grow up close to his family. The last thing he's thinking about is dating, but when Joe runs into Angelica DeForest, the former "Ice Queen" from high school, he can't help but wonder at the change in her.

Despite a successful career as a violist, Angelica DeForest lives a lonely life. Painfully awkward and socially inept, she's spent her adult years caring for aging, bitter relatives. She promises herself she will try to be bolder, to reach out to others and maybe even (gasp!) socialize. She certainly doesn't intend to begin with Joe Vanetti, the high school Golden Boy who was always so perfect, so far above her, no matter that he's even more handsome now than back in high school.

A promising future beckons, if they have the courage to banish the ghosts of their past.

Always a Rainbow: **Book 7 (New to the series)**

Lydia Sherwood has vowed not to marry until she's at least thirty. Her parents' disastrous marriage began too young and ended badly. Only when her mother gained age and wisdom did she build a happy union with Lydia's stepdad, Max. Lydia swears she'll avoid the same mistakes, but she's barely eighteen when she meets handsome Drake Westcott, an Air Force cadet, and he's as smitten as she is. Her commitment is to a career in medicine, his to the military. As time passes and life changes for each of them, what will happen to their individual plans—and to the promises they've made to each other?

The Promise of Rainbows: **Book 8** (Formerly: *Return to Rainbow Rock*)

Eleven years have passed since Marcie Carmody left Rainbow Rock for the big city, starry-eyed and eager to build her future. She found love with a struggling law student—or thought she had. When her boyfriend's rejection also leads to the end of her job, she limps home, dejected and ashamed, fearing harsh judgment from her family and community. Finding unexpected acceptance, Marcie also lands a new job in the law offices of Logan Redhorse, working with a new associate. On hyper-alert to make sure she exceeds expectations, she calls the police the moment she sees a man in a hoodie rifling through Logan's files.

Ryan Fields needs a new start. His wife has left him for a man she met in an online role-playing game and has taken his sons with her. Ryan is experienced in native law, having practiced with a Sacramento firm, and the position with Redhorse sounds like a perfect fit. He does not expect to be picked up as a burglar on his first visit to the office, thanks to a nosy redhead. No way does he want *her* as a legal assistant!

But Marcie's apologies and her office skills are real, and Ryan decides to give her a try, firmly ignoring the glimmer of attraction that hovers any time she draws near. Both Marcie and Ryan have wounds to heal and obstacles to overcome. Surely, they aren't ready to find new love, but Fate, and Love, may have other plans.

Once in a Rainbow: Book 9 (Formerly: *Danny's Girl*)

Running from a man who has threatened her life, Manon DuPre fears even slowing down, let alone stopping, but the Arizona Highway Patrol disapproves of her speed. How can she persuade the handsome trooper that she needs his help, not an arrest?

Raised by a drunken abuser and a terrified mother, young Danny Sherwood grew up to be a protector. Maybe that's why he's such a dedicated patrol officer. When he stops a dangerous speeder on the Interstate, he doesn't expect a beautiful, terrified woman, who claims to be fleeing a killer.

As the community of Rainbow Rock rallies to help, how can Manon and Danny embrace a joyful future when they still must face their difficult pasts, and a potentially lethal threat?

Chasing Rainbows: Book 10 (Formerly: *Roman's Holiday*)

Roman Kincaid has it all: a meteoric rise to fame and fortune as a country-pop performer and now, as an A-list Hollywood celebrity. He also has a demanding agent driving him to exhaustion. Depleted and dispirited, Roman takes an impromptu holiday, disappearing into Arizona's high desert. A chance encounter leads him to Lottie Beale's café and pie shop.

Lottie Beale is humming along to one of Roman's new releases when the man himself walks through her door. Keeping her cool, she serves him as she would any customer, but his presence fills her with happy thrills—and terribly unhappy memories. She has her own reasons to hide.

Roman's offer to travel with Lottie as his guide sounds like an awkward come-on when Lottie first hears it, but he swears he'll be the perfect gentleman and she easily reads his need for friendly, undemanding companionship—a need she understands too well. Their road trip takes them to well-known places like Mesa Verde and the Four Corners monument, and to less famous sites only the locals know.

It also takes them on a journey of self-discovery as each comes to terms with where they've been and where they want to go. Can a famous star and a small-town pie maker find common ground? Anything is possible in Rainbow Rock, romance capital of the great Southwest.

An Unexpected Rainbow: **Book 11** (Formerly: *A Monumental Love*)

An unexpected romance might have the power to heal the past.

Roxelle McCann is eager to meet the family of her best friend, Kyra Redhorse, so she takes a mini-vacation to the Navajo Nation. Roxelle expects to find out more about Navajo language and customs and to be awed by the beauty of Monument Valley. She does not expect to find love among the monuments. The man she meets offers both a tender reminder of the past and a surprising possible future.

SEASONS OF DESTINY ROMANCE SERIES

Welcome to the small town of Destiny, California, where love blooms all year and the bonds of family and friendship last forever. The Seasons of Destiny series features four sweet and clean romances that will warm your heart.

Each story may be read separately, but there is great enjoyment in reading them in order.

Paris in the Springtime: **Book 1**

Paris is back home but not for long. Emotionally gut-punched after losing her job in Sacramento, Paris Cutler returns to her grandmother's home in Destiny, California to take a breath and figure out what comes next. She loves Gran and Aunt Jess and is thankful they're always there for her, but Destiny has never felt like home. Paris is anxious to get back on her feet so she can get back to the city. When she runs into Greg Frantz, her high school crush who's now the high school principal, she can't stop thinking about how handsome and charming he is. She also can't stop feeling like that awkward teen again with the unfortunate knack of blurting out everything she's thinking. And she can't help but wonder why Greg moved back to small-town Destiny.

Greg Frantz can't stop thinking about the beautiful and outspoken Paris. He always admired her gutsiness, especially considering everything she went through as a kid, losing first her dad and then her mom. He's thrilled when the accomplished and talented writer agrees to help with a crucial grant application for the school. Greg knows that Paris sees the small mountain town as a temporary stop, but he'd love to persuade her to take a chance on Destiny.

Sunny's Summer: Book 2

Six months after the deadliest fire in California history, Sunny Ray drives through the rubble and ash of the once-lovely town of Paradise. She's there to document the history of the Camp Fire for her university studies, one survivor story at a time. Sunny has an ability to understand and connect with the devastated townspeople of Paradise, given her own troubled childhood before she was adopted by her aunt and uncle in neighboring Destiny. If only she could help Deputy Sheriff Evan Millett.

Distant and simmering with resentment, Evan refuses to speak to Sunny at first until he sees how the townspeople respond to her. As Evan eventually relents enough to help Sunny with her research he can't help his blossoming attraction to the lovely young woman as his trust in her grows. But when their fragile bond is broken, can they salvage their budding romance, or will it become another paradise lost?

Amber in Autumn: Book 3

Amber Reyes gave up a chance at love to take her dream job as principal of the elementary school in her beloved hometown of Destiny, California. Two years later, Amber has her days full, but her evenings empty. She yearns to marry and have a family, but the lack of eligible men in the quaint small town leaves her questioning if she made a mistake coming home.

Devastated by his ex-wife's volatile life and tragic death, Max Burnett moves his grief-stricken six-year-old twins, Kate and Will, to Destiny, hoping that the town of his youth can offer a healing change. Believing himself too damaged to love or be loved, Max doesn't think he'll ever meet a woman who could be his partner in life and a mother to his kids.

As the principal of Kate and Will's school, Amber takes on the delicate challenge of helping the troubled children adjust, but dealing with Max is a completely different matter. Their initial sparring leads to a powerful attraction. But, as Max and Amber's feelings deepen, so does the turmoil with Kate and Will. How can Amber and Max heal the wounds of the past and build a positive future?

Winter Skye: **Book 4**

Skye Ray had the kind of childhood that nightmares are made of before her loving aunt and uncle adopted her and her older sister Sunny. After many turbulent years, Skye is finally on track and pursuing her dream of completing her degree and becoming a professional artist. She's determined to focus on her goals, but when she meets Peter Koury, Skye wonders if perhaps her dreams could include the tall, dark, and unequivocally appealing grad student and glass artist.

Peter Koury's last relationship was a disaster and he's sworn to focus on his art career. Battling his own tumultuous past, Peter is determined to pour everything into his sculptures. But when he meets Skye, he finds it hard to resist her striking beauty and quirky charm. Blown away by her talent and passionate nature, Peter might just have to rethink his views about love.

CHRISTMAS TOWN ROMANCE SERIES

Welcome to Christmas Town, officially known as Bedford Falls, CA—where the spirit of Christmas is celebrated all year long, and where a wholesome romance is just around the corner. This sweet and clean small-town romance series will make you want to curl up by a cozy fire with a mug of hot chocolate and a plate of freshly baked gingerbread cookies. Enjoy Christmas year round and make Christmas Town your destination for Holiday romance reads.

Each story may be read separately but there is great enjoyment in reading them in order.

A Joyful Eve in Christmas Town: **Book 1** (formerly *Joy Comes to Bedford Falls*)

A new job brings Claire Reiser to Bedford Falls, California, a Sierra resort village widely known as Christmas Town because it celebrates the Holiday Season year-round. Claire arrives just days before Christmas, reconciled to spending the holiday alone.

Ben Scarge is also new in town, whisked in to manage the estate of his late Uncle Simon, a curmudgeonly miser who puts Scrooge to shame. Like Claire, Ben knows no one and anticipates a lonely holiday. Then a furry visitor delivers a gift neither Claire nor Ben will ever forget.

St. Nick Comes to Christmas Town: **Book 2**

Kiley Ross postponed her dreams of a university degree for many years, but she's ready to tackle it now, including the newswriting lab class taught by grad student Nick Santino. Nick's class challenges Kiley in every way. Trouble is, Kiley can't seem to stop thinking about her movie star look-alike teacher outside the classroom.

Nick Santino knows better than to become involved with a student, especially in his first class as a teaching assistant, but he can't help his attraction to Kiley; she captured his attention on Day One.

Kiley and Nick are coping with the rules and getting through the term. When circumstances throw them for a loop, how will they deal with the fall-out?

Kisses and Kittens in Christmas Town: **Book 3**

Amanda Velasquez is weary of attending her girlfriends' weddings when she can't even get a date. Is it her fault she's tall and built more like her linebacker dad than her runway model mom? Marco Fuentes admires the striking woman whose quest for good health brings her to the gym where he lifts weights. A mutual attraction draws them together, but their pride and prejudices keep tripping them up. Can a basketful of abandoned kittens help them choose snuggling over sparring?

Mischief and Mistletoe in Christmas Town: **Book 4**

Emily Draper and Carl Fuentes can't possibly fall in love. New career opportunities have them both contemplating major changes, perhaps even leaving Christmas Town. How can the magic of Christmas and a cute kitten called Mischief make their future warm and bright?

Holly and Hearts in Christmas Town: **Book 5**

Bethany Sheridan has created a comfortable life for herself and her disabled daughter, Gracie. But with the daily demands of her work, her pet fostering, and caring for Grace, Bethany has no time to date let alone fall in love. Richard Hale has just landed a new job with a load of responsibility. He has always relied on a stable routine to manage his severe stutter. But his life turns upside down when he meets the lovely Bethany. How can a wheelchair-bound Cupid, a sweet-but-confused service dog, and an adorable puppy called Holly turn their awkward meeting into a second chance romance?

Visit **susanaylworthauthor.com** to sign up for Susan's newsletter.

About the Author

Susan Aylworth loves "travel, great music, and perfect raspberry jam" and claims addiction to "words in almost all polite forms." Her first book, started when she was nine, "was a rip-off of *Black Beauty*. I wrote eight whole pages!" For her fifth-grade career day, she stated her ambition to become "a rich and famous author." Years later, she is pleased to have achieved the 'author' part of that goal.

Susan enjoys researching backgrounds and careers for the characters in her novels. "It's one way to live many lives all at once." She lives in northern California with her writer husband, Roger. She has also lived on the East Coast and in the Navajo Nation, the setting for several of her novels. Like most women of her generation, she wishes the kids would visit more often.

She loves hearing from readers. Reach her at susan@susanaylworthauthor.com. You may also sign up for Susan's newsletter at her website: susanaylworthauthor.com. Follow Susan on BookBub for updates on new releases. Like Susan's Facebook author page, www.facebook.com/Susan.Aylworth.Author, and/or follow her on Twitter @SusanAylworth. "If you enjoy my books, please tell everyone you know: friends, relatives, neighbors, the person who delivers your mail, people you meet in line in the grocery store, everyone!"

www.ingramcontent.com/pod-product-compliance
Lightning Source LLC
Chambersburg PA
CBHW020051180626
46812CB00006B/2277